Praise for
Liz J. Andersen's Second Novel,
My New Best Friend is an Alien

"Liz Andersen serves up another exciting, fast-paced adventure for animal lovers everywhere. The setting is wonderful, the characters are interesting, and the action keeps you on the edge of your seat right up to the end."

—Jerry Oltion, Nebula winner, and twice nominated for the Hugo

"Tajen "Taje" Jesmuhr, intrepid veterinary student, goes on a hero's journey in this next volume by author Liz J. Andersen.

"Along with fellow vet student and new friend, Giemsan Fane, she is assigned to Big Maxson's Planet in order to study disease prevention in the local animal populations. Because Taje doesn't seem to take the easy way, ever, she quickly becomes entangled with a host of colorful interplanetary characters, some good and some not so good. Fast paced and full of wild experiences (lizard riding! pizza with a side of krazzle!), the story is cleverly conveyed through Taje's inner thoughts and courageous actions. I look forward to reading more about her adventures in the future."

—Patricia Prisbey, Ret. Librarian

International Praise for
Liz J. Andersen's First Novel,
Some of My Best Friends Are Human

"Excellent!"

—Andre Norton, Science Fiction Writers of
America Grand Master

"I finished your book last night. I settled down with it in front of a cozy fire and wound up staying up until 3:00 to finish it. I couldn't put it down! I had to find out what happened to these interesting characters."

—Jerry Oltion, Nebula winner, and twice nominated
for the Hugo

"Teens and adults will enjoy this fast-paced sci-fi adventure! The book is written in journal-style entries of an orphan teen girl named Tajen. The occasional slang words used by her and all of her classmates are really unique. One can imagine that teens coming together from diverse planetary civilizations would absolutely have their own short-hand language to communicate with each other. The descriptions of the isolated world where they learn to survive, their medical technology, diversity of main characters and animals kept the story fast paced and held my interest. I enjoyed reading about the astonishing discovery they made towards the end. Very likeable characters and a satisfying read!"

—Patricia M. Prisbrey, Ret. YA Librarian

"This is a coming of age story set within a distinct and well crafted SF universe which I thoroughly enjoyed.

"The story starts off with a set of orphaned teenagers living in an underground orphanage on an alien world. Life and civilization outside the orphanage is sprawling and contains many varied species; of which the orphans comprise of. The main character is a girl called Taje who struggles to fit into day to day life within the orphanage. Her one love in life which sustains her is her love of animals which shows itself with her many pets and her desire to one day work within a related field. This love is the cause of the main plot point mentioned in the synopsis; namely being the opportunity to go on an ecological field trip. Her route to get there is interesting which is where I'll leave it with plot.

"The most impressive feature of this book to me was the sense of optimism and hope running throughout. The characters are all young and inexperienced but want more out of life than their birth afforded them. They are trying to achieve more of themselves which lends itself to this optimism and forward thinking. It was a genuinely nice experience reading this as it's rare to read a book where the hope of the characters is based on their wanting more from themselves and will not abuse others to achieve this; it's all on themselves and their strengths and many weaknesses."

—Joseph McLoughlin—U.K. Book Reviewer

"I love your book!..Sitting in my 'space lounger' it's a very good reading matter!"

—Caroline Michal, a German fan

Colorful Creatures, Friends, and Dangerous Forests Everywhere

Colorful Creatures, Friends, and Dangerous Forests Everywhere

Liz J. Andersen

Labbwerk Publishing

Eugene

Labbwerk Publishing, Eugene, Oregon 97404
©2025 by Liz J. Andersen
All rights reserved. Published 2025

Printed in the United States of America
Paperback ISBN: 978-0-9988448-6-2
eBook ISBN: 978-0-9988448-7-9

Library of Congress Control Number: 2025945182

Labbwerk Publishing gratefully acknowledges the generous support of:
Editors: Jackie Melvin & Brian Boudler
Cover Photo: by Siim Ainsaar
Back Cover Photo by Liz J. Andersen
Cover Design: Cricket Harper

Names: Author Liz J. Andersen
Titles: Colorful Creatures, Friends, and Dangerous Forests Everywhere

Summary: During the final lab of her junior year of interplanetary veterinary school, Taje nearly gets stuck inside a surgical patient much larger than herself. Her spirits lift though, as she and Giem are assigned an externship on the exquisite planet of Enchantment. Its landscape is pockmarked with craters lined with flower rings where the brilliantly colored crater pups live. They are hunted, captured, and quarantined for the popular and lucrative pet market. Taje and Giem must help in the Quarantine Stations. But the two vet students soon discover the import/export business is far less than ethical, and the hunting is likely to upset the crater ecology. When they speak out about this, the whole planet turns against them. Will they be able to save the crater pups and escape back to school on Olecranon unscathed?

Science Fiction. | Action and Adventure fiction. | Ecology—Fiction. | Crime—Fiction. | Extraterrestrial beings—Fiction. | Survival—Fiction. | Friendship—Fiction . | Veterinary Students—Fiction.|
OCLC Record: 1485487035

Other titles by Liz J. Andersen

The Federation of Intelligent Life Series:

Some of My Best Friends Are Human
My New Best Friend Is An Alien

As Editor

Along the Margins
South Dakota Immigrant Homesteaders
By Hans H. Andersen

This Book Is Dedicated To

**South Sierra,
Marmots, Ponderosa Pines,
& My Very Patient Riding Instructors,
Becky & Lee**

CHAPTER 1

I confronted my patient, an average-sized saury. She towered more than two stories above me. She was obviously tranquilized, standing quietly in the heavily padded clamps of her massive restraining stocks.

I always felt small in my blue scrub suit, since tradition insists that all surgeons are giants. This scene made me feel microscopic.

Technicians on an elevated scaffold had gowned, capped, masked, and gloved up, to aseptically insert a couple of hose-sized venous catheters. These connected to tanks of IV fluids and anesthetic drugs metered by a mobile tower.

Other anesthesia techs climbed all over the scaffolding surrounding the hulking creature, attaching and inserting various sensors. These monitored the saury's vitals and would also assist my suit sensors with supplying data for the hologram that would hover before us. Allowing the whole class to follow my surgery, of course. Sigh.

Our school couldn't afford to let every class member try this procedure in lab. Sauries have come down some in price, what with the new clone farms. The expense of shipping even saury offspring down to the surface of Olecranon still severely limits the number we can work with. The Ag School has promised us a more ready supply from its planetary-based herd—but not before I graduated.

"Ah, Taje, good morning!" Dr. Cretchell smiled at me. His green scrubs made his hair look darker and redder than mine, and stand out even more. His furry pointed ears, short lanky build, and ever-cheerful attitude rarely failed to remind me of a bouncy little leprechaun. An evil sprite who reveled in obscure, nasty, grueling essay exams. Also, unlike most of our professors, Cretchell completely disregarded our precious barrier of vet school anonymity. Somehow he had committed all 163 of our names to memory, and found opportunities to use them to our faces in class.

I tried not to show hostile suspicion on my face, while I wondered how on Olecranon he had managed to learn my nickname.

"We're running right on time," Dr. Cretchell continued obliviously. "We should have the beast scrubbed and opened for you while you're suiting up, if you start immediately."

"I, uh—"

"We'll have a direct access tube hooked up by the time you're ready to exit."

His intimidating, assured manner squelched my desire to clarify a few slightly confusing, glossed-over aspects in the 3D deskcom version of a saury salpingotomy. So instead I obediently found my way up to the prep area, a series of several small rooms on the second floor, behind the stage.

The first was a locker room, where I stripped. I sat on a bench for a few minutes, and watched my heart pound through my thin chest wall, near my left breast.

The second was a shower room. Here I performed my total body presurgical scrub, working methodically from my cleanest body parts to various orifices. Each room had a time meter, and I began to glance at the digits more and more frantically, as I realized I was moving too slowly. I knew I'd forget or fuse some crucial step if I tried to hurry any faster. This would be my first unsimulated surgery, and a real, live animal was expected to survive it, in comfort. I couldn't afford to make any mistakes this time. I'd have no reset command. I threw used sponges at the meter.

At last I reached the final room, where warm air and sterile towels awaited careful application, and a sterile stand held my skin-tight, soon to be pressurized surgery suit at the end of a red pathway. I dried myself in the same order I'd scrubbed. I stood before the brown suit, that had "Prop. of UOIVMTH" printed in red across the butt. It split open to receive me.

I also saw "HF N6&1/2 RH"—human female, size narrow six and a half, right-handed—also printed in black down each shoulder. Now I knew I wouldn't go numb, swim around in my suit, or struggle with left-handed instruments during the surgery. I glared at the suit. One misstep putting it on, and I might end up in a badly fitting substitute sterile submersion suit.

I took my time. Through the split back, I carefully inserted my left foot, followed by my left leg, and then my right foot and leg with my weaker knee. Next came my hands and arms. With every move I had to be certain not to touch the outside of the suit or any of its hoses, which would set off sensor alarms and let everyone know I'd broken sterility. All the scrubbing in the world won't remove all of my integumentary microflora, which can be fatal to the patient.

There. I'd made it. I hoped the suit would deal with my sweat efficiently. I had decided against hooking up to the other liquid and solid waste removal systems. I had good sphincter control, not to mention virtually no breakfast in my system, and it would save time.

I ordered the suit stand to lower the clear helmet, and to seal it and the back of my suit for me. The stand split apart to release me, with a tail of hoses supplying air, sterile saline, power, and communications.

"Are you ready?" came Dr. Cretchell's impatient voice over my helmet com, as soon as each half of the stand swung out of my way.

"I'm all suited up." I gave him a sickly smile. I'm sure he already knew my status.

"We're ready for you. Open the access hatch and go in."

Right. I gathered my hoses and carefully avoided the red path I had walked on in bare feet, as I stepped over to the hatch. I ordered it open, and reset my suit sensors before I climbed into the sterile access tube. From here on out, I could touch most of my surroundings without receiving or causing contamination.

My next challenge, however, was the tube itself. I had a nova fear of heights, so having to crawl through the clear tube to get to the dorsal paracostal incision, in the saury's left flank, was almost scarier for me than doing the surgery.

Instead of looking down two stories, I tried to concentrate on the scaled, dark green, massive body of my patient ahead of me. Four powerful limbs supported her trunk, which extended into a long skinny tail coiled up on heavy padding on the stage to my right, and a long skinny neck confined in the stocks on the left. The neck, in turn, supported a pathetically small head, looking rather relaxed and silly in its padded clamps.

My surgical approach utilized a standing laparotomy, since sauries are too heavy to lie down for any length of time. Their own weight would crush their internal organs. So the anesthetists couldn't make my patient so sleepy that she'd lay down. She'd just feel very detached. If all went as it should.

"Let's hope your classmates picked the right location for their incision," Dr. Cretchell said cheerfully, bless his black little Tliesjian hearts. "Otherwise you'll have a lot more work finding your way around in there."

Wonderful. I didn't bother to reply.

CHAPTER 2

"Don't worry, Taje," came Jan's wonderfully confident voice, "we got the incision perfectly placed for you. Just grab a big egg case, drop in, and get it done!"

Jan had grown up on a saury ranch on the creature's native planet, and she was rather cute, so I resolved to thank her personally as soon as I finished my surgery. I arrived at the equipment bulge in the tube, which ended in a circular opening, still lined with semitransparent peritoneal membrane, the innermost layer of the saury's abdominal wall. It looked like a professional job to me.

I picked up a collapsed egg case from the top of a pile, and clamped it on the back of my suit, where it fit like a smooth hump. My suit possessed no sharp edges or corners, of course. Even my surgery kit was distributed in smooth, rounded compartments, around my waist and down my arms and legs. I selected a scalpel from a pocket on my right wrist, stepped towards the circular opening, and prepared to slice through the last layer.

"Now, remember," Dr. Cretchell said gleefully, "if you need help, we'll send in an assistant. However, I'd prefer to demonstrate how easily an egg impaction can be handled by just one surgeon, even in an animal of this size."

That gave me strength to cut through vertically first try. I sheathed the scalpel, stretched the cut tissue edges apart, grabbed the frame of the attached hatchway, and inserted myself feet first through the incision.

My gloved hands had become more slippery than I realized from handling the peritoneum, and I lost my grip before I could find solid footing. I slid down and back along the saury's inner body wall, away from my strategic entry point. I knew sauries supposedly possessed a lot of wasted space—evolutionarily driven to simply outgrow, not necessarily out-mass their predators. That was why I didn't have to learn how to use a powered, armored surgical suit to force my way around in here. This fall felt ridiculous.

"Taje, what happened?" Cretchell said. "You're going in the wrong direction."

"I know." I couldn't completely smother the irritation in my voice. "I slipped."

I finally slowed my descent by grabbing onto a section of the huge pale net of fatty, ropy omentum, which continued to slide on down with me, until the tissue curtain reached the limits of its own tethers. All my suit lights had turned on; not much help. The abdominal organs crowded me closely enough to block most of my vision beyond about a meter.

Now it dawned on me that all those lecture and deskcom warnings—regarding expert palpation versus visual cues for finding large animal surgical landmarks—were truly serious. Especially starting so far off course, I might really have to remember the number, size, and location of all those folds, indentations, ridges, flexures, muscular bands, ligaments, vessels, and nerves I once crammed for an anatomy midterm. My face grew hot as I used my saline flush to clear a bluish-green blood stain from the front of my helmet.

"Taje, climb the omentum back up to your entry point," Jan suggested.

"Oh yeah." I vac-headedly goaded myself out of my frozen fear. The fatty tissue net was as slippery as anything else in here. I knew it could withstand some punishment, and I went after each hand and foothold very deliberately, determined not to lose any more ground. Just as I spotted the lit-up, circular incision area, with the origin of my suit hoses dangling down from it, my tail of hoses forced me to another halt.

"Taje, you've stopped." Dr. Cretchell stated the obvious.

"I know." I tried to force my way upward, and felt a sickening, tearing give to the lines that snaked down from my suit. My face fried, and steam coated the inside of my helmet. What had I done?

CHAPTER 3

I swallowed hard. "I caught my lines on something, and I think I'd better go find out what it was." Unless you want to tell me? Obviously my prof didn't, nor did he let Jan say anything. So I spidered back down the omentum, allowing slippage to speed my descent, and resenting the ensuing com silence, since my hologram no doubt showed what the problem was.

I found it. In my fall and return climb I'd managed to loop my hoses around a blood vessel about the same diameter as my skinny arm. I felt irrationally relieved to find my tough suit lines intact. None of my suit alarms had gone off. However, I did discover the vessel torn and gushing blood like a broken pipe. For a ghastly moment I worried about arterial blood loss, until I realized it wasn't pumping.

"It's a vein, and it's bleeding!" I couldn't quite hide the panic and dismay in my voice. "I'll have to try to repair it." Easier said than done, as the bluish-green blood began to coat and clot on my suit compartments, while I frantically reviewed the intricacies of sealing the various layers of a vessel wall of this size. Did it have three, or four—

"It's only a minor bleeder," Cretchell said. "Don't bother to fix it. Just ligate it."

Still clinging to the omentum like a story pirate, I considered this fresh insight with some embarrassment. I couldn't believe I'd lost track of the scale I was working at. Of course it was minor. I pulled a couple ligatures from their pocket on my left medial calf, placed them proximal and distal to the laceration, and triggered them to clamp. The bleeder stopped immediately, and as I clambered back up to my starting point, I got to listen to Cretchell quizzing the class to see which black hole could remember what obscure branch of which vessel I'd torn, and what would have happened if I hadn't clamped it. Probably nothing, it was so small.

"Nevertheless, Taje quite properly returned to identify the problem. Although of course you'd want to do that before pulling on your lines. Gentle tissue handling is a must."

I drew level with the tube hatchway, and pulled out my scalpel to cut my way through the omentum. All my scalpels had safety lines running to their pockets, a nice feature, because I dropped this one twice, before I remembered the saline flush controls for periodically cleaning the fat and blood from my gloves. Along with working in crowded near-darkness, I found it shocking to deal with so many slippery, slimy surfaces. No sim had prepared me for this.

I finished my body-sized hole in the omentum, pulled myself through it, and promptly lost my grip and my balance again. This time I did manage to catch hold of the omentum fairly quickly, and only had to climb back up several meters, while I wondered if the whole class was laughing at my hologram. I turned around very carefully. Seated in the rent with my legs woven into the curtain of tissue below me, I palpated the organs in front of me with wide gentle sweeping motions.

If my classmates had placed their skin incision correctly, I should have the left dorsal ovary (sauries have a total of four), or at least adjacent renal tissue, right in front of my face. I needed the ovary to find its respective left dorsal uterine horn, and I needed the tubular horn to remove an egg. That is, if I wanted to do a very realistic job of it, and follow the horn, from its origin at the ovary, down to where it met up with the left ventral horn. At that point the two joined to form the left lateral horn, and I could scoot along to find the juncture with the right lateral horn, at the body of the uterus. That's the intersection where most saury egg impactions naturally occurred. It's also where intestines or even the colon were more likely to get in the way.

I reminded myself the darker kidney tissue should feel firmer and smoother, with deep creases. The pale ovary would feel softer and more lobulated. If I couldn't feel either, I was probably seated too low, and feeling nothing except bowel loops. On my second fall I'd found myself sandwiched between omentum and intestines, and this did seem to feel different. Not as much as I'd expected. And with my poor range of vision in here, trying to distinguish different organ colors wasn't much use, either. I was considering moving lower to make another comparison, when Dr. Cretchell spoke up again.

"What have you got your hands on?" he demanded.

I started to sweat again. "I'm not sure." How vacfully ridiculous. Normally a real assistant or even a medcom would tell me immediately where I was from sensor data, instead of forcing me to rely on memory and wits alone. Why did I feel so guilty? I started moving caudally out of desperation. I could do a small spot check biopsy. However, that would take time—

"Come on, Taje; commit yourself. We're waiting."

"I'm on ovary now!" I blurted out with relief. Moving just a meter towards the creature's tail end had definitely changed the texture appropriately, and even the color seemed paler. At last I could really move. I followed the ovary dorsally and caudally, to the link with its horn. As my heart began to pound, I managed to clamber aboard and kneel on the long tubular horn, above its various suspensory ligaments, without losing my balance again.

I hunched down in the crowded space below the body wall, and began scooting and crawling down the horn, in search of an egg inside of it by feeling with my whole body. The first soft, immature lumps, the eggs most recently delivered by the ovary, had no shells, so I had to skip them. A messy job to extract, they also wouldn't properly simulate the actual surgery. Impacted eggs usually had enlarged or misshapen shells. The real question was how far I wanted to go. Well, I thought, I wasn't proud. Let's just take one of the first eggs with a decent shell, a little farther on—

"Okay, Taje, we see you're on the horn at last. Now that we've waited this long, where are you going to make your incision?"

Somehow I got the feeling Cretchell didn't want me to take the quick and easy way out. "Uh, you want me to go to where the left and right lateral horns join?" Why, oh why, did I even suggest that? Would I ever get out of here?

"I think you'd find that a little too difficult, since her IV fluids have got her surrounding bladders rather full, and we didn't order any saury-sized urinary catheters for this lab. How about at the left bifurcation?"

"Sure," I said generously, hoping my relief wasn't too obvious. I found myself on a down-slope, and would arrive there soon enough.

When I did get there, I almost didn't recognize the connection of the left dorsal and ventral horns, it felt so distorted and lumpy. My dear professor had managed to hand me a real one.

CHAPTER 4

Could Dr. Cretchell possibly special-order a saury in trouble? Maybe that had even made her cheaper. Or maybe our herd had spawned this problem and needed help. Two eggs had decided to compete for simultaneous access from the two branches that meet up to form the left lateral horn. For added fun, the lower egg was abnormally large, and oddly shaped. To carry out the surgery correctly, I'd have to extract that egg. It would surely never make it out on its own. Well, at least it had arrived underneath the other egg. If I arranged the egg case below, the bad egg would just fall into it.

Easing my cramped body over the side of the left dorsal horn, between suspensory ligaments, and down onto the nearest intestines. It felt like stepping on a sentient practice mat. I had to work at rooting my feet, to keep my balance on the twitching, shifting surface, and I wondered what Dr. Cor would think of this unusual application of his self-defense lessons.

Unclamping the translucent egg case from my back, I sealed its inner and outer cutting rings to the uterine wall, just below the offending egg. I activated only the inner cutting ring, so the egg case would remain attached to the uterine bifurcation, while the malformed egg fell with a caudal circular patch of uterine wall into the case's slowly expanding interior.

I suddenly found myself with two more problems I should have anticipated. First, the egg was too large and lumpy for the average-sized case I'd carried in. Secondly, the more normal egg fell downward too, and came to rest on top of the enlarged egg, making it impossible to close the egg case. I felt like an idiot as I frantically climbed up and shoved the uterine wall from behind, to squeeze the top egg on along into the lateral horn.

The egg was heavy and awkward. I had barely enough room to squeeze it over the lumpy egg. I gradually stimulated the tired, rubbery uterine tissue to resume its contractions, and it took over the job before my clumsy efforts broke the shell. What a dangerous mess that would make!

I was embarrassed I hadn't thought to ask Dr. Cretchell for a look at the saury's physical status before I started the operation. I suppose in return he'd considered it fair game not to warn me ahead of time. Jan's enthusiastic suggestion to take a big egg case came back to haunt me. I presume she'd barely gotten that past our prof before Cretchell had stopped anyone from saying anything more. What a fused trick! Only an absolute vac-head starts a surgery like this without reviewing scans first. And my homework references, not to mention Cretchell's lectures, had made no mention of this particular problem.

What to do? My mind began to blank out in white noise panic.

Well, I'd just have to humiliate myself more by asking for help, since Dr. Cretchell had quit handing out spontaneous suggestions. I'd need an assistant to join me down here with a larger case, or I'd have to go back for one myself. Though by that time, the rest of the class would probably have to rush off to their next lecture.

That's when I realized the distracting little red flashing light on my chin panel meant my com had quit functioning. Either that tug on my lines had done some real damage, or Cretchell expected me to extricate myself from this. I couldn't think of any alternative to climbing all the way back out for a larger egg case, and that would take time. As one of my more intimidating surgery profs had drilled into me, "Time is Trauma" in surgery. A good surgeon would already be closing on this one!

CHAPTER 5

My suit grew clammy as I stared at the full egg case, with the lumpy butt of the egg still palpably above it in the uterine lumen. If only I'd carried in a larger case! I just needed a little more coverage to protect the inside of the saury's belly from contamination. The inside of the uterus, that formed the egg shells, connected with the big outdoors via the filthy cloaca. (As some said, why had nature connected the baby factory with the sewer?) The normally sterile abdomen had few defenses against cloacal and uterine microorganisms that contaminate the eggs' outer surfaces.

Not to mention the risk of breaking the exposed egg shell—with the release of egg proteins foreign to mom's immune system—on my way out. It would take prohibitive amounts of sterile fluids to flush out the mess, and I didn't even want to try to imagine the monstrous scope of an egg yolk peritonitis in here.

More coverage. Hmm. How about if I just borrowed some of the uterine wall itself? There was enough to spare, and if I kept the dirty lumen side down on the egg, and the clean serosal side out, I'd satisfy aseptic technique. I took out a scalpel and went to work with shaking hands. Thank the Galaxy I hadn't activated the outer egg case cutting rim. I cut a generous, roughly circular patch cranial, big enough to cover the rest of the egg, while leaving a large hinge attached to the rim.

Timing was crucial. As soon as I cut the flap free from the uterus, I locked up my contaminated scalpel, slapped the loose uterine flap over the egg case rim, and re-activated the rim seal, all before the egg sack fell down and back against intestines.

Next I had to fix the rents in the left uterine bifurcation. The two holes grew in an alarming manner, as powerful longitudinal uterine muscles retracted the cut edges, and I couldn't fight them barehanded. So I pulled out a couple of expandable tissue bridges from a right thigh pocket, clamped them in place just in time, and turned on traction. That created enough apposition for me to staple the egg case cut and my incision. Crude repairs, fast and effective.

I began to regain my pride as I sat down, leaned back against the egg case, and got it to clamp against my back. All I had to do now was rock forward, stand up, and climb out again.

The malformed egg was too big and too heavy for me. A normal saury egg would outweigh my theoretical backpack weight limit by a hefty, intolerable amount—and this egg was far from normal. Why on Olecranon had Cretchell thought I could do this by myself? No wonder surgeons were supposed to be giants! I could hardly budge the full case, much less stand up and move around with it. I probably looked like Jet flailing around on her back after an accidental fall. Only worse, because at least she could stretch her neck out and tip herself back over with her nose!

Now what? I flopped back against the egg case and wanted to cry. Some surgeon! I was never going to make it. Now I needed to call in an assistant, the com malfunction light was still flashing away in my helmet, and I didn't even know how to turn off the fused distraction. I had excised the egg from the uterus. How could I possibly remove it completely?

CHAPTER 6

Wait a micro—what if I ran a drain down to the ventral abdomen? An exit hole for that wouldn't have to be too big.

My drain wasn't long enough to reach from here. I checked. With a lot of effort—all the muscle power I thought I had, and a little more—I dragged the case and myself laterally, until we started to fall together.

As the case and its contents took me for a ride down between gut loops and omentum, my com malfunction light turned off and the com itself returned to life. I don't think I entirely squelched a cynical grin.

"Tajen—" Cretchell finally used my full first name, "you can't take the egg out the ventral abdomen. The risk of postoperative dehiscence—"

"I know," I said. "I'm not going to." I evilly waited for my prof to ask what I was going to do instead. I knew I had him baffled. He didn't say anything more. He wouldn't admit it, I guessed. I didn't care. He probably knew I wasn't one of his better students. I'd show him I could handle this.

I settled like a giant urolith, unclamped from the egg case, and got out a narrow drain. I stuck one end through a natural hole in the omentum and down against the inner body wall, and turned on the cutting edge of the drain.

Abruptly I found myself in the middle of a quake, with giant bowels threatening to crush me up against the body wall, while the whole world rocked and canted. I struggled and yelled inarticulately (fortunately). So it took a while before Dr. Cretchell's repeated "Use a local! Use a local!" got through to me, and a little while longer before I reached the forgotten control on the drain. All the motion slowly ceased, and I could breathe again, albeit painfully. How many times was I going to embarrass myself before this nightmare ended? Forgetting to use a local anesthetic—

Dr. Cretchell cleared his throat. "Sorry, Taje, we thought we had her deeper. She didn't mind the uterine incision. Are you okay?"

"Yeah," I said, and began to smile. Dr. Cretchell apologizing to me—a miracle! I got the drain end out to the real world—air blew in through the other drain end, and I programmed it to seal to the flap cover and to cut on through the egg shell. I sat back on my haunches to wait.

The egg began draining while lying on its side. I rocked it gently to make sure it was getting lighter. My one remaining big fear was that the contents might be too solid to pass enough mass out through the slim drain. The case did lighten enough for me to tip the small end up, and the immature shell inside collapsed. Soon it became more manageable than a normal egg.

Now how to dispose of the drain without contaminating anything? I pulled on the end attached to my generous uterine flap, and found enough slack to staple a double row in the flap above the drain. That allowed me to slice the drain loose between, right between the two rows of staples with a sterile scalpel. I stuffed the rest into the end of the drain with the handle of my scalpel. Holding up the drain end, I used my scalpel handle to stuff the uterine flap into the egg case and locked the rim closed. I locked up the scalpel and activated the drain end closures. I fed the entire drain on through the saury's body wall, and stapled the inner layers of the small drain incision. Someone else on the outside would have to scrub and close the skin. I couldn't help panting from the work I'd already done.

With the egg case clamped again to my back, I returned to my old friend and climbing net, the omentum. I had to squeeze my way painfully up and cranially between it and the abdominal organs. Now my back was two times wider. A dizzy return to a fear of heights, and a few small tremors, threatened to knock me from my slippery holds. However, I was determined not to fall again, and I kept saline flushes flowing over my gloved hands and feet.

"We're trying to let her wake up a bit now," my teacher said. "You'll be out soon—move about four meters more dorsally and two cranially."

I was following my hoses back, although his directions were a kind gesture. I felt too delighted over finding my lighted entry incision minutes later—and I was breathing too hard from exerting muscles I normally sat on in lectures—to think too many more unkind veterinary student thoughts. Indeed, relief from all the stress made me a bit giddy as I dived head-first back into the clear access tube, and I almost forgot to seal the peritoneal and fascial layers of my entry point.

Throwing all pride to the wind, I dumped the egg case with my helmet in the equipment bulge. My bladder was quite full, and Cretchell now had the access tube spiraled down to the stage floor. I sprayed the tube liberally before shutting my saline line off, disconnected my hoses, and made a fast slide down on my butt.

When I reached the ground, only my best friends still waited there to greet me—Sakken, Jekkan, and my roommate, Giem. I scanned most of the class racing to get to our next class in time, while a few noble students, including Jan, remained behind to close skin incisions under Dr. Cretchell's supervision.

"You did it!" Sakken said, as I stood up and smiled shakily, wondering how to find the nearest restroom. "Dr. Cretchell said you did great!" Jekkan added. Giem embraced me in a powerful Ballophonian hug. My ribs objected strenuously, and I grinned to avoid a grimace.

"He was surprised you knew the modified Wogurton technique," Giem said.

"You're a regular black hole," Jekkan teased me.

"I just—made it up—as I went along," I proudly admitted. "I never—heard of that technique before." My ears began to ring, and I had to bend over to keep from blacking out. Had I stood up too fast? Fortunately, everyone stood too close to let me to fall to the floor.

"Taje, what's wrong?" somebody asked.

"Broken ribs?—I think maybe—I'm developing—a pneumothorax."

Suddenly everyone was yelling too loudly. I could hear alarms blaring, and Dr. Cretchell ordering someone to call the med school.

"What is it?" my friends asked as paramedics strapped me into a stretcher. I was trying very hard to control my bladder, while getting one last sentence out around an oxygen mask.

"Just don't—let—any of the med students—operate on me," I whispered, before I passed out and no doubt cut loose.

CHAPTER 7

I found myself on the fallen slab again, in the underground Shielvellen hallway. Weirdly, it hurt to breathe, although I knew I'd smashed my knee in my fall there.

Then I was stumbling through Shielvellen woods, hunting for myself by the light on my belt, with everyones' panic mixed up with mine. Aerrem found me hanging onto a rough tree trunk. She shook me, and she made me go on. Broken animal skeletons back in the hallway gathered around me for a macabre dance with glowing, glaring eye sockets.

Now the eyes glowed down at me from metal dragons curled around the top of lamp posts, lighting a sadly neglected park. I sat on a cold bench in front of a murky fountain. I fingered my soft new mustache, and felt deeply depressed about the Istrannian deportation order. I was good at running. But they'll find you, the dragons reminded me.

Both of us lost hope.

"What are you doing down there?" Giem stood in the doorway, her arms around a bundle under her cloak.

"I was asleep." I felt relieved to find myself in a hospital gown, on the floor, instead of the Shielvellen hallway where I'd almost died. "I must have fallen out of bed." Wasn't it obvious? I was still bruised and sore, and my bad knee did hurt now. Had I landed on it again? I rubbed my smooth upper lip, where I'd never grow a mustache. I noticed I could breathe easily. Something must have gone right—

"Haven't they told you?"

"What?" I groaned as I struggled to my feet, and sat on the hospital bed. Yes, I could breathe, although it still hurt.

"You've been discharged."

"How long have I been here?"

"Just today—"

"Oh, good." Any longer and I would be in trouble. A missed school day meant losing out on at least a dozen species, and a couple hundred diseases. Missing a week or two meant having to repeat the quarter, if not the whole school year. The expense of educating interplanetary vet students is staggering enough without setbacks, so it's no wonder the med students and their instructors felt pressured to get me out of here.

Giem saw my sour face. "Your scans came out fine." She pointed at the comscreen over my bed. "And Dr. Hako has gone nova, waiting for us to show up for our appointment. We're over an hour late."

"So I'm fine, huh?" I peered back at the screen. I'd come close to cracking ribs, with bruised and torn fibrous periosteum. A chair nearby was draped with my surgical immersion suit, looking like a shriveled, putrid surgeon, stinking from dried saury blood. I glared at it with disgust. "What a relief." I choked back dream tears.

"I brought you some clothes." She dumped my boots on the floor and the rest on the bed. "Do we need to return your surgery suit, or will someone else take care of it for you?"

"How should I know?" I snapped. "I wasn't even conscious on arrival."

Giem wrinkled her nose. "Let's leave it. At least you didn't suffer a pneumo, thank the Galaxy. You just fainted. You should have eaten breakfast before you went to class this morning." That was Giem. My roomie, not one for sympathy. I'd commed that much about her, but I didn't know why. She knew I couldn't eat when I was nervous.

"Thanks a lot," I muttered, and I turned away from her to change.

CHAPTER 8

"Fuse it all, I thought I was over him!" I exploded as we left in the Med Center translift. Giem rolled her eyes as the other passengers stared.

"Shandy?" she said.

"Of course."

"He still hasn't sent you one single letter. You should have been over him long ago!" Giem said. No sympathy, remember? "Where are you going?" she demanded, when I limped away from her, as soon as we made it out of the building.

"I need to go look up something. Hako's waited until the last micro again. If he's so anxious now, you go."

Giem tried to grab me by my jacket—her usual trick—and I shrugged out of it so fast I startled her. I flew down a gravel pathway, fighting the chill wind to escape. I had remembered one detail I could check. Then I'd know.

I ran so breathlessly fast that the student barracks ahead of me sparkled and wavered. Perhaps I wasn't as ready as my hasty Real Doctors (as we called them behind their backs) wanted to believe. I tripped on one lonely weed and crash-landed. I wept. I really had thought I was over Shandy.

Footsteps crunched on the gravel path, and came to a halt beside me. I tried to push myself up from the ground with a gravel-rashed right hand. I used my left hand and got to my knees, and Giem's powerful grip under my armpit hauled me to my feet. She handed over my jacket, I pulled it on, and quickly tucked my injured hand into a pocket.

"Taje, this is our last externship together." Giem kept her grip on me. "Don't you want to hear about it in person?" She did a double-take over my tear-streaked face. Like Shandy, I preferred to avoid public humiliation. "What's this all about?" she asked.

I looked away from her. I knew she wouldn't believe me. "Never mind." I wiped my face dry. I needed to hurry. Dream images vanished so easily. "I'm just so behind on studying for finals now that I can hardly think about anything else." I gave her one truth, and an unrelated complaint. "Besides, why does Hako always have to tell us about our assignment last?" Was it to give us as little time as possible to study for it? "I don't see why you can't just go talk to Dr. Hako, and tell me—"

I didn't get to finish, because Giem changed her hold on me. It still looked polite in front, as if she was gently supporting me. Behind my back she had my left thumb in a simple, incredibly effective lock, threatening even my loose joints with intolerable pain. After a whole long Olecranon year she still hadn't forgotten one of Sensei Cor's more sadistic tricks.

"Great Galaxy, Taje, you're such a fused liar. What did they do to you back in that hospital? I can't believe you'd let homework interfere with personally receiving Dr. Hako's prep talk for our last summer assignment. Or are you still bitter about not getting to return to Big Maxson's Planet?"

Oh Great Universe, remind me of another set of friends I'd tried so hard to file away as nice memories, in my less-than-perfect mind. Giem jolted me out of any retort with an extra nasty thrust, to get me into the toasty vet school admin building and march me into Dr. Hako's office. I hissed at her.

Dr. Hako looked up from his typically cluttered desk, and gave us each an amused stare from his brilliant blue eyes, unprotected by eyelashes, eyebrows, or any other epidermal derivatives on his pale blue nonhuman head. "You finally made it."

"I'm not sure all this effort is worth it," Giem said, as she cleared off one of the chairs in front of Hako's desk. "Taje will probably just ship back to Big Maxson after graduation."

"Like you won't launch right back to your home planet?" I said, bending and moaning trying to empty the seat next to her. We'd exited the Med Center in such a rush I hadn't remembered to pick up any pain meds.

"Ah yes." Hako leaned back in his padded chair." My two loyal vet student teammates. Who wish more than anything else to work together one last time this summer, receiving expensive training for Federation of Intelligent Life interplanetary careers."

CHAPTER 9

Giem sighed, stood up, and sat me down in her chair. She moved the contents of my chair onto the mess on the floor, and sat down heavily in it as I struggled to unseal my jacket left-handed. My ears burned along with the rest of my face, due to the transition from the cold air outside, of course. Neither of us said anything more in the silence that followed.

"What? So quiet?" Dr. Hako said at last. "Haven't you any questions about your externship ready on the launch pad? Did I find you a scenic locale? Will you receive a rewarding vacation at the end? What's happened to my two most demanding students?"

"Taje spent too many hours in the dirtside med school hospital, where they ran experiments on her brain. I think she has grounds for suing. I had to kidnap her to get her here."

"Must have been rather a time-consuming kidnapping. I almost gave up on you."

"The hospital was apparently a little late with your message," I said. "I never got it." Of course, I'd probably slept right through it, and I'd left before checking for stored messages.

"How are you doing, Taje? Not expelled from your sickbed too soon, I hope?" Dr. Hako actually sounded slightly guilty.

"I'm fine. The IV did wonders, and it hardly hurts to breathe," I began sarcastically, and belatedly realized I'd better change my vector ASAP. "My discharge orders promised I'll be in fine shape for travel by next week," I added hastily, trying to look a little less crippled up. Sitting up straight hurt, but I managed it. My injured hand had begun to stick to my coat pocket, so I left it there. "I'm just bruised."

Dr. Hako nodded calmly. "I figured it would take a lot more than a little repro surgery lab mishap in a saury belly to keep you from going this summer. I'm still sorry you had to miss shipping out last summer, for what turned out to be a false alarm, and I'm glad it did prove false."

I shivered. "So am I." I couldn't imagine being stranded for the rest of my life on desolate Olecranon. All because I might have developed a dangerous reaction to the latest, most successful technique for preventing the interplanetary spread of diseases.

I did lose one out of three of my very valuable externships, because some rare and aberrant allergic reactions—a few fatal—had begun to crop up in reports on the still relatively new, mandatory microfloral replacement program for FIL interplanetary travelers.

It didn't matter how often you traveled, and how recently you'd left behind the last of your natural microflora. FIL had become so paranoid about foreign disease transmission that you had to convert your microbiome to a fresh set of powerful, benign, bioengineered micro-organisms, on each interplanetary flight. To protect both you and anyone you encountered. And as someone who'd never handled the rebugging very well (although I'm inclined to blame nerves and spacelag), I was considered at risk, and immediately grounded all last summer for extensive and grueling tests. So my nonexistent family couldn't sue FIL after I died of anaphylaxis in a rebugging tank.

Fortunately, all those tests had come back negative. That was my second scariest summer ever. Despite living in fear of never leaving, I'd enjoyed my substitute internship, although I hadn't traveled beyond our orbital veterinary teaching hospital. I also got full credit, rather than falling behind a full planetary year in my schooling. I knew I should thank Dr. Hako's formidable influence for that.

"At least I got to do animal behavior clinics with you, and help with your research," I said to Dr. Hako.

"If Taje is willing to look on the Bright Side of that whole mess, it means she's trying to butter you up," Giem translated maliciously.

"Butter? Isn't that some toxic human dairy food?" Dr. Hako turned his puzzled gaze from his wristcom translator to Giem. "And after you finish senior clinics next year, do you think you'll seek an internship on Ballophon? We shall be sorry to lose you."

"From government service," I couldn't help adding. "Why don't you force newly accepted vet students to sign a FIL contract before they can start here?"

Giem ignored my sarcasm, and tried to answer Hako honestly. "I still have some time to think about it before my application is due." Right, Giem. And you still have the shorter haircut you came back with from Ballophon, where it was all the rage. "I guess some of the clinicians I worked for last summer were impressed enough they want me back."

"They gave you outstanding evaluations," Dr. Hako said. "If you apply, I have little doubt of the outcome."

Giem was an utterly brilliant student. If I hadn't become her assigned roommate and close friend, I'd have envied her for it. I couldn't even swim my way through a demo salpingotomy without getting my chest mashed by a saury's dinosaur-sized guts.

"Well, I just wish I had that much confidence."

I shook my head at Giem. Curiously, the only person who didn't totally believe in Giem was Giem herself. "Dr. Hako means you have the right connections," I offered my own nasty translation.

"Connections—are important," Hako said. "I can't deny it." He was one of the few professors we could talk to with this much honesty, and we admired him no end for it. Although of course we never told him so to his face.

"That's not the question, I guess." Giem's voice revealed her distressed uncertainty. "If I do have a good chance of getting the internship, I want to be as certain as I can be that I want it, before I apply. I do realize how unprepared our training here will still leave us. There's just so much to know and too little time to learn it all!

Another whole planetary year in an internship after our senior year here, before I can enter the Real Worlds, seems an awful lot to commit to. I hope, Dr. Hako, all this doesn't make you regret allowing me to return to Ballophon last summer for my sophomore externship, after I found out Taje couldn't go anywhere."

"I knew how homesick you'd become, and you're not the first student we've risked it with. At least you returned to complete your Interplanetary D.V.M. degree."

"Some don't?" I asked, though I didn't feel nearly as shocked as I would have as a prevet. It was so difficult to get into this school, that until you began to experience the arduous pain of it for yourself, you couldn't imagine what drove students to quit in the middle. And what courage it took to do so, considering the high expectations everyone held for you.

Dr. Hako gave us a human-style nod. "After all, our location isn't exactly the most hospitable. Maybe for good reason—after six standard years, we wouldn't want you becoming too attached to Olecranon to leave. How about it, Taje; are you at least going to stay with the program, and make yourself useful to more than one world, aboard a FIL Ship after you graduate?"

I studied my dust-smeared boots uncomfortably. "I thought we came to talk about our plans for this summer?"

"That was a nova attempt at evasion," Giem said tactlessly. "I admitted my uncertainties. The least you can do is answer his question truthfully."

Oh thanks, Giem, I wanted to say. During an uneasy pause, Hako simply sat patiently waiting for my answer.

"I don't know either," I said at last. "Only I think I'm even more lost. I know I could benefit from an internship for another planetary year right here, but I have to escape this world soon or I'll fuse.

"Anyway, I commed I could continue my education under a senior FIL Ship veterinarian, and I also hoped I'd have a friend in the same Ship with me. Of course, if I have any homesickness, it's for traveling aboard a FIL SEAR Ship. I don't know if I'm ready to go it alone, especially on the spying end of it."

"Shhh—" Giem began to hush me up on that supposedly secret subject—

"It's not really spying—" Dr. Hako once again attempted his euphemistic denial—

"Whatever you want to call it," I said, "since we must go somewhere new this summer, will our next assignment require any use of those extra classes we keep sneaking off to, without the rest of our classmates?"

Dr. Hako's face went blank while Giem's lit up with anticipation. We'd find out whether she'd feel disappointed too. While I'd had an impossibly nostalgic desire for a return to the world and friends of our freshman externship, Giem had longed for at least one more chance at a new adventure.

"Well," Dr. Hako answered me at last, "I'm sending both of you to a very busy station with a lot of traffic, so you might as well practice your powers of observation. If you have any time left for it. I would expect that of you anyway."

Sufficiently ambiguous to allow Giem hope; or was it just a nice little teaser with no substance? Talk about evasions—and Giem didn't even call him out on it.

I sighed. "Where is it? What will we do? I'm sure you know Big Maxson still needs a lot of help," I couldn't resist saying.

"Taje, will you leave it alone, already!" Giem said.

"It's true—"

"You'll work in an animal export quarantine station on Enchantment," Dr. Hako interrupted before we could argue more. "Have you heard of it?"

My eyes widened. "Enchantment is currently the only source of crater pups, a local pest and the latest galactic pet craze." Perhaps being partnered with the smartest person in our class had its advantages. This was big! Far bigger than our little project on Big Maxson's Planet. At least until the latter had become a much more serious investigation. I smiled at my teammate. "Giem, you wanted to work with pets this time, instead of farm animals!"

"They're wild caught, they don't reproduce in captivity, and they don't live all that long," Giem added her disappointed, encyclopedic knowledge. "Crater pups evolved in a geologic formation called the Rash, one corner of an Enchantment continent pockmarked ages ago by a cluster of meteorite strikes. The impact craters also contain spectacular 'flower rings.' Crater pups eat the flowers."

"Also a major export," I said. "Can you believe it? There are people so nova rich they support a whole industry based on the interplanetary export of bouquets. Crater pups supposedly tame easily. Anyway, maybe we'll figure out why they don't reproduce in captivity or live long, and we'll become famous," I said.

"You've got to be kidding," Giem said.

"Well, yeah. Bright Side, Giem, Bright Side."

"I see neither of you has lost all contact with the Real Worlds." Hako at least sounded amused. "I received a request for help from one of Enchantment's export stations some months ago. Like any new quarantine setup, the mortality rate is higher than anyone would like, and the stations are too overworked and understaffed to do much about it. This is definitely junior level work. You'll be expected to apply all you've learned in your class work to improve survival rates, and this project should keep you quite busy indeed."

"You mean it should keep us out of trouble, and give us enough work to make up for our first summer?" I teased him.

"Hmm, yes. Don't expect a lot of free time with this one."

"Trying to make me miss Big Maxson?"

"Taje, can't you *ever* give up on that subject?" Giem said.

"Not until I ask Dr. Hako for a favor." I gathered up my courage.

"Oh?" He widened his view out of one eye, while Giem stared at me curiously.

"Well, seeing as how it was your idea to send us to Big Maxson's Planet in the first place, and noting all the wonderful free work I did for you last summer, not to mention the connections you have if you run into any problems—"

"What do you want?" both Hako and Giem said.

"Dr. Hako, could you please take care of Jet for me?"

"Me?" I'd definitely surprised Hako. "Uh, can't you find a suitable summer student pet sitter?"

"Really, Taje, haven't you tried contacting anyone?" Giem sounded embarrassed.

"Please, Dr. Hako, she means so much to me. I couldn't trust anyone else with a Big Maxson pet, and you're an interplanetary veterinarian—"

Hako looked a bit nonplussed by my pleading. I could guess no vet student had the audacity ever before to make such a request of him. He blinked his electric blue eyes. "Okay." He surprised both of us. "You've made your case. I suppose Dr. Bioh could advise me in a wrench. You'll have to spend time properly instructing me."

"Of course. Thank you so much!" I oozed gratefully, while eyeing my wristcom translator settings nervously.

"Well, speaking of veterinarians," Giem frowned, "we'll have some vets to work under this time, won't we?"

"Certainly," Hako said. "They're mostly very involved in administration—close adherence to FIL animal exportation laws—while simply trying to keep up with the tremendous demand for interplanetary shipment health certificates. It's a tricky balance, caught as they are between suppliers and exporters. So they'll probably expect you to carry a fair amount of responsibility, and work under a lot of self-direction. I'm sure you're both capable of handling that in your own unique fashions."

At this point Dr. Hako's face became very unreadable, which usually makes me suspect he's feeling most highly amused.

"So you consider our working methods rather unique, huh?" I said, frustrated enough by the lack of answers to carelessly forget my very recent gratitude. "Have you planned a new set of baby sitters for us? Want us to ignore any more big-time criminals? Perhaps we should leave our new stunners here—"

"Pardon us, homework is calling." Giem stood and hauled me up by my coat collar, but that didn't quite throttle the rest of my snide remarks, unfortunately.

"Or maybe we should just relax," I said, "since FIL authorities can't seem to hang onto the bad guys we catch for them anyway—"

Dr. Hako slammed his hands down on his desk, and my big mouth froze in shock, while Giem let go of me. We sank back into our seats. We both knew we were in Hako's "hot oil" now. We'd never seen him lose his temper before.

"Bad Guys—that's another human expression, isn't it?" His beady blue gaze burned holes in our faces. Sweat dripped down Giem's forehead and my armpits. "It's despicable! No one—and I mean no one!—ever gets up in the morning deliberately determined to injure the universe. We're all trying to do our best, whatever it may look like to an outsider."

CHAPTER 10

We sat swallowing air, while a couple tortuous minutes crawled by. Satisfied at last by our repentant, mortified silence, Dr. Hako raised his hands, and Giem and I cautiously stood back up.

"What's that?" Hako stared at the blood seeping through my jacket pocket.

"Uh, just a little, uh, riddleberry jam, I, well, spilled on myself, at breakfast."

"Thanks, Dr. Hako," Giem interrupted my strained story, "for putting so much effort into our assignment and—" she towed me through the doorway—"for sending us together, once again."

The door slid shut behind us, cutting off the ghost of a snort, and a fresh odd saying to add to Hako's list—something about being wary of enchanted forests.

Giem turned to me. "Let me see that."

"What?"

"Your hand." She tore it out of my pocket.

"Ouch!" My entire palm was throbbing and bleeding through ground-in dirt.

"Come on. We're taking you back to the Med Center."

I swallowed hard. "Giem, it's just a scrape."

"I won't let you endanger our last trip together!"

"Quit calling it that! We do plan to become a team someday, don't we?"

"If you don't kill yourself from infection or get yourself thrown out of the program first."

"It's not going to become infected. I've had enough protective microbe conversions, before the R.D.s got too scared to tank me last summer. And we all know rebugging lasts longer than FIL is willing to concede. Here, I'll show you." I led her into a nearby bathroom and sluiced the wound. Sure enough, it cleaned up nicely, even if I had to hold back more tears over the raw stinging.

"Convinced?" I choked out.

"Taje," Giem frowned, "I thought you learned how to fall."

"That's blue belt material, and I haven't earned my purple belt."

"What? And a whole school year of elective training beyond me?" she said, as we left the bathroom and headed for the main doors.

"I haven't found my center." I slapped my coat seal left-handed against the wind as we stepped back outside. I was Cor's slowest student, and although he showed me nothing besides endless patience, I didn't need anyone rubbing it in. "And I miss my best practice partner."

"I'm sorry," Giem said in a tone of voice that said she wasn't really. "I just couldn't justify another year of martial arts on top of stunner lessons."

"I know," I'd heard her reasoning many times before, "I just wanted to catch up with everyone else, and earn my orange belt—now where are you going?"

"I think we'd better detour through the cemetery before we return to our homework."

Where Giem would remind me again—with graphic examples—of how short life is, and how worthless it is to spend it worrying. I nodded in defeat.

We entered under the rickety, vine entwined, arched gateway of the old military cemetery, and paced our way up and down aisles of the dead. Endless markers were the only accomplishment of those who'd nearly destroyed this planet, before their living comrades agreed to peace to join FIL. What a cheerless place. A century from now, who would care what any of us had done?

We talked a little about our new externship before we left. Were either of us thrilled? I'm not sure.

When the sun set and the sky darkened, we left. The nearest campus light lit up as we passed under it. Now I remembered a mission beyond my oppressive homework. "Fuse it all. I have to get back." Something about lights. Park lamps? Dragon lanterns!

I ran for our dorm, and for once Giem had to work at keeping up with me. Once we reached our room, I couldn't convince her. She didn't consider long distance esper dream intersection possible, even when I first described and then proved the lamps existed on Istrann, in a park right across the plaza from the embassy where Shandy had grown up. My current roommate annoyed me by suggesting I'd dream-dredged a forgotten detail from one of Shandy's stories, long ago. I said Shandy hadn't told stories about his home. Of course she didn't believe that either.

Giem sat down at her deskcom and sniffled over a message from her parents including a holo of her horse, Swiftsure. She glanced at me. "Nothing from Shandy, right?"

"Right." Rub it in, Giem.

"What about Aerrem? Or Krorn?"

"Of course." I had received a holo from Aerrem, holding Dizzy on a leash. I sniffled and Giem peeked over my shoulder. Krorn played his flute for me.

"So remember you have other friends," she said. "Forget about Shandy."

Easier said than done.

I lost myself in studying for finals, and then we had a lot of packing to do.

CHAPTER 11

I couldn't see much of Port City or its weather from the tiny shuttle viewscreen in the seat back in front of me before we landed. I was feeling too sick to pay much attention to it. All I could tell was that Enchantment had a much more sprawling spaceport than Big Maxson. On its landing pad, our shuttle connected directly to a sealed jetway, extending from the Port City terminal. We had to use our wristcoms with proper medical codes to get through the jetway airlock into the long windowless hallway, plastered with bright, flashing, headache-inducing holo ads for nearby hotels, restaurants, and whatever else tourists might want.

Giem and I followed in a line of passengers to our gate lounge, one of many open waiting areas around the periphery of the bustling, echoing building. There we scanned around carefully for the Altruskan veterinarian depicted in the holo Dr. Hako had given us.

"Do you see her?" I said, as someone yellow-orange and sour-smelling bumped into me, apologized and moved on, and was quickly replaced by a more spiky passenger, less polite. "Ouch." We'd come to a halt in the midst of the outflow into our lounge, and we obstructed traffic. Among all the milling species capable of interplanetary travel, I did spot some Altruskans, none looking like our expected host.

"Dr. Emmel? No, I don't see her either," Giem said, who had a better view, nearly a head taller than me. "I don't think she's here." She sounded surprised, even though our first externship had started this way.

"Maybe she sent someone else to pick us up," I said, as a wave of dizziness roared over me. Please let this end soon, I thought.

"Unless they're late, I doubt it," Giem said. "Our shuttle delivered us right on time."

"Let's sit down for a moment, then. Maybe Dr. Emmel's just running late." People still jostled us, as friends, relatives, and business associates rushed to greet each other between rows of bright pink seats in the black-carpeted lounge. My vision threatened to turn the same dark color as the carpet.

"I'm sure glad this rebug reaction of yours is nothing serious," Giem said, after glancing at me. "Why don't you sit down here and watch for her, while I retrieve our luggage."

"That's a nova lot for you to manage." I objected politely because my luggage didn't have anti-grav, unlike Giem's. I promptly sat down anyway in the nearest seat. Gradually the sparkles cleared out of my vision, and I may even have scanned a distant Big Orange Cube sliding swiftly down an exit corridor. I blinked and the BOC was gone.

"I'll rent a cart," Giem said. "Just don't move until I get back. And hand me your wristcom, so I can claim your luggage. I'll get the local time cycle downloaded into both of our wristcoms."

"Okay. Thanks," I said, although I knew she might also use my wristcom to pay for the cart. Well, it was only fair.

Shifting over a couple seats after Giem left, to one more obviously designed for a human rear end, I leaned back, grateful for a chance to cry a few tears in private.

I hadn't told Giem. More than spacelag, small changes in gravity and atmosphere, and our shift in the last rotation through our paraship's rebug tanks had gotten me this time. Under general anesthesia for the latter, I'd received an even more vivid dream of desolate, wrenching emotion, clearly connected with Shanden Fehrokc.

The dream images had faded as soon as the anesthetics faded from my body. But the feelings had shipwrecked themselves in my brain, where they continued to oppress me. Now I thought I better understood how Shandy suffered from esper-level empathy, without any innate or learned controls or blocks. Great Galaxy, I'd nearly talked myself into deleting the first episode, back on Olecranon, as entirely my own dream.

Giem seemed to take a nova long time. Perhaps she had run into Dr. Emmel? Or maybe it was just my own distorted sense of time—

"I'm back!"

CHAPTER 12

"Huh?" I jolted upright, startled to discover I'd dozed off.

"Good thing neither the good doctor nor any of her minions have arrived," Giem said, parking an aircart filled with familiar luggage in front of me. She sat down in the next seat, and handed over my wristcom.

"Not here? How do you know?"

"Here, take this." Giem tossed me a vending machine carton. "I bet you didn't even scan the holo page I tried, without any success. Go on, drink it. I know you haven't had anything today, and we'll have to travel more soon."

I reluctantly pulled out the clear straw to try it. The juice looked a bit like thickened, opaque bile, and thankfully had only a bland nectar flavor. I asked Giem to explain. Had Emmel at least left us a message under Information?

"No." Giem peeled open a candied nutrition square, that looked and smelled disgusting. "I called the quarantine station—"

"Alright. Direct action."

"Well, I wish. I had a difficult time with their secretary. Dr. Emmel wasn't there and it didn't know whom to refer me to." Giem took a ravenous bite from her machine snack.

"So she's on her way?"

"I didn't get that impression. I think there's some sort of mix-up, and we'll probably have to show up personally to get it sorted out. I found a tube ride we can catch in about an hour. That will take us to the station. I bought us tickets for it, and left an Info message for Dr. Emmel, just in case. The ride will take another couple hours—"

"A couple hours!" At tube car speed? Where were we going? I began to regret not bothering to study any local maps.

"The station's apparently rather remote—at the end of the line, in fact. I think we should move to the tube gate lounge, to make sure we don't miss our ride."

I sighed, folded and stuffed my empty carton into the recycle slot in the arm of my chair. We followed holo signs and crowds across the vast noisy space to a massive row of translifts, and took one across and down several levels.

It dumped us into a broad, busy corridor, lined with the usual loud junky mixture of duty-free shops selling ugly luggage, imported drinks, expensive jewelry and wristcoms, cheap 3D holo thrillers, cephalic pain remedies, and gaudy souvenirs, supposedly edible and otherwise. Suspiciously, port translifts rarely debark directly anywhere important. I felt sorry for the poor little old purple Telmid, with tattered antennae, slowly limping behind her cart, as we dodged around her with the rest of the crowd.

Bright yellow seats and more black carpeting graced our tube gate lounge. I dropped into a seat. I could guess the presence of about an equal mix of locals, business people, foreigners, tourists, and traders, judging roughly by clothing. One couldn't make any conclusions by species, I recalled. A relatively newly discovered FIL planet, Enchantment lacked any intelligent natives or extreme natural dangers. So it was wide open for colonists, development, and all sorts of trouble.

At least, that's what I imagined. In an effort to cheer myself, I gently patted my new little stunner, holstered under my shirt. Probably completely unnecessary. We couldn't resist trying out our newly earned licenses, subtle extra coding in our wristcoms allowing us to carry past various FIL checkpoints. When everything is going wrong, think of it as an Adventure. You can't have an Adventure without Things Going Wrong, I reminded myself. I needed to knock on wood, but unfortunately there was none in sight.

"You've been awfully quiet since our rebugging," Giem said, from her seat beside mine, after giving her armrest screen a cursory review. Full of travel, luggage, and sensory stimulant ads, for those unwilling to pay for actual entertainment. "What's the matter?"

She wasn't vac-headed, and neither was I. I knew she meant beyond my usual spacelag. "I had another— dream—with Shandy."

"Back in the shuttle gate lounge, when you fell asleep?"

"No. In the tank."

"Nobody remembers dreams from the tanks."

"Exactly," I agreed grimly. "This seems a little beyond coincidence."

"Yes, it does."

What did that mean? I didn't want to ask. I hadn't expected her to believe me.

"Well, try to relax," she said. "Soon we'll get to see a whole new planet, one with a reputation for some great natural scenery." Giem clapped me on the shoulder.

We couldn't get seats in the crowded tube car. I clung to a pole, hung my head to keep from fainting, and worked at not throwing up on my luggage at my feet. When we got seats at last, I fell asleep, and suddenly Giem threw my luggage from the overhead rack in my lap and at my feet.

"We're here!" she said.

"CRATER ONE, Enchantment Animal Export Quarantine Station One," lit up over the exit doors.

"There's more than one?" I said, horrified, wondering if we'd even come to the correct station after this much effort.

"I believe our prep data mentioned more than one quarantine station, and this is the main one." Giem confidently led us to a translift that took us back up to the surface. As we exited, bright sunlight and a heavy, sweet perfume hit us in a heady double wave. I blinked as I adjusted to the light sparkling off an unexpectedly extravagant plaza. It was laid out in neat little squares, with swaying blue-green trees, wooden benches, multi-hued flowering shrubs, and sculptured fountains flashing against a clear blue sky.

Giem and I smiled at each other. We wound our way through the plaza to a large pale gleaming building, with metal letters across its front spelling out our destination again.

The clear main doors let us into the lobby, where the front comsec asked us to download our wristcom ID's. It mulled their data for a long minute. "With whom do you wish to make an appointment?" it finally said.

I looked at Giem in surprise, and she shrugged at me as if to say "See what I mean?" She turned and patiently said "Our business is stated in our wristcoms. We have an appointment with Dr. Emmel."

I glanced around the room, and saw no open doorways to the rest of the building. No one sat in the dark-brown carpeted lobby, despite various blue and green chairs, small pale blue tables with clear green vases full of exquisite fresh-cut flowers, and intriguing holos of prize crater pups set into wood-paneled wall niches.

"I'm sorry, your appointment is not on our schedule," the comsec said. "Our apologies for any inconvenience. Do you wish to make an appointment now?"

"Okay," Giem relented. "How soon can we see Dr. Emmel?"

"I'm sorry, there's no such person in my directory. Are you certain you have the correct address?"

"Does your directory include all Enchantment Animal Export Quarantine Stations?" I said.

"I can check my ancillary directories."

"Please do so." Groan. Here it goes. We're really supposed to be somewhere else. How will we get there if the tube stops here?

"I have no such name listed."

CHAPTER 13

What? "Well, how about the head of this station?" I said.

"The Director is not currently available for public appointments. Public Relations Officer Andrek is available next week on—"

"Our business is with the director, today," Giem said, in a dangerously patient tone. "We're interplanetary veterinary students from Olecranon, reporting to start work now for this facility."

"Our Employment Officer is unavailable today. She can be seen—"

"We must see the director," I insisted. "Today. Now. As soon as possible. Tell the director we won't leave this lobby until we do." And with that, we stepped back, to set our luggage on seats beside us, while the secretary blinked to itself and shut up.

"What's going on?" I said quietly. "Did some glitch totally erase us?"

"And Dr. Emmel?" Giem said. "I don't know. Maybe we got sent to the wrong planet—"

"That's impossible—"

"I know. Relax—"she must have heard the sudden panic in my voice—"I was teasing. I'm sure there's a logical explanation. I'm just too tired to com it."

If she was too tired, we were really in trouble. I stood up to stretch my legs, and wandered around the room. The holos were only cheap stills, and still looked cute. Crater pups had lap-sized, plump little tailless bodies, with four short stout legs ending in padded paws. Sharp little eyes peered out from their pointy little faces, adorned with prick ears. The crater pups' most striking feature was their brilliant, shimmering, feathery-textured coats, evolved to blend in with the equally fantastic wildflowers of the crater-pocked "Rash."

However, our anatomy studies revealed crater pup coat structures bore very little relation to avian feathers. Three-sided pseudofeathers rotated on central shafts manipulated by a complex set of interlocking, subcutaneous muscles. When a coordinated nervous system reflex suddenly revolved the whole set of pseudofeathers, the result was supposed to be breathtaking, as each crater pup could in this manner turn one of three vivid colors. The holos disappointed me, not showing this color shift, and I still feasted my artist eyes on the sample hues displayed.

As I studied the last holo on the right, a door nearby slid open so suddenly I jumped back. The secretary simultaneously spoke again. "Please go down this hall, and enter the third office on the right. Dr. Nilod will see you at once. Thank you."

I rushed back to my seat for my bags and, with Giem, entered the empty hallway open to us. The third door on the right slid open.

"Please come in," said an older man's voice. We entered his neat office, found seats before his desk, and dumped our luggage at our feet. The grey-haired, balding, portly human in a white lab coat over a business suit seemed surprised by the packs and bags lying on his immaculate, grey-carpeted office floor, and he looked up with an apologetic expression on his face.

"I understand you are the two junior interplanetary veterinary students Dr. Emmel requested from the FIL training program on Olecranon."

Great Galaxy, he understands. Giem and I just looked at each other in exasperation. Had I felt more alert, I might have thought of a feisty reply. Instead, I more politely didn't say anything.

The man coughed on some embarrassment. I took some secret delight in it, until I heard his next line.

"Unfortunately, Dr. Emmel failed to tell anyone else about her unauthorized request, before she resigned her post at Station Three, and shipped offworld a week ago."

Great Universe, how could this get any worse? A wave of cold nausea crashed into me.

Giem asked a less obvious question. "Are you the director of this station?"

"No, Dr. Morbe's not here today. And he's the Director for the entire Enchantment Animal Export Quarantine Services Corporation. I'm Dr. Nilod, head of Veterinary Services for

Quarantine Station One. I apologize for the time it took our secretary to unscramble the situation adequately to notify me about your arrival. I don't normally handle this sort—"

"The situation," I took a deep breath, trying to draw energy from a small pit of bubbling anger buried deep below my exhaustion and fear, "is this. We are Tajen Jesmuhr and my teammate, Giemsan Fane. We've just finished our last junior veterinary interplanetary final exams and traveled all the way from Olecranon, to serve you in an externship we have to complete, before we can begin senior year clinics. That's a lot of effort just to get this news from you, and we're tired, suffering from spacelag, and in need of accommodations right now. What can you do for us?" Like reinvent a job for us?

I found myself hoping he couldn't see that I was trembling in my seat.

"Maybe you could find some sort of work experience for us here," Giem added. "We're free labor, except for room and board."

"Maybe. I'll have to speak to the Director."

"How soon can you do that?" I said.

"Oh, he'll be back tomorrow."

"Then we should check back here tomorrow—what time?"

"Uh, how about 18:00?"

"Okay, so can you get us an immediate hotel reservation nearby? And tell us how to get there?" I stood up. I could tell I was making Giem uncomfortable with my pushiness. I'd gone beyond caring. I needed a good bed, now!

"Certainly. I'd put you up myself if I had room." He turned to his deskcom. "Oh, good," he said with obvious relief, "our local Enchanted Inn still has vacancies."

CHAPTER 14

"I guess I'm glad you finally woke up enough to get mad," Giem said, as we stepped back outside minutes later.

"You surprised me," I told her. "Weren't you just as tired of the run-around?"

"Sure."

"Then why didn't you blast him first with one of your nova logic attacks?"

Giem gave me a double-take sort of look, and shrugged and smiled. "I reserve those for you. I'm not that bold with strangers."

"Oh, that's generous of you," I said. "And hard to believe. Why, the way you can instantly zap the weak reasoning of anyone in vet school—"

"With people I know and have grown comfortable around, after three planetary years. You didn't see me my first days at Ballophon U. And probably had too many adjustments to make yourself, to remember much about our first days at the U of O. I'm surprised you never discovered I locked onto you for one good, if rather dangerously unpredictable, reason."

"Only one reason? What?"

"You're my secret weapon!"

She had to use her peripheral vision to dodge my attack, on our way down the nearest street.

Every civilized construct on this planet looked brand new—and probably was—I reflected on our six-block walk through the small, fairly busy town, nestled in Crater One. Tantalizing slivers of bright blossoming colors on surrounding crater walls flashed between buildings, and the warm breeze teased our noses with sweet floral scents, as we dodged other pedestrians and passed by shop displays full of camping and hunting equipment, and flashy holo ads for various tours.

We soon realized people must use this little crater city as the major launching point for scenic tours of the Rash. The Enchanted Inn, on one edge of town, also had recreational facilities, including a park, a swimming pool, a duckball field, a rental garage, and best of all, I decided by the sudden change in smells, a stable. The whole complex was built low and sprawling—I guessed building up and down wasn't so urgent on new planets— and we had to do a bit of slow wandering to find the main entrance. We entered a vast, black flag-stoned, sky-lit lobby.

I stopped at a generous, low-walled, pond with a musical fountain, in the middle of the lobby, while Giem strode ahead to check us in. Hypnotizing electric blue, purple, and pink frilly-finned fish lazily swam the channels between crystalline rocks set into the clear water of the black pool.

"Too bad Grek isn't here." Giem chuckled, startling me out of my trance as she tugged on my arm. I objected that the Big Maxson native would know better than to fish here, while she led me to a quiet hall off the lobby. "Of course. Where's your sense of humor today?"

"I think I left it on Olecranon." I tried to smile as I stumbled over the transition to plush grey carpeting.

"Too bad." Giem halted us at long last before a numbered door that recognized her wristcom and let us in. The room was only a little larger than our dorm room, so the two beds, done in flowery purple, blue, and white, nearly filled it. Giem dropped her luggage on the bed nearest a set of clear back doors. Through them, I caught a glimpse of a small raised porch, overlooking a lush backyard garden with a scattering of lacy black metal restaurant tables and chairs.

"By the way," Giem said, cracking a door to stick her head out and sniff the breeze, "I found out at the front desk Dr. Nilod did nothing more than reserve us two of the finest rooms here." She closed the door and turned back around, as the smell of fresh blossoms wafted over me. "We're expected to pay for this."

"Two rooms?" I asked blankly, stashing my stuff at the foot of the bed closest to the front door. I peeled off my shoes, and stretched out on my bed with a satisfied sigh.

"When I found out the bill is on us, I had them switch us to one of their least expensive double-bed rooms." Giem sat down heavily in the one armchair in our room. "It's still no bargain, but I didn't want to put us through a search for a cheaper place today. We can check into that tomorrow morning."

"We can't pay for our whole four months!" I was startled to find myself close to tears. On top of all the other mishaps today, this news felt overwhelming. "I don't care if this was an unauthorized employee request—Nilod should take responsibility for what Emmel did!"

"I know." Giem brushed her thick brown hair back out of her golden face. "If they don't give us proper work, room, and board within a week, we ought to trade in our return tickets for the earliest possible flight back to Olecranon. And I'm sure Dr. Hako will make our school reimburse us for what we do have to spend here."

"Dr. Hako—he should have looked into this better!"

"I'm sure he did his best. Come on, Taje, this isn't the end of the galaxy, you know. You probably just need some solid food in your stomach, to start seeing the humor of it." Giem stood up. "I'm going to shower, and then let's try the garden restaurant out back."

My stomach recoiled at the idea. Although she was probably right, I reflected as I lay on my bed waiting for her. Maybe some nourishing soup would give me a fresh perspective on this whole ludicrous mess. I hoped so.

CHAPTER 15

A few steps beyond our back porch, and down on the black flag-stoned, meandering garden path, we found an empty table surrounded by flowering shrubs. A large bowl of warm vegetable soup and fresh-baked rolls eased their way into my stomach. I had almost forgotten what it was like to soak up some real sunshine, and I feasted my eyes on intricate, colorful blossoms that had fallen randomly on the table.

I almost objected when our autoserver abruptly brushed most of the flowers off the table, after returning with Giem's order, a crater pup sandwich she wanted to try before we got a chance to become fond of the creatures. (Admittedly, Enchantment had meat cell culture vats. Giem was still afraid eating this wouldn't feel right later on.) I gave the back of the retreating server an annoyed look, while Giem picked up her thick sandwich from a bed of chips, and took a healthy bite out of it.

"How is it?" I said politely, although I knew the rebugging tanks made her so hungry she'd probably choke down krazzle claws if the menu had nothing else.

"Great. If crater pup pet-appeal ever fails, their owners can just croak 'em and cook 'em!"

We snickered evilly. Of course we didn't share this typical veterinary humor at other people's tables. It was as vile as it was deceptively callous.

"Truthfully, it does remind me of skelfy from my home planet. And I can't beat this view."Giem sat with her back to the inn. That meant she got to look out between some of the garden flora around us.

On the opposite side of the table, I turned in my seat to gaze at the not-too-distant crater wall, sporting what looked like artificially colored geological layers. These were the famous "flower rings" lining the walls of many of the Rash craters, in bands of color separated by subtle vegetative preferences for various microclimates and mineral layers. The latest rage for holo-posters and tour groups, along with floral customers.

"I wonder how long it'll last?" I said, thinking of the oncoming fall season we'd arrived for. Too bad summer didn't hit every planet at the same time. Although a nova rich bum could use paraspace travel to spend life following summer seasons around—

"Enchantment flowers don't die at the end of summer— they adapt, to all except a few of the winter months," Giem said. "They're more than just reproductive organs, as you'd know if you'd done more of your homework. No one understands their total importance. Even in deep winter they just tuck themselves away for a short while."

"I meant the good weather." My spirits, recently improving from my traveling naps and filling stomach, took a dive with Giem's lack of trust in my prep work. "I did my homework."

"Well, Dr. Hako knows how much you hate chilly weather. Don't you remember his assurances in the prep material he gave us?"

"This isn't supposed to be served cold!" An obviously irritated voice, from behind the towering bushes to my right, interrupted our potential skirmish. I had to grin at the randomly appropriate complaint. "And don't just go back and re-warm it. At this price, I expect a replacement!"

Astonishment zapped my grin. Giem and I stared at each other, only momentarily distracted by an autoserver scuttling briefly into sight, and then disappearing through a hotel service door. I laughed, slapping our black metal table. "It's got to be him. How typical! Always fighting with someone or something—"

"Shhh. He'll hear you. And it can't be him." Giem wasn't laughing as she set down the remains of her sandwich. "The galaxy's too big for a coincidence like this. Davin Mohrogh isn't the only person in FIL who likes to argue."

CHAPTER 16

Giem looked at me meaningfully, so I put a clamp on a verbal retort and scooted my metal chair back. It caught on the edge of a flagstone, and I had to scramble to not go loudly crashing down with it.

"So what do you plan to do?" Giem said, in a hushed voice, as I bent over to pick my chair up. "Practice spying on some innocent luncher through the bushes?"

"Of course," I whispered back cheerfully. "Don't you want to know for sure whether it's him?"

"I suppose anyone who believes in dream transmission through paraspace would consider a nova chance like this."

I didn't honor that with a reply. Instead I squeezed my way between close bush branches, cluttered with big soft green leaves and dusty blue and purple flowers. The dust turned out to be copious amounts of pollen, and a thick blue cluster slapped my face, when I disturbed a spring-loaded branch blocking my view. I sneezed.

And I was abruptly sucked out of Giem's view—quite a sight for her, no doubt—as I was yanked through the bushes and thrown to the ground. Where I lay looking up at the nozzle of my own stunner.

The muscular, black-haired trader bent over me, staring with shocked surprise, and then he laughed.

"It's my FIL vet spy friend from Big Maxson!" Davin exclaimed. "Taje! Where's your partner in crime?"

"Right here," Giem said, as she stomped around the clump of bushes with a scowl on her face. "Davin? Is that really you blowing our cover out loud?"

Davin continued to laugh as he removed his right knee from my stomach and stood up, tossing my stunner up and down with his scarred hand, and gave Giem a disgustingly handsome and dashing look before barely glancing at me. "New toys," he said, "and still getting caught—"

"Shhh," Giem said, and was gently shoved aside by the server, back with a steaming platter it extracted from its belly and set down on Davin's table.

"Ah, that's better." Davin sighed as he tossed my stunner back towards me, and sat down before the large hot meal. In the process of standing up, I wasn't quick enough to catch my palm-sized weapon, clattering to the ground a meter away from me.

"Thank you, sir," the server said. It spun around and hurried off, running over my weapon on its way around Davin's table. I picked up the stunner, and studied it with sick dismay. Its sleek veneer was permanently marred by scratches and dents, and when I released the safety, I checked the green power light doubtfully.

"Not too bright, is it?" Davin nodded in the direction of the server. "Got a loose connection somewhere. Someone should tell the management."

"Who told you to find us here?" Giem said suspiciously, while I tucked my poor stunner back in its holster under my shirt.

"Nobody. I could use some company for lunch, if you would care to join me?" Davin said, with a little less certainty in his voice.

"Looks more like you're having dinner," Giem said sharply.

"Don't mind her," I told him. "Giem's been like this ever since her last trip to Ballophon. Come on, Giem, let's go get our plates and sit with him."

I had to work at not getting clobbered or even just kicked, but I felt too curious to pass this opportunity up. I soon had us installed at Davin's table, despite Giem's somewhat puzzling reaction to the miraculous appearance of her Big Maxson Romantic Interest. In some ways he was pond scum and we both knew it, but we had also endured her periodic bouts of self-doubt and lingering lust over the past couple school years.

"Ballophon?" Davin said as we sat down at his table.

"My home planet," Giem impatiently reminded him. She finished her sandwich, and attacked her chips one by one. "Come on, Davin, meeting like this on Enchantment can't be a complete coincidence."

The autoserver rushed back, belatedly noticing new guests at Davin's table. Vac-brained machine. "Welcome!

Would you like to order?" it asked, without any apparent memory of us.

"No thanks," Giem said. "Go away."

"Drinks, perhaps?" it tried again politely.

"I'd like some dessert," I decided. "Do you have any ice cream?" I liked trying whatever passed for ice cream on different planets. It never tasted quite the same.

"Certainly, sir. What flavor would you like?"

"Krava—no, I'm sorry." I blushed at the slip, another impossible reference to Big Maxson. With Davin here, it just felt natural. "Chocolate, please, if you have it. One scoop in a dish." Chocolate was usually available, anywhere in FIL where there's humans.

"Very good, sir." It puttered off again, as I opened my mouth to correct its faulty gender recognition, and decided not to bother. So I didn't have big boobs. I'd long since decided if that's what a mate wanted, I didn't need him or her or whatever.

"No, you're right, of course. I guess it's not a total coincidence," Davin admitted, as he worked on some type of cloned steak with vegetables, imported tilkfu, and wine.

"You guess?" Giem said, incredulously.

"Well, sure—I mean, I'm just surprised Dr. Emmel never told me she'd taken me up on my suggestion."

"Your suggestion!"

"Yeah." Davin looked up at Giem with a pleased grin on his face. "I came here some half a standard year ago to get in on the early crater pup trade. I sell a lot of my catches at Station Three, and she's in charge of it. Business was pretty wild, and Nirim was always too—uh—Dr. Emmel was just so worn out all the time, from her work. I suggested she order up some vet student assistants, like Dr. Bioh did on Big Maxson's Planet. I guess she knew about the FIL program, and hadn't thought of using it to get help for herself."

"And you gave her our names?" Giem said.

"Sure. I told her I didn't know if you two were still available, that you worked hard and smart—I commed it couldn't hurt."

The autoserver returned to deliver my dessert, to Giem. She pushed it on over to me, and when I spooned up a creamy brown bite, I grimaced. It was coffee—the other ubiquitous human flavor of the galaxy—a flavor I happen to hate.

"Then maybe you can explain what happened to Dr. Emmel," Giem said.

"What do you mean?" Davin stopped eating, a look of alarm on his face.

"The good doctor left her job and this planet a week ago, without bothering to tell anyone else to expect us."

"She was supposed to pick us up at the port," I said. "No one met us, and no one else seems to know what to do with us."

"She quit and left?" Davin was clearly upset. I could tell right away he wasn't going to be any help. "I planned to see her again next week," he added. "I knew she was looking for a better position, and had a possible offer somewhere on Alt Del. I didn't realize she'd leave so soon."

I idly stirred my ice cream in its cold metal dish, and glanced over at Giem as I worked at stifling a smirk. Was she also reading between the lines? She began to appear intrigued.

"So what are you doing here?" she asked Davin.

"I told you—I'm hunting for crater pup pups."

"No, I mean this hotel. Rather an expensive stopover, isn't it?"

"Oh, well. There's nothing cheaper in Crater One, where the local quarantine station for selling pups also happens to be. Like just about everyone in the R&R station on Big Maxson, the residents here tend to thrive on hunters and tourists. As you might guess from the prices." Davin turned his attention from Giem to me, and frowned. "What are you doing to that?"

I glanced down with embarrassment at my dessert dish. I'd idly stirred the ice cream into a soupy mush. "It's coffee-flavored."

"You should have made that vacful server take it back," he said.

"It didn't seem worth it."

"It will when you get the bill with your room. I can't believe they couldn't find somewhere cheaper to board you two."

"You just said there is nowhere cheaper in Crater One." Sure enough, Giem caught that slip.

"Well, Dr. Emmel could have—I mean, I'd think someone should have invited you to stay at their place, or let you use a quarantine station apartment."

"We told you, no one was even expecting us. Thanks to a total lack of communication from your Dr. Nirim Emmel, before she launched—"

That seemed a little unfair—

"Well, speaking of taking off—" Davin glanced at his wristcom and stood up. "I've got an appointment to keep, and a whole load of business to take care of this afternoon and this evening. Want to meet me later tonight in my room?" he asked, looking meaningfully and specifically at Giem.

Was he truly so dense, or just gifted with a tremendous ego? I couldn't believe it. I felt like a forgotten third leg.

"Taje and I just arrived this morning from Olecranon. I think we'll both be asleep by then."

"Oh, well, maybe some other time. I'm leaving early tomorrow on another hunt."

"If we're still around. We may have to return to the University very soon, to try to get a new assignment before it's too late."

"Oh." Davin looked crestfallen as he came around the table, to give us each a quick, strained, good-bye hug. "Beware of Enchanted Forests," he said, trying to act lighthearted. He seemed like he wanted to say more, before he hurried off.

Afterwards, Giem stared down at the crumbs on her plate. "How embarrassing," she said at last.

"What?" I said, startled. "Sure, you were sort of hard on him after a whole three standard year absence—"

"At least he didn't come flying all the way here just to see me! I can only imagine what a vac-head Dr. Emmel must have been, to take his advice. I'm sorry, Taje. It's no wonder our assignment got so fused! Why do I let myself get sucked into such nova relationships?"

"You didn't get sucked in. You had some fun a couple summers ago, that's all. Quit being so hard on yourself, Giem."

We stood up from the table and Giem shook her head, with cross amusement on her face.

"What ?" I said, following her back to our room.

"Look at us. Never peaking or sinking at the same time. You've perked up at last, and I'm down and taking it out on everyone, including you and Davin."

"Why," I asked slowly, the thought of the bed I was headed for ushering another sudden surge of sleepiness so powerful I had trouble finding words to speak, "didn't you consider just having a little more fun with him tonight? I mean, I'm grateful not to have to fight off some jealousy, and, well, I'm fairly certain that wasn't your reason. Is it because of his affair with Emmel? You'd have plenty of time—" I yawned—"for a nap first."

"With Emmel? You think so?" Amazingly, I'd caught Giem completely off-guard, so that wasn't the answer, either.

"What do you think?" I said.

"You have a hormone-driven, sex-starved mind!"

"Hey, that's just a nasty way to get off the subject," I said, in a mock-offended tone. I could easily recognize Redirection, The Vet Student Way, for avoiding questions you can't or don't want to answer.

"Okay, okay, you're right," Giem said contritely, "sleepiness wasn't my reason, it was my excuse."

"So what is it?"

We reached our porch and stepped back inside.

"I was afraid to," Giem admitted, sitting on her bed.

"Afraid?" Giem? I found it hard to believe.

"Of getting involved. Offworld. Again."

I pulled off my shoes, and crawled straight into bed. "You mean off of Olecranon?" my wound-up brain couldn't help asking, as I shut my eyes. "Big Maxson? Or Ballophon?"

I don't remember Giem giving me an answer to that one. Maybe there wasn't one.

CHAPTER 17

The next morning I found myself trudging up the last switchbacks out of Crater One. Giem waved at me from the top. Of course it was her idea for killing time before our meeting, and it did burn off a lot of my adrenaline. When I finally joined her, the view from a soft, blue-green, grassy patch, and our picnic lunch, were wonderful rewards.

I hadn't realized the town of Crater One lay to one side of a small blue lake. Like an oval viewscreen, it mirrored small clouds fluffing their way overhead. I gazed upwards, and saw long-tailed spiraling flocks, almost as colorful as the rainbow-blossomed crater walls below.

We'd heard what sounded like birdsong, among the rocks and blossoming bushes on our way up. I knew what flew above us—huge crater hawks lazily riding the thermals resembling Earth birds about as closely as crater pup insulation resembled Earth bird feathers. My sweaty scalp crawled as one huge blue crater hawk dipped within meters of us. It screamed and soared off, over the undulating, grassy, blue-green and violet hills and rocky ridges outside the crater.

"Crater hawks mostly just eat crater pups," Giem reminded me, with a twinkle in her eye. She had almost finished her lunch by the time I'd had enough rest to even think about eating. I was just starting on a crisp flower bulb sandwich, while my roomie was munching on her chocolate cookies.

"That crater hawk looked big enough to attack small children," I said between bites. "And judging from the visible lack of prey on our way up here, desperation could conceivably drive a crater hawk to attack unnatural—"

"Remember, they're not interested in foreign prey. And we're probably too noisy to scan crater pups. And this is a populated, busy crater. Crater pups are supposed to be shy and good at hiding."

"No wonder," I said, "with predators like that."

"So relax and enjoy the view."

"It is rather spectacular. I guess I didn't pay enough attention to any maps to notice the lake before. Now that we've stopped, I'm getting nervous again."

"A lot of the larger craters have lakes. Natural pooling, I suppose. Let it remind you—mizu no kokoro."

"'Mind like water. Adaptable to the shape of any container, and returning to a calm surface after being rippled," I remembered Dr. Cor's interpretation. "Giem, as usual, your memory is disgusting. That's purple belt material, and you quit after orange."

"You didn't. You should be working on it."

CHAPTER 18

By the time I had finished and partly digested my lunch, we had to practically crash our way back down the long, zig-zagging trail, ending behind the hotel stable. We just barely beat the sunset, in time for a quick shower and change of clothes for our second meeting with Dr. Nilod.

I was engulfed in a cold sweat as we took seats in his office. After all, what was the worst that could happen? He might send us right back to Olecranon. I glanced over at Giem, outwardly so much calmer than me, and I envied her ability to come through the paraflight rebugging tanks without ill effects. An unworthy thought. If Dr. Hako couldn't fish up another assignment immediately, I suppose we'd both suffer the frustration of being held back after senior year clinics, for one last externship before we could graduate.

Mizo no kokoro. Mizu no kokoro. I can't say I knew how to achieve that one—

"—and the Director and I contacted your Dean of Student Welfare, after thoroughly reviewing information from your wristcoms, concerning your proposed work here," Dr. Nilod was saying, clasping his hands over his pot belly, keeping him a set distance from his desk. Weren't there any good lipidologists anywhere within commuting distance of Crater One? Or did he like being overweight?

"You called Dr. Hako?" Giem sounded impressed, and she had reason to be. The paraspace transmission must have cost vastly more than our hotel bill so far.

"For a short consultation, after some rapid com data transmission. We have a much better idea of your function, and we feel we can definitely use you—"

"That's great!" we both blurted out in perfect, and perfectly embarrassing, unison.

"The question is, how to transport you?"

"Transport us?"

"Aren't we working here?"

"I've been given to understand,"—Dr. Nilod coughed to clear his throat—"you are here to get active veterinary experience. And to help improve our survival rates. It's our outlying stations that are most overworked and understaffed, and could gain maximum benefit from your presence.

"However, as you may realize, the tube ends here. Unfortunately, our company cars all happen to be tied up. Furthermore, our budget is rather limited for this unexpected event. Especially for obtaining such last-minute reservations.

"So at best, we can afford to rent you mounts, and we're hoping as vet students, you can handle a week's ride out to Station Three? The trail, I understand, is quite good, and your teacher mentioned something about having brought along your own camping gear?"

Giem and I looked at each other, more utterly delighted than Dr. Nilod could know. A week's vacation before even starting? How could we have planned it any better after all?

"No problem!" I said.

"Just give us a good map and adequate food supplies, and point us to the trailhead," Giem agreed more carefully. I hadn't thought about the cost of food and a map.

Dr. Nilod nodded and smiled with obvious relief. "We'll give you credit at one of our local camping stores. We will also reserve two mounts and a pack animal, for departure as soon as possible from the Enchanted Inn." He made some brief notes on his deskcom. "Oh, and we'll take care of your bill there. I was given to understand your pay is entirely in the form of room, board, and work experience. Well, that should do it. I hope you enjoy your ride out to Station Three."

We whooped with delight as soon as we left the building. Colored lights made the plaza a fantasy land at night.

"We get to enjoy a whole week of Adventure and Excitement before we start work!" Giem said.

I almost added, you forgot Romance, however, I didn't want to hear her whole harangue about alien lovers again.

"We'll ask for horses!" she said.

"And a yusahmbul!" I added, as I leapt over the corner of a fountain.

CHAPTER 19

We learned the next morning that all the hotel stable had to spare on such short notice were three spindly little nicklets, more suitable for Telmids than for humans. We still had an enjoyable day of leisurely planning, shopping, and packing. And by the time we checked back with the hotel stable manager that evening, a cancellation had granted Giem's wish.

I found my spacelag converted me here to an early-to-bed, early riser. So I didn't find it difficult to get up with Giem at our dawn departure time the next morning. Events seemed to be going our way, I thought, rather dangerously, as we hauled our packs into the stable and found the manager.

A dark, stocky human, she eyed us carefully. She nodded at three horses she'd tied up in the main aisle of the barn. "King, Prince, and Jack," she introduced them. "You can groom King and Prince to saddle up, and Jack for carrying your baggage."

Slave labor—this was truly going economy style. A warning look from Giem kept me silent, until I had a closer look at the three geldings. Then I couldn't help it. "These three? Together?"

"Yes," said the manager, expressionlessly. "What's the matter?"

Giem gave me another intimidating glance. She bent over a box of grooming instruments, and picked out a pair of antique-looking devices. "Have a curry comb, Taje," she said helpfully.

"Uh, nothing's wrong," I said, as I took the comb, matched looks with the manager, and realized we were being tested. Well, I'd never seen such a mismatched appearing trio. But what did I know about horses? Only minimal basics, so I followed Giem's lead. What about a yusahmbul? I wanted to say, and managed to keep quiet about it.

Sure enough, as I worked away on circular sweeps against dusty fur with a tool I considered about the same tech level as a bear skin or stone knife, the manager didn't rush off to other tasks. She simply leaned against a fence post with her arms crossed and quietly watched us.

Giem loudly wapped her curry comb against a post to clear the dust out of it, reminding me to follow suit. She'd gotten King, a massive, stocky, sleepy bay, for all appearances right out of an ancient fairytale. My dun mount had a similarly muscular, almost draft horse appearance. Except he was a miniature version, so short I wondered if he could claim to make it out of pony range. King made Prince look like a dwarf. Whereas Jack, a mildly overweight chestnut, was the most average-looking of the lot, so he stuck out like a mahogany mutant between the other two.

Giem, despite having more area to cover, finished King first, and curried Jack while I finished Prince. Next we went for the power brushes—a step above bear skins and stone knives—and after we finished King and Prince, Giem requested hoof picks, while I took a turn working on Jack.

For the first time, I saw the manager briefly smile. Are we passing? I felt tempted to ask. I suspected we were, gradually and perhaps grudgingly, as we saddled and bridled our horses with minimal assistance on final adjustments. Giem conferred with the manager on tacking and loading up Jack.

"Great Galaxy, this is a lot of stuff!" the manager said, as we all began to struggle over final packing arrangements. "How long are you two going to stay out there?"

"We'll work at Station Three for several months, and we heard we'd need to ride for about a week to get there," Giem said as we matched glances, and snickered softly over the same memory. Maybe our lean trip on Big Maxson had led us to getting a bit carried away with our food stock. "The last time we went camping, we didn't bring good food, so we nearly starved ourselves. We tried to buy more food this time, especially since we weren't sure about the quality or how we'd return. Plus we tried to bring enough clothes for our externship."

"Well, I think you succeeded," the manager said. "On top of all your clothes and camping gear, and adequate feed supplement for the horses, it makes quite a load. I'd better retrieve saddlebags for King and Prince. Otherwise poor Jack will never make it."

CHAPTER 20

The sun had risen well above the crater wall by the time the manager had us mounted up, adjusted our stirrup leathers for us, and led our horses out and around the barn.

"I usually require riders to hire a guide, especially newcomers. But Dr. Nilod assured me as vet students, you'd know what you're doing," the manager told us, revealing the extent of Nilod's frugality, and perhaps the reason for her wariness.

I straightened in my saddle, as I tried to unobtrusively refamiliarize myself with the swaying gait, and found myself grateful for a shorter mount.

"Anyway," she continued, "these three horses don't look it, but they make a very decent team. They're long term friends, they stick together, and they know the trails. Once in a while they get a little feisty, and then they get second names—Kinky, Prick, and Jackass—but most of the time they're alright."

We laughed, and the stable manager stopped us in front of a familiar trailhead. "This trail will take you all the way to Enchantment Animal Quarantine Station Three. Just don't wander off on one of the side-branches, usually clearly marked. Follow your map, let the horses lead, beware of Enchanted Forests, and you can't go wrong."

"I think we're only riding these horses one way," I said anxiously, as she handed us our reins, and gave Giem Jack's lead rope. "Who will return them? Or do we keep them all summer?" Forlorn hope.

"Oh, there's plenty of traffic out on the trails, especially between stations. I've received one group and sent out two others, before taking care of you this morning. I'm sure your station will find someone to return them soon enough. Besides," she grinned broadly, "I get paid by the amount of time you have them. Just remember horses require daily supplement when they eat Enchantment grasses. And good luck. Beware of Enchanted Forests!"

"Thanks!"

"Bye!"

The manager slapped their rumps, and her horses moved for the trail at once. They soon settled into a steadily plodding gait, up the numerous switchbacks at a speed that seemed amazing, compared to our efforts on foot. So we sat back and enjoyed the views, and the pleasant rocking motion of strong muscles under our saddles. It's not hard to com why people still enjoy such a slow and ancient method of transportation, and willingly pay for it on their vacations.

We reached the crater rim in less than two hours, and spent the rest of our day on a road-sized, well-used trail.

It wound through rolling, grassy country, with scattered bushes and even scarcer trees. The difference from the lushly colorful crater flora was striking. By our lunch stop, we had seen so little shade we waded into a stream and happily splashed ourselves, while the horses drank in great sucking gulps.

"What do people keep repeating," I said later, between dry mouthfuls of crackers and chunks of cheese, "Beware of enchanted forests? Must be some quaint saying, imported from another planet."

"This planet does have forests." Giem studied our wristcom holo map, and dipped into our trail mix. "Some of the forests here produce several rather popular new types of wood. In fact, compared to the primary industries of this planet, like forestry, fish farms, and mineral and gem mines, Rash crater products are of rather minor economic importance. There are even a few craters along our way with decent stands of native trees. Shall we stay in 'Forest Crater' tomorrow night? It's even got an 'Improved Campsite.'"

"Touché, Giem. What's an Improved Campsite?"

"Dunno. It's just listed that way on the map. Maybe—"

Whhhissshhh!—a small sporty aircar whisked over the trail, fording our picnic stream. Fortunately, the resulting shower felt good in the midday sun.

"Vac-headed tourists!" I cursed anyway. Various aircars and other riders had passed us that morning about every twenty to thirty minutes, and I had begun to wonder how much of a wilderness experience we'd get out here. And why someone hadn't simply arranged for a lift to deliver us to Station Three.

"The crowds will let up once we get a little deeper into the Rash/" Giem read the look on my face. "We're still too close to Crater One."

"Then we'll see more hunters."

"We'll stay in craters set aside for camping, not hunting."

"Why camp inside the craters, where everyone else does?"

"Most have better water sources, and a lot of them rate highly for beauty. Why do you suppose there's so much traffic out here?"

"Okay, so what scenic crater can we stay in tonight?" I began packing up our lunch food, a virtual banquet spread out on the violet grass. We had overdone it. I felt stuffed, and we still had leftovers.

Giem studied her map again. "Here's one—Snake Crater—it's a little off the main path, but I think we can still reach it by late afternoon."

"Sounds terribly scenic, Giem."

CHAPTER 21

Snake Crater turned out to be not much more than a small flowery rift, with a stream running along the bottom of it, so it was one way to avoid crowds. We found ourselves unexpectedly tired out by our first day, and grateful to find no other tents pitched here. We took care of the horses, unloading them and making sure they got their supplement. We set up camp as soon as we could, with our saddle-weary muscles. I positioned our tent to catch the first rays of the rising sun, and we got into bed, with stomachs bloated from dinner, as the first stars appeared.

I had guessed this crater got its name from its snaking streambed. The next morning we found a different answer, after lurching out of our tent on stiff, aching legs, with our tent gear. We nearly stumbled over the thick mass of intertwining, leathery, segmented crater snakes, basking around our tent in the early morning sunshine.

I'd studied a little about crater snakes beforehand, because I had an interest in ecology, and along with crater hawks, crater snakes were the main crater pup predators. Until intelligent life arrived on this planet, anyway. Along with crater hawks, crater snakes also had no reported interest in adding foreign proteins to their diet. The fact that the smallest of them equalled Giem's upper arm in diameter, and twice her height in length, didn't really dawn on me—excuse the pun—until now.

They wern't truly snakes or reptiles, in the human sense of those words. Altruskans might call them trilskands, and come a lot closer than any Earthly comparison. Crater snakes had rows of multiple stumpy legs (knobby, pincered, and currently twitching lightly—in some native form of REM sleep?), and axillary pseudofeathers. Kind of like giant skinny caterpillars with fuzzy armpits and crocodile heads. Nothing to be afraid of. Sure. That's why my hair stood on end.

My scalp crawled as I followed Giem. We had to step carefully between powerfully coiled bodies, to get to our packs and the horses, who seemed totally indifferent. Maybe our mounts were used to the whole scene—bored with it, in fact. Or we'd tethered them far enough away from camp that this didn't worry them.

I began to relax too, as we got breakfast and packed up Jack without disturbance, until it came time for me to saddle up Prince. Then I found the biggest, ugliest, most scarred-up crater smale using my saddle as a chin and front leg rest.

"Serves you right for throwing your saddle on the ground last night." Giem pulled her saddle and pad off a rock, and hefted them up onto King's high back..

"I stashed my saddle on a rock too," I complained, eyeing the proof, my saddle pad still lying on a rock.

"The saddle must have slipped." The creature's long, pink and green mottled snout rested on it. Three layers of eyelids slowly peeled open as I stepped closer. "Come on, old crater smale, move along. I need my saddle."

The crater smale grinned a bit, revealing only its outermost rows of sharp, brown, crowded little inward-curving teeth. I jumped back (number two escape move on Sensei's octagon). "Giem! It's got teeth!"

"For crater pups, Taje, for crater pups. Come on, we haven't got all day. Is that what you're going to tell the senior clinician next year, when he orders you to treat something like it?"

"Okay, black hole, what do you suggest I do?"

"Move it off. It won't attack you. Anything besides just standing there and whining about teeth. I'm nearly ready to go."

I was getting almost as pissed with Giem as with the snake. Suddenly I got an idea for a little bit of insurance. I knew hunters used stunners on crater pups, so presumably crater smale physiology would respond as well. I pulled out my hand weapon, guestimated a setting, briefly released the safety, and fired at the snake's head.

Its jaw and multiple eyelids slid shut again, as I remembered to be pleased my battered stunner still worked. I holstered it, and stepped forward to retrieve my saddle. No such luck. My best efforts couldn't budge it from underneath the unexpectedly heavy, sleepy weight of the creature's head and forelegs.

"Giem."

"What?"

"Could you—umph—help me with this?"

Giem joined in, and even our combined strength didn't move my saddle.

"One, two, three, heave!" I repeated for about the sixth time.

"Uh, Taje—I'm beginning to think—oomph—its neck just doesn't physically bend this way much—hey, look out!"

We both leaped back as the beast shook its head and reopened its eyes. I began to doubt my stunner's power, as we watched the snake quickly regain enough motor control to crawl several meters forward, draping the heaviest-looking section of its body over the seat of my saddle. There it came to a rest, and blissfully sunned itself.

"Nova vac-headed arrogant creature!"

"Comes of having no natural predators, except cannibalism by the largest," Giem said, crossing her arms to study the problem. "And this definitely looks like the great-grandmother of the lot."

"We'll see about that," I said, impulsively stomping along its ten meter length, while still carefully not stepping on smaller snakes sunbathing in parallel. I tried nudging the crater smale's less imposing end with the toe of my boot. No go. Several less tentative nudges (okay, I kicked it) had no bigger effect on the fat old pink and green slug. So finally I just reached down with both hands, and shook the hard tail tip as violently as possible.

Whump! Suddenly I was thrown forward on my belly as the crater smale, probably more startled than it had felt in years, shot forward and disappeared into a dark crevice in the nearest crater wall. All the rest of the snakes followed, a few slithering right over me in their haste.

Giem stood laughing at the spectacle. "Enjoying a new planet?"

I couldn't help smiling too as I brushed dirt and grass from my clothes, until I discovered the source of a bad smell was some sort of excretional streak down the back of my shirt. And when I picked up my saddle, it slipped from my fingers, slimed with a foul oral secretion.

"Poor thing," Giem said wickedly, "probably needs a dentistry. Why didn't you check it first for abscessed teeth?"

I washed in the stream between changing shirts, and used my filthy one to wipe thick stinky saliva off my saddle. Then I went after Giem, whipping her with my disgusting shirt. So the morning wasn't completely wasted.

CHAPTER 22

"Just think, that might be Garth Riddock whizzing past us," I said from the side of the road, after a particularly expensive trail aircar passed by us late that afternoon. The traffic had eased only a little today. Again I couldn't help wondering why Nilod hadn't simply found us a ride. Maybe he had no friends?

"That would definitely make one coincidence too many." Giem turned her wristcom map on again. She seemed to enjoy plotting our progress on it.

"I wonder if Garth thinks about how much we talk about him."

"Are you kidding? He's so fused. Not a bit."

My thoughts churned as the horses clopped along, snorting on trail dust, and occasionally trying to snatch greens and violets from the side of the road. The only other sound came from the creaking of our saddles, and the only pervasive smell was of horse sweat. Sweat-soaked dirt coated my reins and hands.

"Maybe," I spoke at last, "it's like what Dr. Hako said at our last meeting. Hey, is that Forest Crater ahead, over there?" I pointed across the landscape at a dark blue-green pit, opening up in the near distance.

"I think so. Hako said lots of stuff. What are you talking about?"

"When he got so angry, remember? Have you commed what an Improved Campsite is?"

"I think it's a packer group campground," Giem said. "What did Hako say?"

"You really don't remember? I can't remember Dr. Hako's exact words. He said something to the effect that no one wakes up in the morning, and deliberately sets out to injure the universe. He seemed to believe that no one intends to be a bad guy—he hated the expression. He thought we all try to do our best, in our own way. It just doesn't always look that way to an outsider."

"Garth's just a greedy, suave, fallible criminal." Giem dismissed the subject, as she slapped her loose reins in her hands. "That's my best theory to date. Shall we try the campsite?"

I bit my lip. "Sure."

"There it is." Giem pointed.

"What?" I asked.

"The turn-off for Forest Crater. See the sign? And a perfect location for an Ambush. We must Proceed Cautiously."

Gradually we descended from our fantasies out from the sunny, charmed, nearly windless weather of our trip so far, into the somber depths of a completely forested crater. It was perhaps a quarter of the size of Crater One. I couldn't tell for sure, once we rode down many switchbacks, and our horses began to falter with weariness.

"Great Galaxy these trees are weird!' Crowded, dark bluish-green, skinny, bristly trees, bearing midnight blue pods, grew taller as we neared the crater floor.

"Hush, Taje, they might hear you!" Giem said so loudly it echoed, and we both laughed.

Sun-warmed dust had given way to heavily shadowed tree needle leaf mold. The sound of our horses' hoofbeats was nearly muffled in the soft, thick, grey-green duff..

A short smooth path led us straight into the Improved Campsite. This proved to be a collection of several huge picnic tables and storage cupboards, obviously viciously hewn from the nearest trees, surrounding rotting stumps; a massive, rock-lined fire pit, containing carelessly half-burned logs and flanked by an overly zealous woodpile; some patches of cleared and leveled ground for tents; and a sturdy post corral. I also made out a crude wooden outhouse, emitting a multi-species stink, in the leaf-colored, dim and shifting light.

"Welcome to all the conveniences of home," I said. I shifted uncomfortably in my saddle, and a dull, cold body ache invaded me. "I suppose if we look hard enough, we'll find hot and cold running water." I untied my coat from my saddle and pulled it on.

Prince pawed a front foot in the duff and snorted, the only sounds besides my voice, except surprisingly loud creaks from rough-barked tree trunks swaying in the wind. (Wind? Down here?) "A pre-fab site sort of takes some of the rustic fun out of camping," I added.

"I doubt we'll find any plumbing. There's supposed to be a stream. It should wind past the other side of the corral," Giem said, checking her map again, while holding her restless big bay to a stand alongside me. "I can't hear any running water. Do you want to stay here?"

The question didn't surprise me, although it hadn't existed when we first took the turn-off for the steep path down here. "I don't know," I said, with some amusement over my own reaction. "This isn't exactly my style of roughing it in the wilderness. I suppose I could learn to enjoy it for one night."

"Here, tell you what." Giem leaned over, to hand me Jack's lead rope. "I'll go check into the water supply, while you think about it. If the streambed is dried up until the rainy season begins, we'll have to move on."

Dismounting slowly, with quivering riding muscles, I felt very foreshortened on the ground. By then, Giem had vanished on King, in amongst the nearest trees, no mean feat for either of them.

I used quick-release safety clips to tie Prince and Jack's halters to a tree trunk, although they tried to shy from me as if they'd never seen me before, and they jittered on their lines. I perched on one of the big tabletops. It was made of such thick slabs of wood I made almost no sound. I lounged between sticky, smashed, fist-sized tree pods, in varying stages of decay.

Gazing around silently, I tried to think of this packer camp as my current living space. I heard a series of loud groaning creaks and popping cracks. The horses restlessly whickered back. It took me a while to realize the noise came from precarious, huge dying trees leaning on neighbors. They appeared ready to come crashing down, as soon as they could release themselves from the scraping clutches of still-living competitors.

A few of the dead had already made it to the ground. One ancient trunk lay ominously across an tent plot, exposing a painful mass of gnarled roots at one end, some still clutching dirty rocks midair.

Kathunk! I flinched involuntarily, as a tree pod slammed into the end of my table (and not my head, thank the Galaxy). The pod's waxy, dark-blue skin immediately split open. Yellow-green pulp oozed out, and a little yellow-green wormy thing oozed out next, and squiggled towards me. I watched, torn between repugnance and fascination, as it got closer and closer. Then it abruptly ended the question of my having to move, by detouring to a crack between table planks, and dropping out of sight.

I scooted over, to pick up the newly fallen pod by the intact part of its skin. I felt its weight in my palm, as I turned my head to view the groaning, sawing trees. Was there anywhere in here we could safely trigger our tent?

Giem reappeared on King from out of the blue-green gloom, and she dismounted near me.

"So what did you find?" I said.

"Well, there's plenty of water," she said, as King yanked on his reins. "And there's a horse skeleton back there."

"*A whole horse skeleton?*"

"Yep," Giem said.

"Somebody's horse *died here*?"

CHAPTER 23

"Fallen Moon Lake Crater—that sounds intriguing." I made the mistake of picking out that name from several Giem read off her map, as possible lunch stops late the next morning. We were enjoying another warm, cotton-candy cloud day. The clouds had become a little thicker, edges trailing off into steamy tendrils, which led to dramatic shape changes as they rode crosswinds.

"We could spend an extended lunch break there, and if we really like it, we could even spend the night," Giem said. "We're going to beat our ETA if we don't start lingering."

"Fine with me." It would be tragic not to suck the most out of this trip.

Once again the turn-off from the main trail was clearly posted, and we soon scanned enticing glimpses of deep, dark blue, Fallen Moon Lake, filling most of its crater floor. Tall podtrees grew around the lake's perimeter, on up the near side of the crater wall, not nearly as profuse as those in Forest Crater.

Our main problem was the trail, which dwindled out just as the climb down became steep. We had to dismount and lead our balky horses as we tried to pick out fading switchbacks among jagged rocks and nasty brambles. We made our way down treacherous terrain that kept trying to force us off to the right of our destination. At last we arrived, panting and sweating, on a sandy beach. A small, peaceful stream wiggled across the beach, and fed into the nearly silent, peaceful shore of Fallen Moon Lake.

"Looks nice," I said softly, trying not to disturb any lake inhabitants, their presence given away by concentric rings randomly breaking the smooth lake surface.

Not too far from the shallow, lapping edge before us, the water rapidly transformed from a clear light green to a deep dark blue. The lake bed must drop to an unimaginable depth, hinted at by the nearly vertical crater wall forming the far boundary of Fallen Moon Lake. To our left a cheerful green meadow merged with marshy reeds, along the lazily winding path of the tributary stream. To our right I could see somewhat steeper ground with less undergrowth, clear and flat enough in small areas for campsites, amongst a light forest of podtrees and weathered rocks. Nothing scary here, I thought.

Our horses began to snort and stamp with impatience, so we led them to drink from the stream. We removed their gear in the meadow, to let them graze, before we eagerly slipped back to the beach in our shorts.

"It doesn't really look much like a moon," I whispered, because the crater was so quiet.

"The lake perimeter is nearly circular," Giem said. "Maybe the water is so still it reflects Enchantment's moons."

"Think we'll stay here tonight?"

"Maybe. Let's cool off, and explore a bit first." Giem sat down to remove her boots. Sweat dripped from her forehead.

"Good idea." I studied the smooth sandy bottom of the shallow shore. I walked to the water's edge and stuck my hand in. "Youch! Too cold for me."

I watched Giem wade in, sighing with pleasure. Minutes later she shrieked and splashed back out.

"What's wrong?" I raced to her side.

"Something's attacking me!" Giem sat down on the ground to frantically scrabble at her legs and feet. I couldn't see anything.

"What? What?" I bent over to look, immensely curious. "Show me."

All I got was a tantalizing glimpse of a tangle of slimy orange thready things, before Giem had all the little creatures peeled off her wet skin and promptly dumped back into the water.

"Some sort of local leech-worm." Giem frowned with disgust.

"And no warnings posted." I was shocked. "Did they hurt?"

"No. They didn't have time. No thanks to you!"

"I didn't hardly even got to see any of them!"

"That's what I mean. Here I was under attack, Taje, and all you wanted to do was indulge your scientific curiosity."

We both laughed, half out of relief and half because Giem's accusation was all too accurate. We split up to explore opposite directions along the shore for a campsite, although I couldn't see the point of Giem looking beyond the marsh to the left. I didn't dare object after failing to help her.

So I quietly wandered along the rocky hillside, up to the right around the lake. By the time I found a reasonably level area for our campsite—underneath all live trees— and returned to the beach, I couldn't see Giem anywhere.

I stood uselessly scanning the whole lake perimeter, and found a small trail winding on around to my left. It led between the stream and the lake, and initially carried the imprint of Giem's boot soles. I followed the muddy path, and after I crossed the stream a couple times, I began to regret the hike, as the brilliant green foliage closed and snagged me and my clothes. My progress slowed to a near-crawl, to weave my way between tangled branches, thorny bushes (no nice flowers here!), and goopy little bogs. I was almost certain Giem had gone this way, but her tracks vanished as I bumped up against the increasingly steep crater wall to my left.

"That's it," I muttered, wiping sweat from my face. "This isn't worth it. Where did she go?" I couldn't imagine how she'd hiked any farther.

Extricating myself, I reversed course, and returned to the beach, where there was finally some shade. I lounged back on the sand, considered, and then rejected the effort of a wristcom call. If Giem felt that possessed, who was I to disturb her?

I enjoyed the silent scenery for about half an hour, before a chilling thought zapped my brain. What if the lake parasites had injected a biotoxin into Giem? Maybe she had wandered off in a poison-induced delirium. Our map hadn't warned us of any such danger, but it hadn't even mentioned the leech-creatures. This was a fairly recently discovered FIL planet, and everyone knew no matter how carefully the initial ecological surveys were carried out, they weren't infallible. Giem could be in horrible danger—

Just as I sat up in alarm, Giem came hiking back out along the trail. She had an odd look on her weary, dirty face.

"Giem! Are you alright?"

"Hi, Taje," she said with a sheepish smile.

"Where have you been?"

"Trying to climb that." She pointed at the opposite crater wall, where I hadn't looked.

"What?" I was sure I'd either misinterpreted her gesture, or that indeed some toxin had affected her mind. Giem usually behaved so sensibly. I wondered if we had enough time to call in a rescue aircar. Was the nearest emergency service back in Crater One, or farther back up the tube line? And why hadn't we checked that out before we left on our trip?

"Not the whole crater wall," Giem tried to explain. "See the rocky part sticking out at the base, the section that slants up from the left? I tried to climb it to get a view of some of the deeper water. The fish or whatever seem most active there, and I hoped to catch a glimpse of what's causing the surface rings."

I squinted harder. The outcropping of the crater wall she described was only slightly less precipitous, and reached over a third of the way up. Neither of us had ever had any rock-climbing training. "You're nova!"

"You're right," Giem said in an unusually humble tone. "I don't know what got into me."

"Poisons," I said softly, still staring at her carefully. "From the leech-worms or plant thorns or both."

"It didn't look so bad close up." Giem gave me a puzzled look. "When I got up to that crack in the rock," she pointed, "I reached a horrid part where I didn't know what to do. All the handholds had weeds with thorns. And when I made the mistake of looking down, I understood how you can fear heights."

"I must have scanned right past you several times," I said, becoming more convinced of her story. "I just wasn't looking high enough. You should have called me for help."

"I thought about it. I knew you'd have an even harder time climbing up there, and I did work my way out of it, at the expense of some puncture wounds."

Oh great. I wondered if the weeds had any phytotoxins.

"What?" Giem tilted her head, trying to hear my mutterings.

"Talk about endangering our externship!" I said.

"Okay, you're right."

She startled me. I was never right. "We're not staying here tonight, are we?"

"I'd rather not," Giem said, looking down at her muddy boots.

We tried leading our reluctant horses back out by meticulously following trail ducks and tree blazes. About a quarter of the way up, we realized helpful hikers had virtually peppered the slope with useless signs, and it was just as tough to leave Fallen Moon Lake Crater as it was to enter. When we reached the main trail at last and remounted, I glanced once more at the turn-off sign, and the shimmering dark blue water far below.

"Creepy lake," I said.

"Yeah. Someone should just remove the sign."

"Or give it a less romantic name," I suggested. "How about Ambush Basin?"

CHAPTER 24

The deeper we rode into the Rash, the more fun we had, exploring craters of increasing beauty. Yesterday we'd spent a layover day climbing around the rock formations of Emperor Crater, discovering hidden little fairyland meadows and streams. I'm normally a scientific person. However, I swore, as we sat on a short cliff above a wondrous meadow with a silver stream winding around on itself, munched on our lunch, and spied on a couple crater pup families, that I could feel magic wafting in the breeze. I wore a silly smile on my face. Giem just shrugged and enjoyed the view. The crater pups vanished into the crevices of their rocky dens beneath us, and we moved on.

Today we finished lunch sitting on low rocks on a tiny peninsula jutting from our campsite near the shore of Emperor Lake. The opposite crater wall towered over the lake like a craggy castle fortress. We debated whether to spend another night camped nearby, as we looked yearningly at the lake's choppy silver surface. And that was when we met the Ranger.

We recognized her profession by her splendid dark blue-green, multi-pocketed uniform and broad-brimmed hat, and by the way she walked right through our campsite towards us. We didn't have this fantastic crater to ourselves, but the few other campers here were as discreet as us.

"Hi," the Ranger said cheerfully, "plan to stay here another night?"

"Hi." We smiled tentatively in return, wondering rather ridiculously whether we'd done something wrong. An autonomic response to an Official Person.

"I'm just wondering if your campsite is available." She squatted down before us.

Well, that pressed the question even more. We were due at Station Three by tomorrow and clouds had begun to gather in a dark roiling mass above us. We found this whole crater so striking, we hated to leave.

I looked at the Ranger, golden brown, lean, muscular, and radiating health, except perhaps for a trace of a facial scar, revealed when she brushed her long, dark hair away from her almond eyes. Like Giem and most humans, her eyelids bore a trace of an epicanthic fold.

"Uh, we're not sure whether we're staying one more night," I said. I couldn't help thinking about a career that required working out here, and I felt a sudden surge of jealousy.

I caught Giem studying her too, and my teammate glanced back down at our map. "We probably ought to move on today," Giem said reluctantly. "We haven't much more time. But we can just push our pace tomorrow."

We both felt very torn.

The mysterious, echoing, chittering song we'd heard in various craters interrupted my easily distracted thoughts. "What is that?" I asked the Ranger, as I tried to read her nameplate, spattered with mud. "We thought at first it was birds. We haven't figured out where the sounds seem to come from, except the crater wall flower patches." The Vet Student Way again—evade a question you can't answer by asking another.

"It's crater pups." The ranger confirmed my growing suspicion. "Which craters have you seen so far? I assume you're vacationers? I didn't see any cages or stasis equipment in your camp."

"We're FIL interplanetary veterinary students, on our way to work for a while at Enchantment Animal Export Quarantine Station Three," Giem said.

"Ah, FIL vet students! That must be exciting. How do you like it?"

"It—has its ups and downs." I smiled and shrugged, as usual at a loss as to how to convey to an outsider the enormous excitement and fear involved in our schooling. "It's alright. What's it like being a ranger?"

"Oh, it's great! I love it a lot. The scenery out here is wonderful, and so are most of the people I meet. I don't have too many run-ins with unlicensed pickers and poachers. And I'm on vacation today—I just didn't bother to bring along a regular change of clothes. All in all, I'd say it's a smooth career."

How disgusting, I thought, as I died silently. "So you're headed for Quarantine Station Three?" the Ranger said. "Did you come from Quarantine Station One? How's the weather been?"

"Yes," Giem answered her first question, and proceeded to outline our route, along with the weather. "It's been quite pleasant most of the way, fairly warm even during the few showers we've ridden through."

"Fallen Moon Lake Crater, huh?" The Ranger picked it out among Giem's list, and frowned briefly. "Kind of creepy, huh?"

"Yeah," we agreed at once. I didn't embarrass Giem by telling about her nova climb. Instead we described the leech-worms.

"Sucker threads? That's a new one on me. I'll have to check into our life catalogs, when I report back. That could prove serious."

"Forest Crater was also weird," I said hesitantly. "Something odd happen there?"

"I wouldn't say strange, although I never heard the cause," the Ranger said. "More like sad. A packer's horse died from colic there, too far from help. Anyway, speaking of odd, tomorrow I plan to try to hunt up the Chelner cabin in this crater. Have you seen it?"

"A cabin?" Giem said. "It's not on my map."

"What's a Chelner cabin?" I said.

"Oh, some fused Chelnerian apparently discovered this planet before anyone else." The Ranger pointed out a rough area for her search on Giem's map. "She didn't report it. Instead she built a series of little cabins all over the Rash, and lived in them for years before FIL Scouts ever found Enchantment."

"Then what did she do?" I said.

The Ranger frowned as she searched her memory. "I think—I believe she was dead or gone by the time Scouts arrived. Rumor had it she was trying to escape a kragi addiction. The ecological surveyors found all these abandoned cabins, and another one turns up now and then."

We talked about different craters, when the crack of not-so-distant thunder interrupted us rather rudely, and forced me to glare up again at the darkening sky.

"Well, what will it be, Taje?" Giem also stared at the overhead pile-up.

"I think if we don't want to spend our afternoon trapped in the tent, we might as well move on."

The Ranger set up her camp in our spot as we packed, threw on our raingear, and saddled up in growing haste. A fine mist dampening every surface turned into a light sprinkle as we mounted and waved to the Ranger.

She waved back. "Thanks! Stay away from Enchanted Forests, and fare well on your journey!"

That haunting formality, again. I would have liked to ask her about it. It was too late. The lake perimeter trail led us to the first narrow, flower-bordered switchbacks, up out of the crater, just as the real downpour hit. Giem had to nearly shout back at me so I could hear her.

We couldn't help reviewing our regrets. Why had we decided to spend such a large and difficult part of our lives in vet school, instead of becoming rangers so we could vacation in places like this for work?

"Why didn't you stick with ecology training?" Giem asked me, as we rode the last flowery switchback out of Emperor Crater.

"Pre-ecology nearly killed me," I said sourly. "And it did kill my mount, Ked, and I couldn't save her. Why didn't you just stay on your scenic homeworld?"

"I wanted exotic Adventure, Excitement, and Romance!"

CHAPTER 25

When we at last reached the road through the small town of Crater Three, it yanked us back to the reality of our externship. The road left town and skirted the edge of the largest crater we'd seen so far, too vast for any amount of rain to totally obscure. Crater Three dwarfed the town behind us and the quarantine station ahead of us, both perched on its edge like sad little children's toys. We pulled up in front of Quarantine Station Three late that day, in another soaking rainfall that made us almost glad to end our journey.

The dismal weather hadn't helped my mood, and I dismounted with a feeling of foreboding. Somehow, with our brief vacation ending, I was so expectant of more trouble, I found myself sweating under my raingear. We clipped our horses to the rail outside the prefab, low-slung, cheap-looking sprawl labeled Quarantine Station Three, squatting with its back to the crater. Someone had planted podtree saplings in a ring around the building. They looked out of place and many suffered bare branches. We stepped up on a porch that sounded hollow under our boots, and entered the tiny front office, a stuffy, brightly lit room with a miniature black reception desk.

I looked down at the white tile floor, and discovered the mud from our boots simply blended in with a lot more of the same. Before we could announce ourselves, a door behind the desk slid open. A slender young man, with braided brown hair, and a uniform consisting of a cheap blue smock, T-shirt, and pants, greeted us with an enthusiastic smile.

"You're here! You must be the vet students."

"That's right." We smiled happily in reply, grateful at last—someone not only expected us, but seemed glad to see us.

"You must have horses tied up outside." He came around the desk, and rummaged in a closet near the front door. The raingear he extracted and slipped on still dripped from its last adventure, and he already wore wet wading boots. "My name's Temm. Come on, I'll show you to our corral."

We gave him our names as we hurried back out after him, and he directed us to lead our three horses on around the right side of the building.

"Was there an extra one of you after all?" Temm asked, tugging loose the jammed gate of a small, muddy pen. It abutted the building, whose long eves provided the only shelter.

"What do you mean?" Giem said, as we walked our horses into the empty corral. We clipped them to the fence, as far under the eves as possible.

"We heard there were only two of you," Temm said, "and Station Four got one of you. I'm surprised they didn't bring you out here on a transport or supply run. Three and Four have both been swamped with work all summer."

My heart began to descend into my stomach again. Another fuse-up. Wonderful. "You mean they want to split us up? No one even mentioned a fourth station."

"You're right, there are only two of us." Giem turned to Temm. "If Station Four also needs help, one of us will have to ride on from here."

"Sounds like someone got their coms crossed again. Too bad. You'd have had a shorter ride directly from One to Four. Four will fuse!" Temm grinned at us as he unlocked a door in the side of the building, within the corral. He stepped inside, and seconds later I could hear a trough near us filling with water. He came back out with an armload of hay for a manger under the eves, and nodded back over his shoulder. "You can store your tack in there—I'll give you a hand in just a moment."

He helped us carry our luggage to one of a small series of close, numbered doors, way around on the other side of the building, beyond a set of garage doors. I noticed some healthier podtree saplings outside, and Temm said, "Gnaf keeps them watered." He showed his wristcom to one of the doors, and with some difficulty, ordered the control panel to accept our wristcoms. We crammed our way into a room barely larger than a walk-in closet.

"Sorry it's so small," Temm said, "but we weren't expecting two of you, and at least it's free and convenient.

I have to pay rent to get a larger place in town, and it's a long walk from here. Anyway, that back door leads to a little hallway to the bathroom."

We hung our raingear in a slim closet, dumped our stuff on the floor next to the tiny bed that filled almost half the room, and then we followed Temm back outside and around to another door. "This seems a bit confusing at first, I know," he said, unlocking the door and leading us through a dusty storeroom to another door. "You'll get used to it soon enough. I got lost several times my first couple days."

We walked through a series of dim little rooms, variously stacked with old cages, a couple defunct-looking bioscanners, and jumbled plumbing parts and roof patches. At last we reached a larger storage room with feed, carts, and cages. On the other side of this room Temm led us into a huge, well-lit, flooded cage room. "It's not always like this," he apologized again. "It's just when the rainy season first launches—"

Rows and rows of banked cages hid the sources of some angry voices. They were loud enough to interrupt Temm as we waded in up to our ankles.

"This is ridiculous! You realize we lost over a hundred pups to drowning this morning? Why didn't any of the sensor alarms go off last night?" The accent was Altruskan male.

"I reported problems with the sensors over a month ago. I still haven't gotten an okay on my order for new parts—" This one was human female—

"Well, why haven't you at least pumped out all of this water? You and Temm have had all day."

"Temm's busy saving pups and doing manual cleaning, while I've had so many leaks to fix—"

"What pups we could save were moved this morning, and the autocleaner systems should have been one of your first—" The yellow haired, elderly, white-coated Altruskan halted his tirade, as we splashed down his aisle. Opposite him stood a dark-haired, stocky woman, wearing brown coveralls and a packed tool belt. Both looked angry and miserably wet, and the discomfort of our timing distracted me from a close look at the clear cages' inhabitants.

"Dr. Morbe, our vet students have arrived," Temm said, with what sounded like forced cheerfulness.

Giem and I exchanged embarrassed and curious looks. Dr. Morbe—wasn't he supposed to be the director of the whole quarantine service?

"There are two?" Dr. Morbe said. "I only agreed to take one student!"

"An extra one was sent here by mistake."

"Well, no matter, I guess. Glad to have you! My name's Dr. Morbe." He reached out his dark green, gnarly, yellow-nailed, four-fingered hand to shake with us human style. "And you must be—?"

"Giemsan Fane."

"Tajen Jesmuhr. Glad to meet you." Right.

"Yes! Well. Let's go to my office for a better introduction. Gnaf and Temm, I expect you to clean up this mess before you go home tonight."

Gnaf, the coveralled woman, gave us such a stony, silent stare that I felt a shiver shimmy up my back, as Giem and I followed Dr. Morbe out of the slippery aisle.

A zigzag around more swamped aisles and some dingy halls brought us to Morbe's office. A contrast in comfort, cleanliness, and luxury, if rather haphazard in appearance. We had to leave our boots at the door, to spare the thick black carpet that didn't quite meet two of the walls. From scars on the latter, I guessed this used to be more than one room. I took the velvety grey-green armchair closest to the beautiful picture window—so new some of the guts of its controls were still showing—to the left of Morbe's finely carved, wood-grain desk.

I couldn't help staring out the window, beyond a stunted podtree, at the stormy panorama looming over majestic Crater Three. The last purple shades of sunset vanished over its vast, flowering, craggy surface. I forced my attention back towards Dr. Morbe as he took his seat behind his broad desk. Giem sat down in the plush blue-grey armchair next to mine.

"So," the Altruskan began, as he scratched the base of one of his two trimmed horns, poking out between his yellowed bangs. "Station Four still expects one of you—which one?"

Giem shrugged.

"We were supposed to work as a team," I said, without hiding my resentment. I was still damp and cold, and not eager to stay in this warm room long enough to remedy it. A hot shower and a change of clothes, and I'd even feel ready for the miserable little bed assigned to us. I wondered if I'd have to fight Giem for it.

"Well, you two can take the night to decide who wants to stay and who wants to leave," the doctor said obliviously. "It doesn't matter to me, and we certainly don't want to send one of you off in this storm tonight. We can wait until morning."

How very generous. Giem's forbidding look cut me off, before I could say it aloud and spoil our introduction. It wasn't fair she was bigger than me.

Dr. Morbe leaned back and lowered shelf-like yellow eyebrows at us. "How much were you two told about us?"

Neither of us could help giving him baffled looks. It wasn't as if we hadn't done considerable preparation. Even if we had crammed most of it after finals, packing, shuttling, and boarding our paraship—in fact, while waiting for our turn in the rebugging tanks. Uh, I thought, you're an Insidious Criminal Organization, and you had Dr. Emmel Eliminated, before we arrived. She secretly hired us as Undercover Agents, to Infiltrate your Dastardly Schemes. I thought about the reaction I'd get from that fantasy—

"You provide quarantine services," Giem said curtly. "For crater pups—local, very populous, pesty flower-eaters, and fortunately the latest galactic pet rage." Fine. Anything to get this interview over with before bedtime.

"Fortunate is a good term." Dr. Morbe leaned forward again. "We're a private, commercial enterprise. You both come from a government school where admin works a little differently, so I think I should emphasize that. The only connection we have with the Federation of Intelligent Life is the laws they make us follow."

Maybe that was a challenge. My eyes teared up as I only partly suppressed a huge yawn. I think Giem's eyes had started to roll.

"What's our quarantine period?" Morbe demanded abruptly.

"Four weeks," we answered promptly. We were both good crammers. And that was the easiest test question we'd encountered in ages.

"Right. Do you know why we have to quarantine?"

My turn, I suppose. "To prevent the spread of interplanetary disease—" I blurted out, and then stumbled. I must have grown too tired. "Wait a micro, rebugging should take care of that during shipping—"

"Yes, the microfloral readjustment tanks." Dr. Morbe tapped a horn sagely. "So much has changed so fast. During my schooling, such a process would have been considered impossible. The whole field has grown so complex it's hard to follow all the new developments. One wonders if the new reports of allergic reactions will end the whole silly mess as quickly as it started. Until then, one might also think stations such as this would be outmoded."

I had lost track of the number of times Dr. Morbe made us flinch with his spiel. He continued without appearing to notice. "Nevertheless, FIL authorities decided we were still necessary, to assure consumers of a healthy product overall, medically sound as well as free of infectious diseases.

"The most expedient method to achieve that is to allow the sale and shipping of only those animals that have survived one month of captivity, as well as passing pre- and post-quarantine check-ups. Since the first captive month is apparently the most stressful, it's a harsh test. I understand you're here to help us reduce quarantine mortality. We welcome that help. We're basically middlemen, buying crater pups from hunters, and in turn selling to offworld exporters. Obviously, the more crater pups we can sell at the end of quarantine, the more profit we make."

CHAPTER 26

"Pompous old vac-head," Giem muttered, struggling to unlock our door. At first it didn't want to recognize her wristcom. Next it jammed partway, and we just forced it open. We walked through the narrow space between the bed and wall, and sorted through our luggage on the floor. Giem dug out her brush to work on her thick auburn hair.

"I thought he'd never shut up." I sat down on the bed at last. It was lumpy. "If I hadn't felt so tired by the ride here, I'd have halted his harangue sooner, with the right answer." I lay down and sighed.

Giem glanced around the little room. "That's alright. I knew you had the correct idea crammed into your brain somewhere, even if you failed to rescue us from his speech. What I want to know is, where's the food dispenser in here?"

I put my hands comfortably behind my head. "I dunno. Who gets the bed tonight?" I commed I'd cleverly achieved territorial rights, as my eyes wandered lazily over the sparse bedside controls set into the left wall. "Oh, here it is, right next to the comscreen."

"I get the bed, so don't make yourself too comfortable. What's on the menu?" Giem leaned on top of my right shoulder, nearly crushing me as I reached left-handed for the controls. "Not much of a choice, huh? You get the bed? Why? Funny how most of the entrees include crater pup meat—it can't be an economic measure, can it, regarding this morning's drowning victims?" I made a disgusted face while Giem ordered her dinner. I massaged my shoulder when she stood back up.

"Maybe I'll be sorry I'm trying crater pup meat so soon here," I said.

A cubby opened next to the miniature screen, and I reached in to hand Giem her food tray. I had ordered my first crater pup burger, and hoped it was really a clone cell vat product.

Giem sat down on the foot of the bed, on top of my feet. "If I have to set out on another camping expedition in the morning," she said between mouthfuls of a steak smelling suspiciously similar to my burger, "the least you can do is let me sleep in a real bed tonight."

The only chair in the room was an unpadded stool, so I yanked my feet out from under her, but didn't push her off. "You're riding on to Four?" I said rudely, through a mouthful of food. The bread was stale, and the pale meat was dry and oddly sweet. "We haven't even fought over—I mean, discussed it."

"Hah, Taje! You think you could find your way to Four by yourself, with your fused sense of direction?"

Blast, she won. "So I get stuck with old Dr. Morbidity."

"How do you know I won't get stuck with someone worse?" Giem said, with cold logic.

"The odds don't seem likely. How could this get much worse? With my luck, the vet in charge of Four will be your perfect mate."

"I think we can make room for your sleeping bag on the floor alongside the bed, Taje."

CHAPTER 27

The next morning I awoke after I realized the persistent nudging against my arm was from Giem's foot, not from the krel nose in my dream. My neck had a cramp in it.

"Ohhh," I groaned, trying to focus on my wristcom. I'd left it on my wrist, rather than risk losing it amongst the sea of our belongings sharing the floor with me. "Look how early it is! Not even sunrise. What's the big rush?"

"Not my idea," Giem complained. "Temm's on the room com. He wants to talk with whomever's staying to work here."

Giem left for the bathroom, so I was able to sit on the bed to see the screen. I rubbed my eyes, the better to see Temm's wide-awake, slightly less happy-looking face. I gave him a reluctant hello. By the time Giem returned, I was leadenly dragging on my clothes, my hope for even a quick warm-up shower dashed.

"What did he want?" Giem found her pack and pulled out some clothes.

"Someone to help him out of a bind, before the Big Green Boss arrives later this morning. Temm stayed up until midnight last night with Gnaf, and still didn't get all the chores done as ordered. So it's heroic Taje to the rescue. What are you doing?"

Giem was leaning half-dressed over the bed. "I'm ordering breakfast for me and tea for you. After I finish dressing and eat breakfast, I guess I might as well pack up and saddle up. I don't think I could get back to sleep, and I suspect the sooner I reach Station Four, the better my reception. Here, drink this before you leave."

I took the steaming mug from her, and found it a little difficult to swallow. "I still think it sucks vac they're separating us," I said, after sipping hot ginger tea. "That wasn't part of the original deal. We should have fought it more."

"As far as these characters are concerned, the original deal never existed," Giem said, over her breakfast tray. The smell of food this early in the morning was too vile for words, and her reasonable attitude was a little difficult to stomach too. "So cheer up," Giem said, "be glad we have work, and we didn't get shipped back to Olecranon. Besides, we can call each other whenever we want. We'll have to stay in close contact, to properly correlate and compare our findings, of course."

"Of course."

"According to my map, I should make it to Station Four within several days. Give me a little time to settle in. I'll call by the end of the week. I promise. Goodbye, Taje."

"Bye, Giem. And beware of Enchanted Forests!" I bravely tried to end on a silly note.

I left, before she could see my teary eyes. It wasn't fair, working apart again. The only vet school roomies in our class who hadn't mauled or married by now.

I trudged through mud and a light rain to what I thought was a short-cut door, and wasted a frustrating amount of time inside on little halls, balky doors, and rooms that led nowhere. I resorted at last to going back outside, entered by the front office, and paged Temm to meet me there. He apologized for getting me up early, as he led me back to the previously flooded cage room. Most of the water had drained away, leaving only a few shallow, slick puddles.

"Gnaf stayed up even later than I did, and removed most of the water—she does a good job," he said, tugging absentmindedly on a braid. I tried to remember if his red, blue, and gold, triangular earring meant anything in this sector of FIL. "She won't return until later this morning, and she hasn't had time to get the automatic cleaning systems restarted in the bottom cages. So I've got to do them all manually, before I can move pups back into them." He led me down the first aisle, to a large cart near the end where he'd obviously started working.

"You want me to help with it?"

"If you hand-feed some of the pups still too upset to eat on their own, while I get their cages ready, that would help a lot. A few among the youngest do better with some coaxing, and the ones that got chilled in the bottom cages will probably need that too."

"Sure. Just show me how."

"Oh, it's easy," he said, stopping before a bank of three cages. Each cage was separated into three sections. "Look for the ones moping, and check their feed trough meters. Here's one."

Temm touched a control to the side of a cage. One section slid open, and he gently swept up a roughly two kilogram, brilliant orange pup under his left arm. He took a handful of faded purple and green mashed flower petals, leaves, and dried insects from the full trough—the clash of colors between pup and feed was incredible— and used his right hand to gently stuff an amazing amount into the pup's mouth.

The pup blinked with some surprise, and chewed and swallowed slowly. I stroked its cheek, soft and smooth one way, and prickly in the opposite direction. When Temm put it back, I wondered how the pup felt, exposed in its completely clear cage.

Temm pulled out its cage mate in the next section. "Think you can do it?" He placed the depressed orange pup into my hands. Suddenly, the prickliness multiplied an order of magnitude, as the critter chose that moment to rotate the shafts of its insulation. After a brief, garish scramble of orange, blue, and pink, it presented me with its deep blue coat.

"Fantastic!" I said. "That's the first time I've ever seen this."

"They are beautiful. I've been working here almost a year, and I still get a thrill out of color shifts. Go ahead and try to feed it. Don't worry—they don't bite hard. It's not part of their natural defenses."

I gave the pup a cautious amount of fodder, that disappeared through a small facial orifice, into a surprisingly cavernous oral cavity. "I know that," I realized. "Neither do they run much. Just hide in their forage during the day, and slip into their rocky dens at night."

"That's right." Temm ejected a foul-smelling tray from the empty bottom cage, and exchanged it for a clean tray from the cart. "Once you get it to start chewing, stuff its cheek pouches, put it back down here—I doubled it up yesterday to keep it from drowning—and move on. Otherwise we'll never finish."

"How many pups do you have in here?"

"Nearly a thousand."

"I see." I took a deep breath. I reached for the cage release of the next lethargic pup down the line.

"Aren't you going to ask how many cage rooms we have?" Temm smiled teasingly until he exchanged the next tray, emptying a dead pup into a stasis compartment in the cart.

"Oh no!" And I wasn't exclaiming over the pathetic little drowned corpse.

"Yeah, we have four cage rooms, one to empty out and rotate onto receiving at the beginning of each week. This batch is due to sell out of here in five days."

I learned to work extremely fast, in very short order, while Temm happily spewed out crater pup trivia. It turns out crater pup parents raise their litters on regurgitated food, in their aforementioned dens. The pups aren't allowed out until they're old enough to forage for themselves. That's why they don't usually have to be handfed after capture, but will accept it if forced.

Temm had obviously put all the knowledge he had of crater pup habits to good use, in a caring manner that had me admiring him by the time Dr. Morbe arrived to check on us, midmorning. We hadn't made it out of the first room, but we had nearly finished it. And since this was the only room that had flooded, according to Temm, the rest of our work should go fast.

Dr. Morbe became livid. However, as soon as he saw me he tried to act polite. Having grown up with some Altruskans, I could tell all was not well by the blue flush in his green cheeks.

"Temm, you haven't seen to the other three cage rooms, have you? There's dead—uh, hello, Tajen. I'm glad to see you working with the team! Temm?"

"No, sir, we've had to spend some extra time in here resettling the pups upset yesterday."

"You should have all the pups attended to by this time. How often have I had to remind you how important it is I get a preliminary report from you, as soon as I come in? How much longer must I wait this morning?"

"Oh, we won't take much longer. The other rooms will go much faster."

"Where's Gnaf? She isn't answering my page."

"I think she may be working up on the roof."

"So long as she isn't oversleeping. I catch her at that again, it'll go on her record." Dr. Morbe turned his glance again towards me, while I wondered if he could possibly already have a complaint to yell at me.

"So you've decided to stay with us, eh, Jesmuhr? You're probably starting to realize how much you can learn from us. Anyway, I'm pleased to see such early enthusiasm for the job on your part. I wasn't sure what to expect from students on a required assignment like this. Make sure Temm shows you all the details of our routines today." And with that he turned and left, leaving me almost too dumbfounded to feel insulted.

We didn't see him again until nearly noon, when all of us met in the receiving bay for new captures. Gnaf operated the cranky garage doors, and directed the line-up of trucks waiting just outside. Temm and I alternated helping hunters with unloading cages, and assisting Dr. Morbe at a series of examination tables.

I found it stressful learning on the job, over the next couple hours, the check-in procedure for nearly a hundred pups. I was sure by the end of it, the pups felt the most stress. Each one had a cursory, none-too-gentle hands-on exam by Dr. Morbe. Followed by an attack of body fluid and waste samplers, with needle and suction cartridges that could have used more frequent changing. A rather false economy measure, I thought, as I loaded one of the black "Reject" carts with pups that wouldn't even need its humane euthanasia services.

The hunters seemed oblivious, however, as they waited anxiously for Morbe's medcoms to download credits calculated from exam and lab scores into their wristcoms. So they could rush back into the field and catch another load for the evening check-in.

Yes, evening check-in. I'm glad I didn't know to anticipate it that day, even if it meant I hadn't paced myself for it either.

"When's lunch?" I asked Temm, as soon as we were out of Dr. Morbe's earshot, and running full carts in through the back doors of the receiving bay. By now I was very hungry.

"Normally after noon check-ins," Temm said. He led me on through the halls and a set of double doors, "Quarantine Room Three" spelled out over them. "We'll have to eat fast today, to allow enough time for afternoon autopsies and quarantine room checks."

"Hey," I said, following him with my line of carts. "What about the bioscanners?"

"What?" Temm stopped alongside a row of empty cages, and began to gently, rapidly unload his carts.

"Bioscanners. I saw a few old ones around here somewhere, my first day. Don't we need to run these pups through a scan before we quarantine them?" Bioscanners were such an integral part of modern physicals, I'd taken their use for granted. The only part I couldn't com, in all the hurry back in receiving, was why the scans weren't done first, and included in price evaluations.

Temm just looked at me blankly. He had no idea what I was talking about. In shock, I had to rush to keep up with him. We transferred all our cart occupants into clear cages. We stuffed down a greasy lunch from a measly employee lounge, before moving on to the necropsy room, and another set of antiquated tasks on a percentage of the day's massive losses.

Temm had this down to a very fast routine with his cutting and sampling instruments—standardized organ observations and tissue sample analyses. Of all his tasks, he appeared to understand these the least, and I had to take them on faith. It was all he could do to show me how to obtain and enter the results for the quarantine com to tally, before we had to run through the cage rooms again.

This did go a lot faster than morning—fewer cage malfunctions to deal with and report, and fewer anorexic and dead pups to handle. Again we barely made it to the evening hunter check-ins on time, another noisy scramble, as hectic as the noon session.

I was exhausted for this final piece of business, and had trouble not creating more work than I was doing. I ended up accidentally leaving not one, but two cages open, and two times many of us had to drop whatever we were doing to chase the occupants down. I was just lucky the poor little pups were slow, and prone to freezing up when scared.

I was simply relieved to be checking out with Dr. Morbe at the end of it, never mind the speech I'd prepared in my head, during the day, on what my real job responsibilities should entail here. I could live with a day's crash course on normal operations. Just let me go to bed, please.

"Well, thank you, Tajen," Dr. Morbe said, distractedly. "Temm, before you leave, don't forget I need your final room reports. Also, the Crater One rental horse won't need any further care. Xaffe's hunting group agreed to haul it back for us, tonight. And Gnaf, I'm still getting some leaks in the bathroom behind my office. We need to stop them before they reach my new carpet, so you'd better fix them tonight."

Gnaf gave him a frozen glare he didn't seem to notice, though it would have turned me into an ice cube. "I told you earlier, I'll need help to do that. There's a bunch of jobs I can't get to until we hire another assistant—"

"Gnaf," Morbe entered the ocular icicle contest, "I'm getting very tired of your excuses. Use your head. Tajen is here. Learn to utilize her if you need someone. The more she learns about our business here, the more she can help us."

I gave Gnaf a numb, bewildered look. What did I know about plumbing? She returned the favor with what could only be an expression of thinly disguised disgust. Too late I realized it was a familiar response. She'd been unhappily drafted into helping with the pup chases too.

I spent the next couple hours fumbling to hold odd plumbing parts in position for Gnaf to adjust and seal, in a dim, stuffy, smelly closet. She hardly said a word beyond impatiently curt, orders, and by the end of it I felt about two centimeters tall. I got lost afterwards trying to find an indoor route to my room, instead of going back outside in the first place. When I at last fell on my bunk, I hit a dinner order, undressed, and slid under my covers.

I awoke to my morning alarm, and a stale, untouched food tray sitting in the delivery cubby.

CHAPTER 28

"I think Gnaf hates me," I confessed to Temm. I tried to keep myself awake, as I frantically fed anorexic pups, my last evening of my first full week at Station Three. And I mean *full*.

Weekends didn't seem to exist at Three. Each employee got one different day off during the week, simply burdening the rest of us more, because the main variation in the daily schedule was what new disasters we had to fix. And Morbe hadn't assigned my day off. Somehow it had simply evaporated from his mind. At least on his free day, we didn't have to do check-ins. Instead, we worked doubly hard the day before, to assist Morbe with his post-quarantine check-ups. So we could spend the next day loading exporters' trucks and taking their credits, without his help.

As it was, it took me nearly the whole week to com I should get a day off, instead of looking forward to the weekend. And having started with a sleep deficit, only growing worse each day, all I could do was count the hours, and minutes, until the one reward I had coming tonight—Giem's first call.

"No, you're wrong about Gnaf," Temm said, as he pushed our cart ahead for the next dead collection on the aisle. Room Two had a little more work than we'd been able to finish by evening check-in physicals. So we dove back into it, before we could get dinner and go to bed. I quickly loaded the pup I'd just fed back in its cage, and scanned for the next needy pup, as I secretly admired Temm from the rear.

After a week of his tutorship, I knew Temm wasn't an incredibly brilliant person—he wouldn't be trapped in his present position if he were—and he was also younger than me. He was sweet, and endlessly kind to his charges, in spite of all the unkindness blasted at him.

"I've had to help Gnaf half a dozen times this week," I said, "and she still won't treat me like a normal person." I pulled out another pup and yawned into its startled face. It shifted very slowly from green to red, and I somehow felt insulted.

"Gnaf acts that way around everyone," Temm said, who was also nice enough to talk to me as no one else here did. We'd worked a lot together and had grown fairly close. Neither of us would have ventured this discussion earlier this week. "I think she's just shy."

"Gnaf! Shy?" I thought she was a horrible snob, and nearly said so as we finished up this row, and rounded the corner into our last aisle. What held me back was the memory of a similar error made by Center residents, judging me at a younger age. "Well, maybe you have a point."

Speak of the devil. Gnaf appeared at the other end of the aisle, and rapidly strode toward us as I made harried calculations concerning distances to doors and acoustic factors. The look on her face didn't give me any clues. As usual, she scowled.

However, her dripping raingear and laden tool belt led me to guess what she'd come here for. I mentally groaned. So much for being minutes away from dinner and Giem's comcall. I was in for another thankless repair job assist, probably out in the wet and cold. I shuddered to think we could have avoided her by finishing just a bit sooner.

"It's starting to blow badly out there tonight, and I've got to have help with some more roof patches," Gnaf said as she stopped before us. "Or we'll have to deal with more flooding tomorrow morning."

I couldn't believe she was looking at Temm with this announcement. I had started to feel singled-out for attack, and I almost had my defenses ready this time. Instead, I found myself studying Temm's face with concern. This was about the most upset I'd ever seen him, a surprise, considering his obvious loyalty to station work.

"Oh, Gnaf, not tonight! Didn't I remember to tell you I can't stay so long today? My day off is tomorrow, and my partner will be so unhappy, if I can't help pack for the special trip we've planned. It's our first since the baby!"

Partner? Baby? Maybe we hadn't become as close as I'd thought. My weary brain reeled, even as one subsection of it leaped impulsively to the rescue, crushing a rebel sector willing to quit caring about anyone, just for some privacy and sleep.

"I'll help you out, Gnaf," I heard my traitor self say. "We're almost done here. Temm can finish up and go on home, while I get my raingear. Okay?"

It was worth it momentarily, just to see Temm's look of sheer gratitude. Not to mention the brief shocked reaction Gnaf tried to hide on her face. I headed for an exit, holding my hand over a wicked grin on my face.

"Taje," came Gnaf's irritated voice from behind.

I turned around, my face a mask of innocence. "What?"

"It's shorter if you go that way." Temm attempted to squelch his smile, as he pointed towards the exit doors in the opposite direction.

"Blast the whole Galaxy!" I lost my shout to the night wind, blowing icy sheets of rain in my face, back outside on the way to my room. A half week of sunshine, glimpsed at check-ins, had made me complacent about raingear.

I unlocked my door, just to the right of Gnaf's, and I retrieved rainpants, hooded coat, and gloves from my tiny closet.

"Why in the Galaxy am I trying to impress a station tech?" I muttered, as I closed various seals and pulled down my visor. Why hadn't I commed before—or asked—why Temm stretched his no-doubt thin pay to rent an apartment at the end of the long walk back into town, instead of taking a free room like Gnaf and me? How could I have assumed that simply because he was younger than me, Temm might be available, and couldn't possibly have a family?

I had to remind myself that prolonged schooling had stunted my social growth, as I stomped my boots back on. I returned to the muddy, treacherous night, and headed around the building. "This is insane! I'm cold, hungry, and tired, I'm missing Giem's call, I hate heights, and I haven't gotten to do any real veterinary work."

"Here I am!" Had she heard me this time over the howling wind? Gnaf's flashlight shone down from the roof on a set of slick, wet, cold, metal rungs I could only climb safely by removing my gloves. She had to help me up over the edge.

Gnaf had a demonic grin on her face, lit from below by the light clipped to her belt. I felt completely humiliated. Here I was, a FIL veterinary student, stuffed with incredible and expensive quantities of difficult information, nearly defeated by the simple climb up the side of a building. I felt sick.

"Let's get to work," Gnaf said.

I had to hold down various loose panels and patches, flapping violently in the wind, while she ran a sealer around their edges. It was simple, tedious, bone-chilling work, allowing me plenty of time for more regrets. I should have changed into warmer clothes under my raingear, I couldn't see through the rain on my visor so I lifted it, and more rain leaked through too hastily adjusted seals. My face caught the full brunt of the storm, and cold water ran down around my neck. I wondered if Gnaf could hear my stomach growling or see my arms trembling with fatigue.

After we did about ten panels, it finally occurred to my numb brain that I could just stand on the cheap, vacful things to hold them in place. I also stopped counting, making the whole business seemingly go a little faster in my haze of exhaustion.

I watched recorded com messages late that night, as I peeled, shivering, out of my soaked clothes.

"Taje, this is Giem, as promised, remember? Sorry I'm a bit late. Give me a call as soon as you get in. I've just finished my third day at Station Four, and I'm very tired."

"Taje, Giem again. Where are you? I'm heading for the shower, and I will try once more after that. I'm eager to exchange stories."

"Forget it, Taje. I have to get to bed. I'll try again tomorrow night."

I felt very sorry for myself as I ate a small, hot, lonely dinner and crawled into bed. It didn't occur to me, until right before I drifted off to sleep, that Gnaf could have just as easily stood on those nova patches herself, while she was sealing them. Funny how insights like that don't zap your brain until too late.

CHAPTER 29

"So, was he cute?" Giem asked, the next night. We had both turned up our coms, to overcome the music that blasted from Gnaf's room nearly every night, through the thin wall between us. I'd given up politely asking her to turn it down or wear ear bugs. She suggested I simply ask Dr. Morbid to change my room. Sure.

I retrieved my dinner tray from a prone position on my bed before I answered Giem's question. We'd just exchanged the effusive greetings of marooned and long-lost friends.

"Who?" I said.

"Whomever you spent last night with," Giem teased, in spite of looking as weary as I still felt. "Was it another alien?"

"No." I made a face. "She was a mean, slave-driver."

"Taje, you have very strange tastes." We both laughed half-heartedly.

"So what made you so late?" I challenged Giem, before she could ask for tiresome details. "How do you like the folks at Station Four?"

"They're understaffed to say the least, but they're not bad. You should see the station vet—quite dashing, and very kind too. I think you'd really like him."

"It coms." I stabbed a chunk of my crater pup and vegetable stew. Maybe Giem had a different reason for looking so tired. I knew Giem was skewed very human hetero.

"Don't get too jealous," she broke down. "The vet tech here is his husband, and they're locked tight."

"Oh."

"So haven't you launched after that cute station tech who greeted us—what was his name?"

"Temm's married and has a baby, Giem."

"What in the Galaxy were you doing last night?"

I had to work at not making it into a long, defensive story, especially since I wasn't feeling very agile. I outlined last night's adventure, on top of what enduring a week at Station Three was like.

Giem nodded. "The schedule's much the same here, except maybe a little slower, since this station is newer. Their maintenance person quit a couple months ago, and they still haven't got a replacement. So until I came along, the vet and his partner tried to do it all themselves."

"You're doing repair work?"

"A lot of it. Half a week here and I'm exhausted. I had a similar job as a teenager back on Ballophon, to earn some pocket credits. You complain about doing more tech than vet work. Well, I'm doing even more maintenance than technician duties. These stations obviously weren't built to last."

"Why should they be?" I said, bitterly. "If pet crater pups remain this popular—and short-lived—in a year or two commercial clone companies will take over production. And if crater pups don't continue to sell well, at least some of these stations won't be needed anymore."

"That does sort of put a damper on our significance here."

"I want to go home." I stuffed my decimated tray back into the food cubby, and slapped a control to make it go away.

Giem was still eating her dinner. She looked up from it. "Sure, Taje. Have you got enough credits for a long-distance call to Dr. Hako?"

I would have guessed she was joking, if I hadn't seen her face, which shocked me. "Do you mean it?" The new thought of escaping our trap excited me. "I think I could afford it, although it would probably wipe out my life savings. They're clearly abusing our free labor, and I'm not sure Hako will even consider this acceptable experience."

"Oh, I don't know," Giem said moodily, setting down her utensils. "I know this wouldn't be the first externship used to replace hired help. I suspect Dr. Hako will just expect us to make the best of the situation. No externship is perfect."

"You think so?" I tried to stifle my disappointment. I'm sure I didn't look or sound too happy about it.

"Well, I've noted some obvious animal stress we could alleviate with a few basic suggestions, even without any fancy studies."

"Like what?" I immediately thought of the clear cages, the lack of disinfection between handling different pups, and the amount of trauma they underwent during check-ins and check-outs.

"Coat the clear cages solid, for starters. No doubt the BGB wouldn't be willing to just replace the cages, but what a silly set-up for a species so dependent on camouflage." Giem echoed some of my thoughts.

"The BGB?"

"You know, you called him that our first night at Three, the Director of Enchantment Animal Export Quarantine Services, and temporary head of Station Three, Dr. Morbe, The Big Green Boss. It caught on fast with Dr. Steffin and his husband-slash-tech over here."

"Hey, they sound better all the time. Just tell them not to let the source of that nickname get back to Dr. Morbid. He has no sense of humor. I didn't know he was that big."

"Sure you did. Dr. Nilod told us about him during our first interview."

"Giem, I wish I had your memory. That explains why Morbe seems to dislike staying out here so much. I've heard rumors his deluxe aircar flies him roundtrip to Crater One for his day off. I thought he just did it to check in with the whole operation. Why hasn't he gotten another replacement for Dr. Emmel out here?"

"Rumors concerning her sudden, unexplained death have scared away all prospects."

"Really?" How intriguing—

"Taje, you're so gullible! The job pays fused credits, especially considering the long hours and isolation involved, for a professional, no less. Dr. Steffin and his partner only hired on because they're nova about the Rash, and this is the only way they could afford to stay here together."

"Oh." I thought that made sense. "Uh, want to hear my suggestions for improvements?"

"Sure. Launch away."

"Well, I agree, of course, with the cage idea. Although I'd prefer to see a whole selection of appropriate cage colors, or even better, sensor-adjustable—"

"You're dreaming, Taje."

"I know. I just couldn't help myself. I'd also like to see color-matched feeding. I know they'd never accept the expense of sorting feeds—"

"You know it! Steffin can't even convince the BGB to purchase a few bioscanners, that would cut the stress and increase the accuracy of physicals. Color-matched feeding? I have trouble buying that one. What's your rationale?"

"All I have currently are ecologically based suspicions," I admitted. "I won't have any biochemical back-up until I get one of our bioscanners running."

"Bioscanners? You have *bioscanners*?" Giem yelped.

"It's your turn for a faulty memory." That made me feel perversely better. "They're languishing in layers of dust, in one of the little storage rooms Temm led us through our first day here, remember?"

"I don't think I noticed them. Maybe at the time I just took them for granted. Medical grade?"

"I hope so. I'm priming myself to insist on a meeting with Morbe, where I'll demand a proper amount of time for my studies. I'll also try to get permission to use the scanners."

"Good luck. Just in case you do succeed, how about getting a hunter to drop one off over here?"

"I don't even know if they both work, Giem." I yawned. "I'll do my best. So how about at least instituting hand disinfection between pups?"

"Huh?"

"Crater pups aren't rebugged until they're shipped offworld. A good number might be dying from native infectious diseases, worsened by stress, and we could be spreading problems every time we handle them."

"We use the hand-sterilizers in the carts," Giem said. "Don't you?"

"No one told me the carts even have them. I don't think our vet tech knows about them, and Morbid hasn't said anything, or ever used them in front of me either. I can't stand this place!"

"Steffin tells me Three has the best survival rate of all. Something about what a great tech you have—that Temm really knows how to handle the pups."

"He hand-feeds the sickies. Is that what you mean?"

"Is that all? Why don't all of the stations do it, if simple hand-feeding helps so much?"

"Because it's so labor-intensive? I don't know," I said, exasperated. "What other obvious improvements are we missing?"

"How about housing littermates together, to improve morale? By all reports, these are social animals, with a preference for living in small family groups."

"You'd have to offer the hunters a financial incentive, to bring them in that way." I shook my head. "The BGB was educated in the Dark Ages, and has a very vac-headed sense of economy. None of this will ever make it off a launch pad."

"Well, I'm sure Dr. Steffin will allow me to try some small, controlled experiments. He's sympathetic, even if overworked."

"Giem, how can such a new business be so entrenched in its own vacful rules? And why does such an obviously successful business have to be so miserly? Where's all the profit going?"

"I don't know." She appeared more gloomy than ever.

"I bet I do," I said, cynically. "And it's not into R&D. More likely R&R, for a select few."

"You may be right."

CHAPTER 30

"Dr. Morbe, thank you for agreeing to meet with me," I said in my sickening Eager Student Voice. I felt more tired than ever from trying to help both Temm and Gnaf. And from stealing scraps of time over the last week to prepare and push for this long overdue meeting, on Morbe's day off.

"No problem, Tajen, no problem. You've earned it. You've been a huge help at an especially trying time for us, what with the sudden loss of this station's on-duty veterinarian, the rainy season starting up, and several of our automated systems unexpectedly failing us. So what's on your mind?"

According to Temm, all the satellite stations suffered from chronic employee turnover and mechanical breakdowns. That wasn't what I had in mind to discuss, and I knew Morbe felt rushed. He'd cancelled today's check-ins so he could make it to Station One and back here. I wanted to make use of any free time to start some real work this evening, along with maybe even having some real fun.

"Well, Dr. Morbe," I tried a tactful approach, "I've become familiar enough with your station operations to discuss some initial positive suggestions, and to propose some preliminary directions for my morbidity and mortality study here."

"Suggestions? For your study? Haven't you started?"

By that did he mean he considered me some sort of super student—capable of working simultaneously as a vet student researcher and a station tech—or was the latter the only real job specification he had ever had in mind for me? I had trouble giving him the benefit of any doubt.

"No," I answered patiently, "I've had too much to do, just helping out with all your maintenance problems, to launch a serious study. While doing tech work here has given me a few helpful ideas—"

"Excellent! You're catching on. I know—I've seen the results from your work. Certainly, Tajen, if you have some constructive suggestions, go ahead and transmit them to my main office at Station One. We can coordinate from there."

"Well, I thought I'd just mention some of them right now. They're fairly simple changes that can be made soon, and could almost immediately reduce your daily losses."

"You must go through proper channels, Tajen, proper channels. Otherwise the whole organization falls apart. Speaking of which, I'm going to have to depart soon." Dr. Morbe looked at the time meter on the comscreen set into his desk. "I must make it back to One soon for a meeting."

Dr. Morbe stood up, and I went into panic mode over my nearly untouched agenda.

"Dr. Morbe—"

"Yes?" He had made it halfway to his door.

"What about my study?"

"Oh, go ahead with it. You don't need my permission, as long as it doesn't interfere with business. Just report your results as you obtain them." He was at the door, and threatening to lower his yellowed, bushy eyebrows on me, should I dare to detain him a micro longer.

"I'll need equipment," I persisted. Not to mention time—"

"Equipment? What's wrong with what we have here? Our budget won't allow for any special purchases."

"For starters, I really need at least two medical grade bioscanners," I said as politely as possible, considering I'd never expected to have to explain that to a practicing veterinarian. "I think you've got a couple here I could use, if you'll permit it. And in the long run, incorporated into your physicals, they could save lives."

"Bioscanners? Here? I think you're mistaken. We can't afford the expense or time involved with scans, on our marginal profit, and they aren't required. If your study doesn't take economics into account, it won't be of much use to us. If I were you, I'd concentrate on our current laboratory results, and possibly on some of the necropsy data."

That suggestion was laughably obvious. I didn't laugh as I said goodbye to Morbid's back. Well, so much for trying to get official permission to experiment with the equipment in storage. On the other hand, he hadn't said no, and he had left my study guidelines open.

I quietly followed the BGB to the front door, and nearly snickered when it stuck briefly, and he almost walked right into it. Outside, he glanced back around at me nervously a couple times as he headed for the garage and his private aircar. I calmly walked on, following some recent instructions from Temm, past the dorm rooms, and around to the door he had led us in our first day.

"Wow, two real bioscanners!" I said, a few minutes later, surprised I could find my way back to the obscure little room, and relieved to discover I hadn't wishfully hallucinated them. I brushed away some of the dust from one, and reached for its handles, only to find I could barely budge the scanner. "Great Galaxy, how ancient *are* these?"

I found my way to the supply room, retrieved an aircart, and managed to slide each device onto it by bracing my boots against the wall. Where to take them? Somewhere Morbe wouldn't walk in on me, until I was completely ready to present my case. My room? Not enough space to work and live in. I'd go nova.

My stomach growled. I was overdue for lunch. The employee lounge! Of course. It was beneath the BGB's dignity to step into our grubby little recess area. When he needed us from there, he used a com.

Temm was disposing of his lunch tray, when I pushed the aircart in, and squeezed it between a sagging sofa and a dented coffee table in one corner.

"What's that?" Temm wiped his hands and face with a towel. All our food selections here tended towards grease and ooze. Gnaf was licking her fingers over a tray in her lap, in a lumpy chair on the other side of the coffee table.

"Bioscanners. Like I told you about." I sat down on the sofa in front of my prizes and thumbed more dust off a label. "Medical grade too!" I sneezed.

Temm reached for another towel and handed it to me. "Thanks."

He smiled. "What did Dr. Morbe say? Will you get to start doing your research soon?"

"Yeah," I said distractedly, using the towel to wipe off both machines more meticulously. "He gave me the go-ahead." Gradually I revealed a small animal compartment on the left, and controls and readout screens on the right of each scanner. I set the filthy towel down and looked up. "Uh, he wasn't interested in the details. But he did give me free rein. And I'm afraid that to get anywhere, I'm going to have to cut back on the amount of help I can give both of you."

Temm finished some fruit juice. "Oh well." He shrugged. "It's not as if we didn't manage without you before. We'll do okay."

"Thanks, Temm." I surreptitiously eyed Gnaf. She seemed to ignore us. Good. I'd given her a dose of her own silent treatment for the past week, ever since I'd commed her deliberate ploy to overwork me on the roof in a heavy storm. Maybe she had begun to com it—she'd left me alone more since. I looked back at Temm, who was headed for the door.

"Leaving? Break's not over."

"I know. I'm going to get started on the autopsies and rooms, so I can leave extra early, and take my family to the town park before sunset."

He waved, and I waved back. "I'll join you at work a little later," I couldn't help volunteering. He left with his smile back in place.

I returned my attention to my precious finds, one of the foundations of modern medicine. With coordinated multiple scanning modalities, these machines could integrate data all the way from microscopic biochemical, electrical, and enzymatic levels, up through gross physiologic and anatomical states, into active graphic displays of an animal's complete physical status. Obviously, this is a necessity for analyzing all new exotics, before attempting any serious treatment. Not to mention giving us the ability to rapidly diagnose most ailments even in well-known species. Medscanners could read almost everything except thoughts. (And if Dr. Hako's research succeeded, maybe someday we could even do that, to better help our inarticulate patients.)

I began playing with the controls. I was curious to see how fast I'd learn to apply my recently acquired lab knowledge of newer models. I couldn't get anything to light up on either machine, even when I stuck my own hand in for a readout. They'd probably sat around so long they needed new power units, I thought, searching for some sort of power indicator. Unlike Giem, my lab partner in school, I wasn't so good at the trouble-shooting aspect of these devices, and I quickly became frustrated. I'd hate to have to give her the first turn at these, just because—

I caught movement out of the corner of my eye, and looked up to see Gnaf standing over me, her tray abandoned on her seat.

"You'll never get those junkers running." She brushed a greying, dark brown strand of hair out of her darker eyes with a beautiful golden hand.

I looked back down at the scanners. "Thanks. That's a big help." I tried a few more random controls with growing annoyance. "Have you got a couple fresh power units you can spare me, Gnaf, or haven't I earned that much?"

"Sure. I can sneak a few out of supply for you."

I looked up again, too startled over her sincere tone to cover up my surprise. Before I could speak, a suspiciously amused look grew on her face.

"They won't do you any good, though."

"Why not?" I was sorry I'd allowed myself to become gullible with her. "Think I can't com on my own how to exchange power packs?" Was she going to start playing with me, after a week's abstinence? I'd call a Port City library or a biomed corp com, before I'd ask her for any more help.

Gnaf surprised me by sitting down alongside me and thumping the top of the nearest scanner. "Because Dr. Emmel tried the same thing," she answered earnestly. "These scanners haven't worked right since the day they arrived, and it turned out they both needed new parts. Emmel could only afford to order cheap used bioscanners, and that's exactly what she got."

I leaned back on the sofa, and just stared at Gnaf for a moment. I came up with so many questions I found it hard to know where to start. I realized I was dealing with an interesting character, like Garth Riddock, only different. Something, some earlier experience on Enchantment, maybe, also tickled my brain. I couldn't quite lock on to it.

"So why are you telling me this?" I said.

She shrugged. "You earned it."

I earned it? What did it matter to Gnaf, what got done around here? Seemingly, not even the BGB intimidated her.

"Uh, so why didn't Dr. Emmel get spare parts?" I tried next.

Gnaf answered that readily too, although a trace of a scowl returned. "I suppose she gave up, and ran out of time. She left for a better job elsewhere. Dr. Morbe never authorized the original order, and it was all on the sly, on her own credits too. It didn't matter anyway. She wasn't particularly mechanically minded either."

I was fairly certain that last remark was at least another mild zap aimed at me. I tried to ignore it. "Could you fix them, with the right parts?"

"Probably."

"Did you offer to do that for Dr. Emmel?"

"No."

"Why not?"

"None of the vets who've worked here seem to know the difference between me and an automatic cage cleaner."

So no one asked her, and she hadn't volunteered? That led to another rather personal question I couldn't restrain any longer. "Why in the Universe do you keep working here, Gnaf? When Morbe insults you, why don't you just walk out the nearest door, and never come back? It would serve him right."

Gnaf glanced at the door—to make sure it had slid closed all the way?—and at the nearest comscreen—shut off—before answering me. "I ought to. The pay, the hours, and the attitude around here have all gone utterly nova. We do build up a pension plan that would fuse, if I quit anytime soon. And for those of us who've become attached to the area and another resident, it's almost impossible to give up a rare local job."

Once again I caught myself with an unfounded assumption abruptly overturned. So much for another possible single person working here. "You have a partner out here?" Why did Gnaf live at the station?

"A wife. I know you met her. You rented horses from her. We get to see each other about once a month. It could have turned out worse. I almost had to take a job way back in Port City."

Ah, yes, I thought, I know what had teased my brain. Gnaf's wife was the stable manager who'd deliberately tested Giem and me before she allowed us out alone with her horses. Despite—or maybe because of—Dr. Nilod's favorable recommendation. It was all starting to com. My night on the roof with Gnaf was probably just another test.

I hated undergoing secret tests, and I'd had it done to me too many times. I felt it showed a gross lack of trust I didn't think I deserved, and it still had an insidious effect on my self-esteem. If I had to be tested, maybe I wasn't good enough. And that exposed a raw nerve.

"I saw her last week," Gnaf said, "and she said she liked how you handled her horses. We were both surprised. We haven't liked any vet out here so far. We forgot you're just students."

I don't know if Gnaf added that last bit to mollify me. I doubt it. I found it equally insulting. I couldn't help reflecting on the two nova veterinary practitioners I'd met on Enchantment. They shamed my profession.

After a minute of hard silence, I took a deep breath and changed the subject. "So, could one be cannibalized for the other?" I said, as calmly as possible.

"Huh?" Gnaf blinked.

"The bioscanners. I'm assuming I shouldn't risk getting caught adding expensive vintage parts to a station order. Could one machine provide spare parts for the other?"

"Oh. I suppose one could probably be used to help fix the other. That would leave you with no cross-checking capability."

She knew to worry about that? Even I was guilty of underestimating her. "One working scanner is better than none," I decided. I probably didn't have enough time here to try to secretly order and wait for obscure, outdated parts, even if I was willing to use my own credits.

"Okay, let's do it," Gnaf said, standing up again.

I gazed at her with undisguised amazement. That was some test I must have passed.

"You will still owe me one more favor for it," she added, as she released the cart's brakes and steered it towards the door.

"What's that?" I followed after her, and thought of more forays into storms and swamped back rooms. "And where are we going?"

"To my workshop. I'll try my best to get one of these running, if you'll promise not to cut back too much on helping out Temm. I'll be okay. Temm would never tell you what an impossible bind he's gotten himself into, with the extra pup-nursing he started some months ago. It raised survival rates so significantly, if he quits it, he'll lower his own efficiency rating and lose pay or his job. His family depends on every bit he's earning, yet the longer hours involved have put a strain on his marriage. You've provided a very lucky break for him."

"If the pup-nursing is helping so much, why doesn't Morbe hire at least one more tech to really take advantage of it?"

Gnaf just gave me a look that meant she had expected better of me.

"I know." I sighed. "Nova question. Dr. Morbe doesn't even acknowledge the extra work as the cause of the improvement, right?"

"You're learning."

"Why did Temm ever start doing it in the first place?"

"Misplaced compassion."

"You know, I've never worked in a place like this before," I quietly admitted.

"That's becoming increasingly obvious. Welcome to a Real World."

CHAPTER 31

I have to admit, I didn't know Gnaf had a workshop in the station. Holos of famous Rash craters decorated the grey walls. In some of the holos, Gnaf and her wife posed at the brinks on various mounts—I recognized King in at least one—and they wore smiles happier than I'd ever seen on Gnaf here. I tore my eyes away to avoid rudely staring, and concentrated on helping Gnaf get the cart maneuvered around mechanical clutter to a work bench.

An hour later, Gnaf had the scanners dismantled. I was feeling totally useless, she was cursing steadily, and her com interrupted with a call. It was Temm, sounding disappointed.

"Bad news, Gnaf. Is Taje still around, do you know?"

"Blast! I'm sorry, Temm, I promised to come help you—" I crowded in with Gnaf over her deskcom.

"That's all right. It's just that one of our best hunters had his truck break down this morning, so he's here with his load, for check-in."

"Did you call Dr. Morbe?" Gnaf asked.

"Yes. He wants us to go ahead. He says Taje can do the physicals this time."

"Alright. We'll meet you in receiving in a few minutes." Gnaf shut her com off. "Come on. Looks like our free evening is over."

"I can't do that," I objected, as I followed her out. "I'm not a licensed vet."

"Morbe will review your work tomorrow morning and endorse it."

"It's still not strictly legal," I said, and began to suspect they'd probably done this before, without even a vet student on the premises. I wasn't surprised when Gnaf didn't bother to answer me. Considering Morbe's greed—he frequently ran check-ins overtime, if it meant more business—so this was a logical extension. To what depths would I land to, before this ended?

Temm met us at the top of a ramp for the indoor garage entrance. "Thanks for coming. Dr. Morbe would fuse if we ever turned this hunter away."

Gnaf quickly opened a truck door, while Temm and I dashed to the exam tables to turn on the equipment. A green airtruck backed up to the elevated dock—the whole floor of receiving was as high as the average airtruck bed—and all three of us lined up to help the hunter unload. The sooner we got this done, the sooner we could finish our other chores for the day.

The clamps holding the cages on the truck bed clicked open, and I recognized the hunter as soon as he stepped out of his cab.

"Davin! I might have known it would be you, spoiling our one free evening."

"Well, fine way to say hello to your old buddy, after all this time," he said jovially. He lunged forward to give me a brief hug, completely unfazed by my sour greeting. "How's life at Station Three? Where's Giem?"

"Miserable. Giem's at Station Four. They decided to divide our labor."

"Four!" Davin appeared outraged, while Temm and Gnaf seemed dumbfounded by our familiarity. I couldn't help enjoying the whole scene, to a certain extent. "They split you two up?"

"Yeah. They haven't been very nice," I said. "That is, except for my friends Temm and Gnaf, here, who need to finish up as soon as possible. Mind if we start right in?"

"No. Sure. I'm ready."

Temm and I moved the first cage over to an exam table. While we worked on the first fiery-red crater pup pup we extracted, Davin and Gnaf finished unloading the cages.

I hardly had to search my memory to do the external visual and palpation exams, and call off qualities and defects for Temm to record in the medcom as I went along. I'd watched Morbe do hundreds. I found myself trembling with responsibility. I hadn't done many physicals in school—I'd begin that in earnest next year— so I tried to tell myself that surely I could do at least as well as Dr. Morbidity.

Next came the auscultator. I ran it while Temm used the temp probe. He manually restrained the pup, while

I used samplers to collect circulatory fluid and waste products, and I injected a tiny subcutaneous ID chip. We placed the first pup in a receiving cart compartment and went on to the next, another of the same color.

"Your hands are shaking," Davin said, with an amused chuckle. He and Gnaf had joined us and stood watching. "Haven't you ever done this before?"

"Not outside of a few labs, with professors, and some practice with classmates, under residents." I didn't try to hide my annoyance. It covered my embarrassment in front of Temm and Gnaf.

"Well, you have to start somewhere," Davin said cheerfully.

"This is hardly how I'd choose to begin. Have you and the other hunters any idea how stressful this process is for your new captures? Don't you ever wonder why some of these pups die before they even reach the euthanasia cart?"

"We figured they're probably just too sick to start with, I guess. You mean all this isn't necessary?"

"Not if we had a batch of bioscanners in here."

"Like doctors use—on us? Scanners work fast and don't hurt at all."

"Right. Davin, why don't you com it around?" The idea zapped me. "The stations lose you credits, with such poor service. Maybe if the hunters get involved, you'd force some improvement, or stimulate better competition."

"Taje," Gnaf interrupted me, with a curious expression on her face.

I was almost too distracted to notice her. "What?"

"I don't think you need me in here anymore. Can I— get back to work?"

"You're asking me? Yeah, sure. Thanks, Gnaf."

"Sure." Just watch your back, you little fool, I could almost hear in her voice. She left without another word.

I worked silently with Temm, both of us sweating from the muggy air washing in through the open garage door. "How many pups have you brought us, Davin?" I said, frustrated. Since I refused to duplicate the complete superficiality of Morbe's exams, time crawled.

"Nearly fifty. A fair haul, huh? So, any word from Giem, on how she's doing?"

How about me, Davin? "Almost as fused as me," I said curtly. "You realize this load is keeping me from my one chance to explore a bit of Crater Three? I can't believe I'm living on the brink of this gorgeous crater, and I'm stuck working indoors from dawn to dusk."

"So get some time off, join me on one of my expeditions, and I'll show you some real scenery."

The part I truly wanted to see? I grinned at him. "You mean it? I should probably get out in the field at least once soon, with a hunter, so I can learn about the other end of this business firsthand."

"Sure. See if Giem can join us too. I can't give you a definite schedule. I should make it back here in a couple weeks. Will that give you enough time to arrange it with the doc?"

Right. That would probably take more doing than I wanted to think about. "Maybe. Say, Davin, are any of these littermates?" Back to serious matters, as Temm and I continued to work away. I had begun to notice color patterns in Davin's cages, and while I was in control, I might as well take advantage of it, to set up my first study.

"Almost every cage section is a litter," Davin said. "I catch most that way, of course, and I hear they survive better if kept together."

"Is that a common practice among hunters?" I asked, amazed any hunter would put that much thought into their work. I injected a brilliant green crater pup, and sifted through its pseudofeathers to see all its colors: green, blue, and purple.

"Yes," Davin said, sounding equally startled, as if I ought to consider his answers obvious. "We want them in good shape, for the best prices from you."

"Well, why don't the stations keep litters together too?" I said, while Temm got the next pup out of the same cage section for me. I checked its coat before I started. It was currently a deep blue, and its pseudofeathers had green and purple sides.

"They don't?" Davin said. "We just assumed they did. Is it nothing but a nova rumor after all? I could save a little effort, by not bothering to sort by litters."

"Probably an unverified idea, although not necessarily nova. It's one theory Giem and I would like to check into. Temm, be sure to load these pups into our carts the same way."

"Okay."

When we finished a couple hours later, I had verified the pattern I'd noted earlier. "Davin, each of your litter groups shares identical plumage color combinations. There's a little variation in shades, there's the blue-green-purple litter, the orange-pink-yellow litter, the red-blue-yellowish green—"

Davin laughed at my ignorance. "You really do need a trip out into the Real World! Of course they all match. They always do. Every crater pup hunter with half a brain has noticed that."

"You're sure? Always?"

"Always. It makes sense, since litters hide together. What's the matter?"

"I don't know." I had the feeling this could mean something very important. Maybe if Gnaf got a bioscanner running, I'd com it. "It's just a very unusual hereditary pattern, for a species with such overall variability. Perhaps it's an absolute dominance pattern? Or maybe each litter is simply a set of multiple identical twins. It couldn't be sex-linked—"

"Still avoiding sex?" Davin smirked, and, after I'd zapped him with an intense glare, he changed the subject. "How'd I do here? I really have to get going. My schedule's just as fused as yours."

I turned to the medcom and asked it for the final score, translating into a good number of credits for Davin. I didn't have the BGB's release code.

I glanced over at Temm, who said, "It's okay. Davin knows we can't give him credits until Dr. Morbe returns to work tomorrow morning. Morbe doesn't allow us to handle payments."

So he trusted us with the veterinary work, and not with the currency. At least Dr. Morbe's priorities seemed consistent. I wondered what the BGB would think of my scores, and whether he could alter them. Hopefully, he would at least carefully recheck every physical first.

"You did very well, Davin, take a look here," I decided to urge him. "Don't let Dr. Morbe lower these scores without a good reason. Only two of your pups fell completely below acceptance level. Want them euth'ed, as usual?"

"Yeah. I can't remember exactly where to return them, even if I had enough time, and I don't need any sick pets of my own. Must be the worst part of your job."

"One of them, anyway," I said gloomily, surprised at how depressed even his imminent departure made me feel.

Davin left shortly, after another nice hug. To my extreme exasperation, another airtruck pulled up immediately, before we could close the stubborn garage door. Two humans quickly jumped out of their cab.

"We commed you changed your minds about closing today, when we scanned Davin's airtruck headed this way from town," said the pale, taller man, with thinning red hair.

"We figured you could slip us in too, and save us an overnight stay," added the shorter, stouter, dark haired man.

"Well, you commed wrong," I said. I felt less intrigued than I normally would have—I couldn't remember the last time I'd seen a human, besides myself, with red hair and pale skin.

"Taje—"

"Never mind, Temm. We have other business we have to take care of. We're closed. Come back tomorrow morning, on schedule." Unlike greedy Morbe, who would have stayed, I had no incentive for this. And I was in no mood for any further accommodations. As it was, all our plans had gotten launched into vac.

"Well, how did Mohrogh rate such special treatment?" the dark haired one argued angrily, making me mad I had to waste time arguing back.

"By calling us ahead of time and making a special appointment." It wasn't too much of an exaggeration.

"Where is Dr. Morbe?" the redhead insisted. "Call the doc from here. Tell him Xaffe and Briegal came in with a load. He'll pass us through."

They'd brought pups here before. I remembered reading their names on a station com list, but I stood my ground. "Sorry, our boss has left for the day. Please move your truck out of here, so we can close the door without causing any dents."

I'd made a false threat, due to safety sensors, of course. I acted like I meant it, as I deliberately turned my back on their curses, and helped Temm move our full carts down the indoor ramp and into Room Four. Funny how the pups in the newest room always looked the brightest, I noted distractedly, trying to keep my mind on the job at hand. Temm kept giving me nervous glances as we unloaded the carts.

"Remove the cage separators, so we can put littermates in together," I told him as I did the same. "Do it for some random groups, too. I want some controls."

"Taje—all of this is so—I mean, Dr. Morbe won't like any of it."

"He okayed my research, didn't he? And I doubt he'll even notice. I've heard him brag the separators are beyond FIL quarantine standards. I suppose it's the only requirement he's ever exceeded—did the cages just come this way? If you're still worried about it, I'll take full responsibility."

Temm worked on in silence, and I reluctantly worked my way up to the Reject cart.

"Temm. This euthanasia cart. You haven't cycled it, did you notice?" Somehow, I'd never learned the nasty job. It probably took about two control settings.

"I know," Temm said, as he got the last lively pup settled in. "What were those pups rejected for?"

"Uh, the first has serious congenital malformations, and, um, the second has symptoms of a respiratory infection."

"Unload the second one."

I gave him a puzzled look. I went ahead and opened the cart compartment to scoop out the depressed yellow pup. Its eyes and nose were crusted with pus, and its breathing was rapid and labored. I wondered if it had pneumonia.

"Here. Give it to me." Temm took the pup under his arm, and worked the cart euth controls.

"What are you going to do with it?" I nodded at the pup he'd saved.

"Take it home with me, and try to nurse it back to health. A few of them survive, with extra attention."

"In your spare time?"

"How do you think I've learned as much as I have about taking care of them?" He tried to smile as he headed back to receiving.

"How many crater pup pets do you have?" I said as I kept pace behind him.

"I don't think I want to discuss it—whew. They're gone."

I noticed the pounding of my own heart, by its sudden subsidence, as we closed the garage door. How ridiculous. What was I expecting, a big fight?

CHAPTER 32

Dr. Morbidity found Temm and me the next midmorning, in Room Two. "Temm, you're behind again. Tajen, could I have a word with you?"

"Sure, Dr. Morbe." I hoped my voice sounded calmer than I felt. I didn't stop my work, so Morbe had to step closer.

"Tajen, I want to thank you for the check-ins yesterday. I know it was a lot of responsibility all at once, and I'm sorry you didn't have a chance to practice under me first. I will have to make a few adjustments in the scores. I've just rechecked the new arrivals in Room Four, and except for a natural beginner's tendency to overrate, you did fine."

I had to bite my tongue forcefully. He was so predictable, I almost laughed. At least now I could feel theoretically legal. He claimed he'd rechecked my work. I had another favor to ask, and I drew a deep breath to try to achieve mizu no kokoro, before I spoke up.

"Why thanks," I told the BGB, as I stuck the pup I'd been feeding back in its cage. "Davin Mohrogh's a friend of mine, so I was glad to help." I moved on to the next sickly pup. "And in return, he'd like to do us an extra favor."

"Really?" That seemed to fuel his interest.

"Yeah. To properly help you, I need some field experience. Davin's offered to take me out on a hunt the next time he comes through here, in a couple of weeks."

"Oh dear, I'm afraid that's out of the question. We simply can't spare you, especially while we're still looking for a new veterinarian. Why not wait until your vacation week, at the end of your externship here? We've scheduled that."

Because Dr. Hako made you, I thought angrily to myself, and it should have been two weeks unless pettily counting the week they made us waste getting here, from Station One. At least we had managed to treat it like a little vacation. I cleared my throat.

"Because I need to learn more about natural behavior, and how the crater pups get here," I persisted, trying to reason with him, "as background for my research."

"I'm sorry. It's just unacceptable. Have you tried com reference programs for the information you need? Port City has some very good library programs, if Station One can't supply what you need."

"I have," I said, my intelligence insulted once more. "Nothing can fully substitute for real experience—and I've even got extra ecology training that could make my observations especially helpful. Davin just casually told me about some important field observations not on record anywhere. How much more am I missing?

How else am I going to make a significant contribution towards reducing your morbidity and mortality rates, if I don't have a complete understanding of all the possible factors?"

"By not interrupting your services here, when and where we need them the most."

I had launched right into that, I realized, as the BGB walked away.

"And it sucked more vac from there," I told Giem, over my room com, at the end of that week. "Morbe called Davin after that, and Davin asked about taking me out too, no doubt irritating old Morbidity even more. And the BGB transmitted a significantly lowered payment to Davin, making Davin nova, and I guess they got into a fused fight. Morbe paged me into his office to tell me, and I quote: 'I'm sorry, Tajen, if you leave on an unauthorized trip with Davin Mohrogh, I'll have to flunk you. Your work with us has improved our survival rate. We can't afford to have you go traipsing off on a vacation with Mohrogh.'"

"He really said that?" Giem's shock combined with the bags under her eyes to make her appear totally zapped.

"Word for word. I couldn't believe it. After all the uncomplaining labor I've given him. *A vacation!* How short-sighted can you get? If he doesn't get any real research results from us by the end of our externship, none of our help will have any lasting effect. There's more. He went on to reprimand me for exaggerating the payment score in favor of a friend, and he regretted he couldn't trust me with the physicals ever again."

"Which he shouldn't have asked you to do in the first place."

"Right. And then—" I took another deep breath,"—then those two other hunters I'd chased off, the night before, showed up for late morning check-ins. They proceeded to spend the whole session complaining, loudly, about how rudely I'd turned them away. That was the final zap. Morbe went nova, and he's been going out of his way to make my life miserable ever since. He believes I'm trying to drive away his customers, because I'm mad at him for not allowing me a 'vacation.' He doesn't even have the sequence of events correct.

"So how's life at Four treating you, Giem?" I said through clenched teeth.

"I also have too much work trying to keep Station Four operating, and too little time for my research. No wonder Hako said this assignment would keep us busy. I have trouble even finding enough time for such nonessentials as sleeping and eating. I haven't much in the way of news."

"You look miserable, Giem."

"I am also a little tired of feeling like the odd one out, for once. Steffin and his husband are quite close. I do think they're very sweet. And unlike you, I can't complain they don't treat me right. Please try not to get yourself flunked out of here. I wish we could do more together than calls, but it's better than nothing."

"Hey, I'll just come and join you if I am flunked. It sounds much nicer over at Four. I do have one bit of tentatively good news."

"You've been holding back on me. What is it, Taje?"

"Gnaf's almost certain she's got one of the bioscanners working for me. I don't dare personally test it until Morbe's day off, but I'm quite hopeful."

"Isn't she the tech that had it in for you?"

"Uh, I guess not, since I worked so hard for her. Anyway, she did a lot of work for me on the scanners, so it looks like my work for her paid off."

"That's great! Maybe we can get a real start on disease statistics."

"Yeah. And then we can go home." It wouldn't shorten our stay, but somehow it made the end seem more tangible.

CHAPTER 33

A few days later, I got my chance to try the scanner. I set it up in our lounge again. A couple of the scanning modalities didn't work too well, but Gnaf hadn't promised me more, having parts from only one other fused scanner to work with. Otherwise this one seemed to perform okay. I had Temm run in carts of what he thought were the healthiest pups first. Of everyone working here, he had the best feel for the species. I needed to build up a backlog of normal data before I could start trying to diagnose abnormalities. And that's where I got stuck. I couldn't seem to get any reasonable normal ranges. Crater pup "normals" weren't practical. They just weren't statistically useful. Except, rather unhelpfully, for littermates.

It was the biggest discouragement of my week. Not the final one. As Morbe picked on me ever more ruthlessly, Temm and Gnaf avoided me in an increasingly obvious way, even when the BGB wasn't around. That hurt. We hadn't known each other that long, but I had thought I'd managed to earn more respect from the staff than their nova boss. To lose it now, when nothing else seemed to be going right, made me feel more alone than ever.

I almost called Giem early, just to whine. I wanted so badly to impress her with some progress that I held off. Why couldn't I get any decent average data? Too many of the figures kept forming ranges that were simply too broad. And that applied to information as mundane as respiratory rates, as well as obscure data like minor enzyme levels from what I regarded as the crater pup equivalent of a combined liver and kidney.

Maybe many of even the healthiest-appearing pups were too stressed, and sick with many different, subtle illnesses. That's all I could com, as I labored over statistical calculations one last time, the evening I was due to call Giem. I worked slowly, because I kept fading into escapist daydreams about our vacation travels, and into glamorized scenes of work as a planetary field ecologist. Maybe the latter zapped me with my idea. Anyway, it got me so excited my fingers shook over my com controls.

"You look happy," Giem said, somewhat resentfully, when I got her on my screen. She looked ready for bed.

"I've been miserable! I think I've got an answer, Giem!"

"Okay, Taje, don't keep me in suspense like a Mek Ikkol story, before I have to hitch a ride over there to strangle the answer out of you."

"What story?"

"You know, popular SF by Gornathe Merrea."

Why did that name sound familiar? "Giem, I haven't got time for that stuff. I've got a working bioscanner, and

I suspect the different color sets of crater pups are entirely separate species! They probably originally evolved from one species and diverged, like in island ecologies, or the space-borne seeds of the ingret, that showered across the many planets of one solar system. Both the Rash craters and even the varied colors of different flower rings form geographic barriers.

"I really tried, but I can't get statistically meaningful normal values for various physiological parameters for pups with different colors, and especially from different craters. Except among littermates, who always have the same colors, and must match colors to hide in the same flower ring. And they're not identical twins. I've checked." I could see Giem's objections overwhelming her face, as she kept trying to interrupt my rapid lecture.

"Each of the different color combinations are different species?" she gasped. "Humans have made too many mistakes categorizing animals by color!"

"You were also concerned about lack of reproduction in captivity. That may be due to trying to breed separate species," I said. "Plus shortened life spans. They don't get their native, color-matched foods as pets. Who can afford to order specific bouquets for feed? Have you tried any color-matched food trials? The crater pups may even have a symbiotic relationship with their flower rings!"

"I haven't any time for experiments like that! And how can eating blossoms off a plant be symbiotic?" Giem said, with disbelief.

"Crater pups can't eat too much of their own shelter. Plus they eat insects that prey on their flowers," I said.

"Taje, do you have any idea what you're implying?"

"Of course. This could shut this whole rotten operation down, to prevent major ecological disasters and violation of FIL species protection laws. Therefore we need to explore this further, ASAP!"

"How sure are you?" Giem demanded. "If we get this wrong because your bioscanner is cobbled junk, we're in hot oil for sure! Don't even think about contacting the Enchantment Ecological Protection Department about this, much less calling Dr. Hako. Remember he doesn't believe in 'bad guys' either. What can we do to investigate this better?"

"We should observe mating habits in the field, because physical or behavior blocks mating between different species, and we ought to find a way to run some DNA analyses."

"We can't do either, unless I ask some friendly hunters to bring me some adults for lab mating observations," Giem said. "Dr. Bioh isn't here to run DNA."

"Lab mating would take too long and it's too inaccurate," I said. "Horses and donkeys can mate, and so can glippers and grappers, yet the only result is a sterile deadend. I can go into the field for this, and also to learn how serious the situation is—"

"And get yourself flunked!"

"On what grounds?" I said. "I'll sneak out of here only during Dr. Morbe's day off, and like I said, I could just come join you at Four, if the BGB catches me."

"First loan me your other bioscanner, Taje, so I can get Dr. Steffin to verify your findings. Call it a second opinion," she said, after seeing my face.

"Gnaf snatched parts from it to get mine working."

"So you have no cross-checking ability for any of this!"

"Giem, doesn't what I'm saying make a lot more sense of this whole nova mess? I can try to get Davin to truck my scanner over to you after our field trip—"

"Taje, T is for Trouble." Giem shut off her com.

CHAPTER 34

"Why did you mark my pups down so much?" a feisty blue Telmid hunter demanded of Morbe, a couple days later. Typical of her species, the Telmid wasn't much over 120 centimeters tall, and that was counting her feathery antennae. I'd done my share of gaping, when she leaped out of her truck alone, and did her share of the unloading. Maybe, like Shandy, she was a transmute, with a few genes from a stronger species, instead of an empath. Whatever. I used her argument as cover to sneak a look at the receiving schedule on one of our coms.

Morbid made some sort of pseudoscientific excuse, and she promptly cut him off. "Davin's a good hunter, and he says you're a cheat," she said. "You'd better calculate a higher score or give me a better explanation, or Davin won't be the only popular hunter spreading the word about you."

She glared at Morbe while he made a minor adjustment, and she stomped off to her truck. Morbid spluttered, in front of several other hunters restlessly waiting for their turns. I stifled a snicker, and a triumphant grin.

Davin had gotten himself scheduled for a check-in the evening before Morbe's day off, near the end of this week. Just like I'd suggested in the only comcall I'd had Giem relay, out of an overabundance of caution. (I had remembered Gnaf's suspicious glance at her com, and wondered if the station kept records of our calls. Beyond that, I found it hard to believe Morbe managed to hack our calls, or used the com system to spy on us.) Finally, a break. Especially since I could see, more than ever, that a rematch with the BGB on a trip with Davin was hopeless. When I'd launched Davin, I had no idea what I'd created and turned loose on the Rash—

"Tajen! What are you doing over there?" Morbe turned his anger on me.

"Uh, checking some com data—"

"I don't think you recognize the seriousness of our business in here. Perhaps you should return to your research this evening."

I could tell he wanted to look polite in front of his clients. Maybe he even feared what I might add aloud to the Telmid's argument.

"I'm dismissed from receiving tonight?" Morbe had banned me from physicals, and still made me help in receiving. That forced me to watch his idea of examinations. I don't know if he intended it as punishment, but that's what it felt like. So I reacted with surprise, and added a dash of amusement, that silently said Indeed you have reason to worry, Dr. Morbidity.

He glared back at me. "Yes. You may go." His eight trembling fingers were turning blue.

I found it easier to choke my laughter down, however, as I passed Temm and Gnaf and their frozen stares on my way out.

CHAPTER 35

Morbe used time for my research as a new excuse to keep me away from more hunters and their check-ins that next week. That was fine with me. It gave me more time to run scanner checks, and to load up a day pack before Davin was due. Early the evening he was due, I carted the bioscanner into my room, since I was no longer in contact with any other hunters who might deliver it to Four. I didn't risk calling Davin directly. I had Giem tell him I'd catch him at check-ins or right after. We'd arranged for him to pick me up later that night or the next morning, after Morbe had left for One.

When he could, Dr. Morbidity tried to find some other work for me during check-ins that week. I suspected he resented any time he did give me for my research. So I felt no surprise nor did I fuse over it when he sent me to Gnaf's workshop to retrieve some repaired cage components, just minutes before receiving on the evening Davin was due to arrive. I commed I'd go get the parts, maybe even start installing them, with a monitor while I worked. As soon as Davin finished, I'd slip outside and meet up with him, before he drove off.

I found the usual mechanical mess in Gnaf's workshop, and nothing loaded and ready to go. So I returned to her front door, to retrieve a cart. However, the door refused to slide open for me. Another station malfunction? Right. I turned to another door. I didn't fully catch on until I found all the doors jammed, and I couldn't get the com to turn on, to call for help.

At first I blamed nova coincidence, despite the fact that this was Gnaf's special territory. Coms were so widely available, throughout the station, I'd gotten out of the habit of wearing my wristcom every day. I didn't want to run it repeatedly through the cart hand sterilizers (even if I was the only one who used them). Instead I had neatly stashed it in an outside pocket on my day pack. I tried everything again, twice. I got *mad*. I returned to the front door and kicked it *hard*, several times. I put a few dents in it, without doing any good, except working off some anger.

At least I'd had enough training to avoid breaking my toes, I thought ruefully, as I sat down on a stool at Gnaf's work bench, and commed it out.

I could probably never prove this was deliberate, although I felt almost certain of it. I did wonder how long they'd leave me in here before they "discovered" me, and let me out.

I suppose if I'd been a tech-wiz I could have broken out in very short order, with the tools at hand, but I wasn't and I couldn't. Getting locked in here seemed an extra big taunt from Gnaf, who must have helped to set this trap. I sneered at her smiling holos on the walls, and thought about using one of several torches in a rack to flame my way out. No one here could possibly guess I'd trained in torching through entire ship hulls.

However, that would probably set off a fire alarm, and I didn't want that much attention this evening. Maybe if they tried to leave me here overnight—

They didn't. Gnaf showed up some hours later—probably after check-ins had ended—just as I was trying not to imagine torching her holos.

I heard her slap the front door a couple times, and yell faintly, "Taje, are you in there?"

I didn't answer. Let her sweat it out.

I heard her tinkering, and the door slid halfway open—one of my dents kept it from sliding any farther. My kicks had at least developed some power. Gnaf squeezed her way in.

"Sorry," she said, looking about as sincere as Giem usually looked, saying that word. "You know how the doors around here lock up sometimes."

"Sure, Gnaf," I said, on my way out—no squeezing for my thin frame. I strode through the halls for the nearest building exit. Gnaf crammed her way out to follow me.

"Where are you going?" I said scornfully, over my shoulder.

"Where are *you* going?" she said in return, in a quiet, steely voice.

"To my room."

"I'm going back to mine too."

Yet she followed me right out the wrong exit. It took a moment to realize I'd stepped out into the muddy, stinky, empty corral, on the opposite side of the building. Was Gnaf following me just to laugh at me? I couldn't see her face clearly in the dark. Or did she have a more ulterior motive? I didn't ask.

Instead, my paranoid thoughts wandered on, to another question—how quickly had my rental horse had been returned to One? Not that I'd had any time for recreational riding. Nevertheless, an interesting feat, after the amount of time Giem and I had needed to get here.

"I've always wondered," I said as calmly as possible, trying to step around old manure piles. "Why did Nilod give us such slow transportation out here?"

Gnaf didn't answer me. She followed me out of the corral and around the building to our rooms.

"Has Temm gone home?" I tried another question, while we both unlocked our doors. I didn't expect an answer to that, either. I had begun to read conspiracies into everything.

"Yeah. Why?"

So I won't run into him on my way into town, you nova jerk, I thought. I still had a chance Davin might stay there overnight. "I just wondered if Morbe tried to keep Temm late with work again. I could give him some help." I said this as a test as well as cover. Gnaf just gave me a last cold look in the light from our rooms, and stepped into hers.

My door had slid open for me. Almost too late I realized I hadn't thought to tuck my day pack or the scanner cart out of direct view. The walls were cheap and thin. I worried Gnaf would hear my door sliding again when I left.

So what could she do about it? Call Morbe in his aircar, on his way to One? And how could he stop me in time, especially if I waited long enough to eat some dinner? Shivering, coatless, in my doorway, I stepped inside to get an order for my growling stomach. If Davin stayed in town overnight, I could afford time for some dinner. And if he'd left, it wouldn't matter.

CHAPTER 36

I wondered about my paranoia, while I ate. After all, they couldn't imprison me here. At least, not for long. I was glad to hear the blast of com music I'd come to expect, nearly every night, from Gnaf's room. I threw my tray back into the dispenser, hit disposal, and decided to add a little last-minute drama by strapping my stunner on, under my coat. I slung on my pack, turned on the cart, and opened my door, under the cover of Gnaf's music.

I parked the bioscanner cart outside and turned around to make sure my door closed. Sometimes it acted up a bit—

Whumpf! I slammed face and chest into the door. It slid open again for me a second later, and I landed on the floor between my bed and the wall, crushed beneath my pack and a much heavier opponent. So much for trying to extricate the stunner denting my belly. I had to concentrate mainly on breathing, a lot of the air punched out of me.

"I like you, Jesmuhr." Gnaf's gravelly voice muttered. "You're okay. So where did you think you'd sneak off to?" She'd gotten hold of my left arm, and was cranking it back behind my pack at an awkward angle. Being in the middle of a respiratory crisis didn't help.

"Like—me?" I gasped out. "This is—an odd way—to show it."

"I thought you were good on your word. For helping Temm more, since I fixed you a scanner. So I didn't believe it when Dr. Morbe said you might try to leave tonight for a vacation with Mohrogh."

"Not—a vacation. You know—Morbe's a liar. It's—research, and only—for a day. He won't—even notice it." I exaggerated my condition a bit, as I tried to think out some sort of escape move. The problem was, I'd never had to practice self-defense with a heavy knapsack, and I rued my inability to pack lighter for a day trip.

"Only a day!" Gnaf snorted. "Only a day to get yourself flunked and me fired."

"You? Fired?"

"Dr. Morbe decided if you left, he'd fire me. He made me responsible for keeping track of you. Get it?"

"I got it." I finally allowed my tensed muscles to relax, and Gnaf let go of me and stood up. I rolled over on my back, on my pack. I slid down it to pillow my head, and I lay there breathing deeply. Gnaf scowled over me from the doorway.

"Look, Gnaf," I tried to reason with her, "how will he even know I left, if I'm back by tomorrow night?"

"He records quarantine room work over the coms." She put her hands on her hips. From the floor she looked like an especially intimidating opponent. Now I suffered a new fear. My big nova mouth.

"Is that even legal?"

Gnaf shrugged. "Officially he uses the coms to monitor pup health."

"Does—does he have the whole station bugged?" Oops. Maybe even this room?

"We're not sure how thorough he is. Why? What have you got to hide?"

"Nothing! Gnaf, you've got to believe me. My research is urgent, and I have to do a small part of it in the field."

"What's so urgent about it that you're willing to cost me my job? You know Morbe won't use anything you find out. He thinks you're trying to ruin his business, and I don't blame him."

I should have realized the potent reasons that kept Gnaf and Temm in this miserable situation would lose me their support, at the slightest hint Morbe might fire them. As if he could afford to lose them too. If we all stuck together—oh, dream on.

What now? I looked at Gnaf's hands turning into fists on her hips, and noticed she'd cocked her thumbs professionally, to avoid breaking them during a punch. My sensei had emphasized repeatedly that fighting was a last resort. It meant you'd made at least a couple of serious mistakes, and you might get hurt by someone more skillful than you.

Gnaf was taller, heavier, stronger, and meaner than me. I hadn't wanted to let the news leak prematurely, before I had more proof to protect myself. I didn't think I had a choice. I tried to explain.

"Gnaf, I think I may have discovered we're creating a terrible ecological crisis for the crater pups—each different color combination may be a separate species, in danger of immediate extinction. I have to see exactly how they live in the craters and how thorough the hunting is. You must realize this is more important than your job or my externship!"

Gnaf gave me a disbelieving glare. "All you vets have such inflated egos! You seriously believe working in here has given you more information than all the FIL surveys used to set up hunting regulations? The rangers don't even catch many poachers. Can't you do any better than that nova excuse?"

Wow. Clearly, explaining was hopeless. I guess I'd gotten used to not being believed, and it seemed that Gnaf had closed her mind, probably for her own self-defense. Well, I did have one last trick to pull out. I drew my stunner, as her look of hatred turned to alarm. "Maybe this will protect your fused job," I said and quickly stood up, using her frozen shock. "Morbe can't possibly blame you for this." I shot her.

CHAPTER 37

I grabbed Gnaf as soon as she slumped, to keep her from hurting herself. But she was so much taller and heavier than me, all I could do was fall with her onto my bed.

I disentangled myself, and decided after that to stuff all the rest of my belongings into my full-sized backpack, which seemed to take a nova long time. I dragged my packs outside. Gnaf began to twitch and gurgle curses as my door slid closed behind me and I locked it. I put my day pack on the cart with the bioscanner, and heaved on my backpack. I dashed on down the road with the stolen cart.

I hadn't much time before Gnaf would regain enough muscle control to use my com and call for help. When she did, I honestly hoped Morbe would direct his rage narrowly at me. Gnaf had tried to follow his illegal order.

Clouds partly hid the stars, and the air felt heavy and muggy. By the time I found the only motel in town, I was hot, sweaty, panting, and bruised from tripping more than once on the unlit perimeter road. At least I had no difficulty finding Davin's door. I recognized his green airtruck, parked in front of a room belonging to the one small motel. Thank the Galaxy he hadn't left town. I had no Plan B.

"It's me, Taje! Let me in, Davin!" I had stepped in sensor range and punched the buzzer more than once. I could hear voices inside, as I shifted in my heavy pack and dripped sweat.

"Morbe told me you decided not to come!" came Davin's surprisingly outraged voice.

"He lied! Come on, it's an emergency! Let me in! I don't want to be seen out here."

"Alright, alright! Hold your launch for just a micro."

It was more than just a micro, and when the door slid open, I caught an angry glare from a woman who sealed her hunting jacket on her way out. Davin reached out, grabbed me by my collar, and hauled me inside. Davin wasn't wearing a shirt, and he grabbed one.

"This better be good, Tajen. If you've interrupted my business to try to avoid trouble with the law, I want no part of it."

"Why would you suspect that?" I frowned as I hit my strap releases, dumping my overloaded pack on the floor. "It's Morbe who has trouble understanding the law, as well as telling the truth. Since when do you believe him over me?" I studied his churned-up bed, and barely suppressed a grin.

"Since he paid me up properly, apologized for an honest mistake, and let me know a certain bored student has caused him a lot of grief."

"And if you believe that," I said, "he's got some stations he'd like to sell you soon." I stepped back outside, to move the cart out of public view.

"What's that? Stolen station property?" Davin appeared increasingly stubborn and angry. I'd better fuse my flippant approach, my pup-sized brain decided, as I set the cart brakes in one corner of his room.

"It's just some private property Dr. Emmel abandoned," I said. "Look, Davin, Dr. Morbe had me locked up in a workroom when you came over this evening. And blackmailed an employee to detain me afterwards. Isn't that illegal? Must be important to keep me out of the field, huh? Will you help me, or should I hunt up that little Telmid? All I want is one day out there—"

"I suppose you never got around to inviting Giem, either?"

"Well, no, she doesn't have the time to spare—Four is even more understaffed than Three. Come on, Davin, what do I have to—"

"Alright, alright. I'll take you out with me tomorrow, and bring you back. That's it! How about getting some rest—"

"Davin, I think we should leave tonight."

"Why? What did you do over there?"

"Why doesn't anyone trust me tonight?"

CHAPTER 38

"That's it. Aim at the smaller ones. You don't want to leave the breeding adults vulnerable to attack," Davin said, while his stunner rifle shook in my arms. It was easier to aim than my hand stunner. It had a built-in life scanner that wasn't nearly as sophisticated as a medical bioscanner, nor did it have the resolution of field ecology units I'd used before. I was having trouble making out my targets, as my arms trembled and my neck cramped.

"Why are you bent over the rifle like that?" Davin shifted my arms and head to correct my stance. "Straighten up and you'll see better. Relax!"

My problem wasn't just the early hour of the day, intended to beat the legal morning hours for disruptive flower harvesting. I suddenly realized I was also afraid of the rifle. To cover enough distance at a fairly wide sweep, and still have enough power after scatter, Davin had set the power on high. That meant if I accidentally shot Davin or myself at point-blank range, death from cardiac standstill was a real risk.

I began to wish I had slept in. I'd had trouble falling asleep last night, and I could have faced this in a more alert manner in the second round of hunting hours, during early afternoon, before evening flower harvests. Davin claimed more crater pup families poked out of their dens during dawn. Nevertheless, I'd only managed to get him to leave town last night, without scaring him, by arguing I wanted my one day of truancy to be as full as possible. So I had to struggle on early this morning without complaint, leaving our camp, set up late last night.

"Can't you see any of them?" Davin whispered impatiently.

"Uh, yeah, I guess." The viewer showed a muddled holo overlay of several color-coded sensor modalities, shifting periodically. Obviously, it took some practice to become skillful with it. The flashing scope and overpowering floral scents wafting towards us combined to give me a blinding headache.

"You guess? Hurry up and shoot them, and we'll find out. Just don't forget to sweep fast over as many pups as you can at once. They'll usually just freeze up if you scare them, until you get close. Then they'll slip into their dens, and it's hopeless."

I depressed the trigger, and tried to spray the beam through all the smaller blobs of life, hidden from direct sight within a long clump of yellow-flowered bushes. I hit the safety, slung the rifle over my shoulder, and tried to remind myself that no one would grade me on this. Was it school that gave me the impulse to insist on perfection if possible or, failing that, to not try at all? Not a good attitude for most new experiences in Real Life.

We each hauled two collecting cages over to my targeted victims. We were working our way around one of the smaller craters near Station Three, a shallow little bowl in the ground. So the terrain wasn't bad. We quickly reached the dazzling golden shrubs, shading stunned crater pups, easy to see by their scrambled, roughened coats.

"Not bad for a first try. I think we've got at least two litters here," Davin said, gently laying a limp pup in one of his cages. "I think you hit several of the parents too."

"That's okay," I said, kneeling over one of the adults to examine its colors: yellow, orange, and green, identical to three pups lying nearby. Crater pup pseudofeather control must be voluntary, to scramble like this with a stun. "I want to compare a few families. You can do the rest of the shooting." We loaded seven pups among ten stunned crater pups, all with identical coat color combinations. As we turned to leave, I spotted a couple small crater snakes slipping in on their crouching, multiple short legs, while a flock of crater hawks circled overhead. The hair on my scalp prickled painfully.

"That's why I don't like stunning any I don't intend to take," Davin said.

I flinched as I watched a snake chomp into one of the stunned scrambled adult crater pups, while a hawk dived in to fight a second snake for another easy live meal. I hoped these attacks were rapidly lethal. Stunners were misnamed. They didn't provide any anesthesia—just paralysis. I began to feel sick. "Davin, are most hunters as careful as you about not hitting the adults?"

Davin turned away, looking a bit green himself. "It's more efficient to just shoot a whole bush down. I doubt most hunters think about it. Except maybe in craters this small, where the commotion from predators might scare all the other crater pups back into their dens. Come on, we'll have to cross over to the other side, and hope it's far enough away from this slaughter."

"How many pups are we allowed to take from here?" I said, working to match his long, hurried strides.

"Up to fifty percent. That is about the most you could hope to clear out of a small crater, or a subsector of a larger one, in one day."

"Great Galaxy, really?" Presumably that was a safe level set by ecologists, but I knew their calculations assumed only one crater pup species. "What happens if more hunters come here tomorrow? They get to take fifty percent of the remainder?"

"Not legally. I'm required to leave a two-month warning beeper here, before I leave today."

"Only two months? That must still assume quite a reproductive rate."

"That's why harvesters consider crater pups such pests," Davin said.

We stopped near the center of the crater, to exchange full cages for empties among our cache, and for Davin to take the rifle back from me.

"Is there any seasonal decrease in pup litters?" I said as we started off again across the crater.

"There's supposedly some during midwinter. I haven't stayed here long enough to speak from experience." Davin slowed his pace and lowered his voice. "Guess I'll find out in several months or so, if I stay on Enchantment that long."

We approached a long line of brilliant orange bushes, a hemi-circle wrapping around the crater, all the way back to the yellow bushes to the right. A line of green blossoms finished this lowest crater "ring" on the left, and other colors formed several more rings upslope.

"I wondered how long you'd stay planet-bound," I whispered. "I'm surprised you didn't get into the export end of this business, with your own ship."

"It needed quite an overhaul, after I got all I could out of the Big Maxson Minidragon market. Selling sterilized eggs that didn't require quarantine made business from there a lot easier, until the big suppliers started cloning the critters. That's what will end this market soon, if it remains popular. I'm taking advantage of the crater pup craze while my ship gets worked on, in an orbital repair dock. I needed a change of scenery, anyway. I'll carry out an export load for sale, when I decide to leave."

I wished I was wealthy enough to buy a ship to go adventuring in. I had to overcome another bout of silent jealousy, to get back to more urgent questions. "Davin, how is it decided who gets to hunt which crater when?"

"It's first come, first served. So it's probably good you insisted on an early start last night. I think we're camped near a harvester group, and where harvesters find good pickings, hunters can usually find plenty of pups."

"And how are quotas enforced?"

"By the threat of random ranger inspections and simple physical limits. The allowed technology doesn't go beyond what I'm carrying, and there are so many craters with so many crater pups, it's difficult to go overboard. Hush—we're getting almost close enough—"

"You're hunting by flower ring—does everyone do it that way?"

"Quiet!" Davin hissed, setting his cages down. He raised his rifle, released the safety, and fired. He was fast.

"Good. I think this area is still undisturbed." Davin slipped the safety back on, shouldered the rifle, and picked his cages up. "Come on. Can you imagine, in all practicality, doing it any other way? Climbing up to higher flower ring levels, for more color varieties, would waste too much time, and scare more crater pups off. No one's buying specific color combos either, at least not so far."

"You always find the same crater pup color combination within one flower ring?"

"Just about. Come to think of it, I can't remember any exceptions. A little surprising, huh? You could expect littermates to match, because they have to live together while they're growing up. Why not have an orange-red-green family, neighboring this orange-yellow-green one? The next ring up has red flowers," he pointed out.

"Davin, exactly when do you think you'll leave Enchantment?"

"Maybe when winter comes around, or when the cloning companies launch, or when I get tired of this planet. Whichever comes first. Why? Has something gone wrong?"

"You've told me enough," I told him rashly. "Consider it a favor, a little business tip—I'd leave as soon as I could afford to, if I were you."

"Care to tell me why? Having my ship overhauled isn't cheap, and I planned on doing much better than breaking even this time."

Now I'd done it. I didn't know if I could trust Davin with information so potentially explosive. Did he have intimate hunting friends he'd feel he had to warn? And if so, could they be trusted to keep quiet, until I had proof?

Having experienced three standard years of the vet school's inescapable gossip grapevine, I knew how fused this could get. If my theories somehow didn't prove out in the end, could I be held personally responsible for ruining crater pup business? I almost stepped on a paralyzed pup, as I waded around in the orange-flowered mass of foliage and my own confusion.

"Careful!" Davin said. "Just what is it I'm vac-headedly helping you to prove out here? Is Morbe right, that you're trying to destroy the pup trade?"

"I'm just trying to get the facts straight, Davin. And all I can say is, they're not looking so good."

Davin wanted me to be more specific, and I refused, so our conversation deteriorated from there. By the time we'd filled a lot of the cages, and the flower gatherers started hiking in with their power cutters and stasis containers, we'd almost quit saying anything at all. Davin hauled cages back up to his truck, while I stayed to watch the harvest. That turned out to be another all-too systematic process of ring decimation. It was obviously easier to walk along and cut the lowest ring of flowers than to hike higher up crater walls. If the crater pups weren't decimated, their habitat was.

I turned away from the crater pups' thinning cover, and squinted up at a growing number of hovering crater hawks. I felt sick at heart, watching possible species extinction in action, as I helped Davin carry the last of the cages up to his airtruck.

Davin rushed ahead of me, in response to an urgent beep from his truck com. So I finished loading and clamping cages on the truck bed. I packed up our camping gear, and I saw a furious look on Davin's face as he began throwing the gear in the back of his truck cab.

"What is it?" I asked, reluctantly. I made sure my bioscanner and folded cart made it in with the rest of our gear.

"Do you really not know?" Davin said angrily. "Get in the truck."

Davin launched the truck as soon as we buckled into our harnesses. "Did you really assault a station tech?"

"It was self-defense and I didn't hurt her!"

"You were accurately described, and those harvesters probably saw you. Do you realize I'm supposed to turn you in?"

"That's your decision, Davin."

"If I want to stay out of trouble here."

T is for Trouble, I almost quoted Giem, as I massaged my pounding head. "Look, Davin, can you at least take me to see Giem at Station Four just long enough to drop off the bioscanner and let her know what's happening?" I commed he wanted to see her anyway.

"We're not stopping until we reach the Crater One Ranger Office," he insisted. "That should be neutral enough territory for you and your boss to calmly work out your differences."

"Davin!"

"No arguing. And don't try pulling that vacful little stunner out from under your shirt, either. You're not fast enough."

He was probably right. I shut up, and frantically tried to think, instead.

It was an act of kindness Davin wasn't taking me directly back to Station Three or to a local police station. If I got a chance to explain my suspicions to rangers, they might carry my case for me to Enchantment's Ecological Protection Department. Even if someone successfully hushed me up for a while.

I knew I couldn't rely on any help from local officials dependent on crater pup hunting and flower harvesting, however indirectly, for their jobs. Nor did I think the threat of species extinction would change Davin's mind any more than it did Gnaf's.

"Davin," I pleaded one more time, "just a micro at Station Four first."

Davin just scowled and continued driving, the scar on the back of his right hand showing unusually white against his golden skin. I watched him for a while, noticing when the sunlight through the windshield struck his hair just right, I could tell it was dark brown, not black.

The Call of Hormones? Surely not, and I felt anger driving away any hint of it. Too much was at stake, even if I ever had a chance with Davin, and I knew I didn't. He'd never looked twice at me before, and now he never would.

I decided to make a move for the front of my shirt with my right hand, ostensibly to scratch my stomach. I'd have to act fast—before Davin thought to put the truck on auto.

"Hands at your sides!" Davin glared at me, before turning his eyes back on the road. I folded my arms across my belly, in a "make me" posture. That again distracted Davin momentarily from his controls. So I gave my emergency door release a sharp right backhanded punch. As the door practically sucked itself open in its haste, Davin cut short an attempt to turn on me, to fight instead with automatic safety controls bent on slowing the truck down as rapidly as possible.

I had no intention of staying long enough to try to overpower him, or to even wait for a full stop. I hit my harness release and threw myself out the open door. My shoulder roll definitely suffered from the lack of a practice mat in place of the dirt and gravel road.

I had the speed of the truck added in, so I did a somersault back up to my feet faster than usual—and almost on over again. As I scrambled into a dizzy run away from the road, the truck rushed nicely on past me. By the time it stopped, I had dashed over a short, rolling meadow to—oh lovely sight—a small, wooded, flowerless crater. No witnesses here.

Almost tumbling down the nearest dirt and rocky slope, I dodged bristly blue-green saplings, skidded over midnight blue pods, and lunged behind a rough, grey-brown tree trunk, barely wide enough to hide behind. I halted there to catch my breath and draw my stunner. If I could get Davin first, and take the truck—

The latter drew up at the crater rim at that moment, not where I expected it. Davin parked about a quarter of the way around the perimeter and exited on the opposite side. He ducked behind the front end of his truck, with his rifle. I slipped around my podtree trunk. At this new angle I found it harder than ever to keep myself completely covered, and I had no clear shot at him.

"I know where you are, Taje. You might as well come out of there and give yourself up," he shouted.

He was probably right. I didn't think my cover would deceive his scanner, even if it could block his rifle beam. I glanced down at my boots and spotted a yellow-green wormy critter winding its way up one of them.

As I fought a reflex to kick it off, I thought I heard Davin's trigger click, and I drew back my tingling elbow. Had he grazed me, or was it just a fresh road burn? I peeked out, for a desperate long shot with my weaker hand stunner, and had no luck at all. Davin's rifle remained steadily pointing my way, over the front of his truck. Wonderful.

"Come on, Taje. This is your last chance!"

Yeah. I'd really fused it. I should've risked trying to stun him in the cab, or chased after the truck until it stopped. Some ace vet student spy.

"Look, Taje, either surrender now, or I'll drive off without you."

I briefly entertained the notion of letting him do just that. I had some justifiable pride in my wilderness skills. Without a decent sense of direction, or a road map, I didn't know if I'd find my way back to civilization in time for myself or the crater pups. And with the bulletin out on me, hitching a ride was out of the question. I looked up between dark branches to the cloudy noon sky, and shivered as I considered spending the night in shirt sleeves. I'd have to find or build some sort of shelter—

"I mean it!" Davin hollered. "I won't have to worry about you—they'll send professional trackers with my directions!"

Lovely. I decided I'd had enough of poorly equipped wilderness adventures, anyway. Playing quarry all day and night, on top of that, felt like far more than I wanted to handle.

"I'm making this your very last chance. Come back now, or stay out here!"

"Take me to see Giem first!" I yelled back. It was useless. I had to give up. I hadn't gained anything from all this maneuvering. When would I quit acting like such a vac-head?

"No bargains. Get back up here, or spend the night playing tag with the rangers!"

I stepped out from around the tree, and hiked slowly back up the slope. Towards Davin's rifle, still aimed at me as he stood up. "Get that stunner holstered, and put your hands on your head," he said nervously.

My armpits grew slick as I went through the proper motions, and struggled to keep my balance as I continued to climb with my hands on my head. Less than a meter beyond the edge, my footing grew stable enough for one last try at him. Davin immediately realized I still had my stunner hidden under my hands on my head, and he shot me first.

I fell down the slope with no control. The world whirled around me, and I could hardly blink. Much less avoid rocks poking out of the dirt, or the youngest saplings I mowed over, before a larger trunk slammed into my belly. I felt it all, but couldn't move a limb of my battered body. I felt my chest move in slow, shallow breaths.

I should have guessed Davin didn't have time to adjust his rifle for close range—just enough to recognize my weapon on his scanner, probably. And I had seen ample evidence his reflexes were much faster than mine. My vision began to sparkle by the time he pulled me away from the tree and turned me over on my back.

Fear of respiratory or even cardiac arrest drowned my immediate pain, and my list of errors. Davin's look of total alarm turned that fear into complete panic. Davin put his ear to my chest as I tried uselessly to scream at him. I'd experienced conscious apnea once before, and I never wanted to go through it again. I was afraid if I blacked out, and Davin managed to resuscitate me, I'd wake up nova.

Davin didn't end up having to give me cardiac massage. He just gave me mouth-to-mouth to supplement my poor breathing. He didn't quit until I regained motor control, maybe ten minutes later, and I fired off some remarkably strong random kicks and punches. He backed off, and I guess it was his gasping sobs that brought me to my senses.

"Davin," I choked out, "it's okay. I'm sorry, I'm sorry!"

Davin stumbled back into a tree. "*You're* sorry!" He wiped his eyes with the back of his hand. "Great Universe. I never did that to anyone before!"

I rolled over, and grimaced as I pushed myself off the ground. Something had snapped in my right knee, the joint with some fake parts, and it didn't feel so good

"Come on, Davin, you'd better hurry up and turn me in. I'm too dangerous to run around loose out here."

As I started for the truck, Davin picked up our stunners, his face so pale, I turned cold just looking at him. Was anything worth all this stress?

He set the safeties as he followed me, stashed our weapons in the back of the cab, and we got in and returned to the road. Five minutes later, Davin set the autopilot and leaned back in his seat. He looked so grim, I turned my face away, to study the green and purple scenery zipping past my door. So my heart nearly launched from my throat when he suddenly grabbed me by my shoulders and shook me, hard.

"Blast it, Taje, that was totally vac-headed!"

My teeth rattled, and I couldn't answer. Besides, he was right.

"What are they teaching you in that nova school of yours? How to not survive for graduation? And I'm not even a professional criminal, much as you'd like to turn me into one!"

Rattle, rattle. I was shaking so hard on my own, I didn't need his help.

"You fused, nova vac-head! Don't you ever try to pull a stunt like that again!"

At last he released me. He also released the airtruck from auto, presumably so he'd have something much more worthwhile to occupy his attention. I sat quivering in my seat, and reviewed a long list of character defects and hopelessly inadequate excuses and apologies.

CHAPTER 39

Neither of us spoke another word until almost an hour later, when Davin pulled off the main road onto a smaller one, with a sign for Station Four. I tried to decide whether to feel overjoyed or totally embarrassed with the change in plans, while Davin parked his airtruck in the shade of a small grove of podtrees, just off a bend in the driveway for the station. He looked at me, and I decided on complete embarrassment.

"You'll wait for us here," he said curtly. We both knew we couldn't afford to let any of the regular station crew see me, but there was more than that in his command. He reached behind the seats for our stunners.

"Sure," I said, gulping on a dry throat. "I'm not going anywhere."

"And who will get into trouble if you're lying to me? Hold your hands up, together."

"Huh?" For a moment I panicked as I did what Davin asked. I was afraid he'd decided to risk stunning me again. He reached up to an overhead rack, and used one of its straps to bind my wrists to it. He got out of the truck, dug out the bioscanner and its cart, and headed on down the driveway.

As soon as he disappeared from sight, I started working on the strap. It didn't take long to realize he'd done a loose job of it. With a little patient effort I could slip my skinny wrists free. It had the stink of a final challenge, and I quit struggling. I wasn't sure how much I valued Davin's friendship, but I decided it didn't matter. I might still need his help beyond here. So I sat back to wait.

Time dragged, and as blood drained from my arms overhead, I wondered what might take so long. Maybe Davin and Giem had gotten into a fight—or maybe the opposite. I began to sweat, and then to shiver. I couldn't see the face of my wristcom. I must have endured at least an hour, before Davin walked back down the drive with Giem.

Giem opened my door and leaned against her hands on the cab roof to talk to me. She obviously knew a lot, and she didn't seem too delighted to see me. Yet the first thing she said was "Well, you could be right about crater pup speciation."

That promptly destroyed my final desperate attempt to appear casually calm under the circumstances. My jaw dropped.

"The more I've thought about it, the more it makes sense. Lab and necropsy data haven't provided us any consistent answers," Giem said. "Davin brought the scanner in, and Dr. Steffin and I both became very curious about your results. So we ran a bunch of our pups through your scanner. Maybe the numbers are too small—obviously we'll need to run a lot more scans—but Steffin agrees your idea needs further investigation. Before we get involved in a major ecological complaint.

"You know you're taking a fused risked coming out here? Morbe is out for blood. Why did you put poor Davin through that nova little adventure today, and did you really use your stunner on a station tech?"

"Yeah—"

"We'll lose all credibility with everyone!" Giem slapped my door closed, spun around, and marched back to Station Four, before I could explain anything. I yanked at my hands, a reflex to try to chase after her. That vac-brained move just tightened the straps.

What a depressing reunion. Davin returned to the driver's seat, and tossed the stunners in back. I rode in silent misery, while my hands fell asleep and my head hurt worse than ever.

CHAPTER 40

By the time we arrived at the ranger station, I'd been doing ten-count breathing on and off for an hour, to fight the needles of pain stabbing my head, along my arms, and inside my right knee. I kept quiet. Davin drove us around a long, excruciating Crater One perimeter road. I barely noticed the wash of brilliant floral colors as we later rode down a switch-backing road into Crater One, bursting with fresh vegetation from recent rains..

Davin pulled in at the large Crater One Ranger Office. He inhaled a deep breath before he got out. Then he walked around to my door, opened it, and released my wrists. My arms fell uselessly to my sides.

I got out clumsily. He grabbed my arm, snagged my hand stunner from behind my seat, and poked it between my shoulder blades. We marched that way up onto the porch, into the station, and directly to the main desk, on the right. Davin's hold was so strong I didn't have to worry about my lame knee.

The dark-haired Ranger looked up from her desk comscreen, and her eyes widened as I tried to shrivel up. Had my holo appeared on everyone's com?

Davin cleared his throat. "I heard there's a warrant out for this person's arrest. I can't risk trying to get her farther up the line, to the nearest police station. I know you have a lock-up—I suggest you use it, until you can get the police to pick her up. She's definitely dangerous."

To herself, at least, I thought.

The Ranger glanced involuntarily back at a weapon rack, on the wall behind her. She noticed how Davin had a death-grip on me, so she just stood up. "Yes, of course. This way, please."

I had to suppress tears of pain, partly from my arms trying to needle their way back to life. I couldn't even see the holding cell, in one back corner of the room, until I was nearly in it. It had cheap metal bars around its two open sides, like a cage, instead of a modern force field.

The door clanged shut on me, just like in old 2D movies. I stumbled over to the little cot filling most of the tiny cell, and gently massaged my arms.

"We only use this once every couple months or so, to hold a poacher or a rare local lawbreaker, until police arrive from farther up the tube. So it should do the job until they come for her," the Ranger reassured Davin. "You will need to fill out some forms before you take off—"

"I'm not filling out anything," Davin said. "Get her to fill out your forms. She's wanted, and she can just say she turned herself in. Right?" He turned back towards me.

"Right," I said dismally, and rubbing my jangling hands on my dirty pants. I wondered if I looked the part. The Ranger's expression made me suspect so. "I—guess, this is goodbye—" I remembered just in time not to identify Davin. No sense in getting him into trouble with me.

"I hope so." He turned and strode out. He immediately returned, and dumped my backpack against the Ranger's desk. "I found this with her."

"Beware of Enchanted Forests," the Ranger said politely, and Davin left without another word.

A minute later, she handed me a screen and stylus. I looked at my arms, and willed them to work. I dropped the screen on my lap and started shakily filling out my name, address, occupation, description of dispute, persons involved, et cetera. I noticed the Ranger still standing just outside the cell, her face puzzled.

"Why do you look so familiar?" she said, as I hesitated under her gaze, which also seemed a bit eerily familiar.

"I was one of two vet students you met in Emperor Crater." I had hoped she wouldn't remember, the micro I scanned her. Oh well. Might as well get all of my embarrassment over with at once. "We gave you our campsite at the lake." About an eon ago.

"Oh, that's right! How did the rest of your trip go?"

What an odd question to ask. She still stared at me strangely.

"Okay," I said. "We arrived at Quarantine Station Three the next evening. How was yours? Did you find the Chelner cabin?"

"Fine, although it rained too hard to find the cabin. Station Three—oh, that's why you match the description I received."

So that explained it. "Yeah, they brought some nova charges against me out there. It's all fused out of proportion, so I'm just as eager as anyone else to get this mess straightened out. I won't cause you any trouble," I said in a rush.

When I handed the screen and stylus back to her—realizing I should have just told her to fish my wristcom out of my backpack for a lot of my data—I once more admired her official dark blue-green uniform. Studying her planetary service patches, I wondered what in the Galaxy had inspired me to end up on this side of the bars.

I squinted more closely at her name tag. "Nessel Niktreckin?" My heart started beating faster, and my face drained of blood. It just didn't seem possible—

"Yes, Ranger Ness, at your service," she said lightly, glancing down at the screen, and her eyes bugged. "Tajen Jesmuhr? I should have recognized your name, when I received the warning—"

"Ness? Not Wind's partner—"

"Taje! The JD Branem had to put up with—"

"—in Drehx Tarnek's pre-ecology class!" we finished together, equally astonished.

"Wait till I tell Giem about this coincidence. What a small Galaxy!"

Ness laughed. "I might have known it. The redheaded class delinquent—"

"Wait a micro." That wasn't fair. I'd been exonerated on nearly every count. Why did my reputation suffer everywhere, all the same?

"I heard you'd transfered to prevet aboard our SEAR ship, and made it into vet school when the rest of us graduated as FIL ecologists," Ness said. "I should have recognized you back at Emperor Lake. What brings you here, of all places?"

"I could ask the same of you," I said, defensively. "I thought you stayed with the program."

Ness turned back towards her desk and her blinking deskcom. "Wait a micro. I've got to send this in."

Shocked, I had to remind myself that Ness had never been one of my closest friends. And our intense class loyalty had always showed its weakest face to me, Trouble-maker Extraordinaire. Nevertheless, my reunions seemed filled with ill-luck today.

About fifteen minutes later, after several quiet conversations I couldn't make out, she returned to the front of my cage. "Dr. Morbe and Dr. Nilod will stop by here this evening, after work, to see you. I presume you know them?"

"Yes." I sighed and rubbed my aching face. "What about the police?"

"Apparently they're waiting to see whether you folks can work out your dispute."

"Oh, lovely. This should prove exciting."

"Not for me. I'll have to cancel a date and put in overtime," Ness said, starting to turn away again.

"Oh," I said, stricken. "I'm sorry, Ness." How many people could I hurt in a few days?

She turned back again. "Did you really stun a technician, and lock her up?"

I could have told her that's what certain members of our class got away with doing to me once, but I wasn't sure she'd believe me. "She attacked me first," I said instead. "I've uncovered what may be a very serious threat to Rash ecology, from pup hunting and flower harvesting. It's a problem that apparently soared right over the heads of the initial surveyors, and no one seems to want to hear about it—"

"I'm listening," Ness said, abruptly.

"Huh?"

"Taje, you asked what brought me here. I did follow through on my training, and I participated in the team that performed the original ecological surveys here. When it came time to leave, I discovered I didn't want to. I'd lost my lust for planet-hopping, and found a world where I wanted to belong. When this job opened up, my qualifications beat out all the competition. So if you've got a complaint about the current ecological regulations, I want to hear it."

Oh, great. Me and my nova mouth, again! And of all the people to have to try to recruit for my cause! I could just envision telling Ness about all the hundreds of species she'd missed in her life catalogue. There she stood, waiting for an answer. I took a deep breath, and tried to extricate my boot from my mouth, very carefully.

CHAPTER 41

Maybe I did do something right that day, because after hearing out my concerns, Ness returned in a thoughtful silence to her deskcom, where she sat looking up information. I could at least hope she was reviewing her team's original survey work. She didn't quit until all the station windows went dark. She turned off her deskcom and stood up to stretch, waking me up from a catnap.

"Want some dinner?" she said, glancing toward a small snack counter along the back wall. "Have you even had any lunch?"

"I'm not very hungry." I thought about my upcoming meeting, as I rubbed my sore knee and forehead. "I could use a painkiller though, and some distraction." Like what did you find out, Ness? Anything? I didn't want to push her any harder.

Ness pulled a first aid kit from her desk and brought me a pill, and a water bottle from the snack supply. She returned to her deskcom. "I think I've got just the item to entertain both of us while we wait."

Entertainment?

"The next issue of my favorite science fiction periodical is out today, and it's supposed to have the latest Mek Ikkol story in it. Have you read any of Merrea's science fiction?"

"No. What is it like? I am an SF fan."

"Oh, it's mostly pure escapism—adventure and romance—I like her naturalist's slant, especially in her Mek Ikkol stories. Mek's sort of a super-ecologist secret agent heroine. She travels from galaxy to galaxy, and occasionally to other dimensions, to perform good, daring, and dangerous deeds, for endangered species and environments everywhere. Between various romantic and sexual interludes, of course."

I laughed. "No wonder Giem likes her. Do you mind setting it to read aloud? This sounds good."

"Okay. This new one's called 'Battling the Evil Agents of Entropy, Inc.; or How I Saved the Partially Civilized Worlds of the Krazzle Solar System from Certain Extinction.'"

With that enticing lead, the front door suddenly slid open, and two men in muddy white raingear with DVM badges came in from a dark purple downpour. Ness turned off her deskcom at once, and politely greeted Dr. Morbe and Dr. Nilod. They barely bothered to acknowledge her, as they unsealed their coats and approached my holding cell. They stood smugly in front of the bars, and seemed to expect me to stand. So I stayed sitting cross-legged on the bed.

"Hello, Dr. Morbe, Dr. Nilod," I said, nodding at each, and having to work at not calling them Morbid and Nil.

"Tajen Jesmuhr, you are in a great deal of trouble—" portly Dr. Morbe began.

"—a Business Meeting was called, and Alternatives were Deliberated," Dr. Nilod said officiously. "We could easily have you incarcerated on Enchantment, and that would no doubt set you back scholastically—"

"Possibly permanently—"

I let them babble on a bit. Battle of the Blathering Agents of the Dark Ages, Inc.; or How I Saved the Less-Than-Entirely Civilized World of Enchantment from Terminal Boredom—

"Jesmuhr, are you listening?" one of them asked suspiciously, breaking into my irreverent thoughts.

"Uh, well—"

"So what do you have to say for yourself?" Morbe's face had turned an angry blue.

"What do I have to say for myself? Who ordered a station worker to illegally detain me in Station Three?"

"That's ridiculous! Gnaf would never obey such an order, even if I were to make such an absurd request—"

"So it was you!" I grinned at Morbe. "And you did order Gnaf to detain me."

"We merely discussed making sure you carefully thought out the consequences of leaving your externship without permission."

"I'd hardly call blackmail a discussion."

"Name one important finding you hoped to gain from your frivolous interlude with Davin Mohrogh." Dr. Morbe crossed his arms and gave me a self-satisfied, green-lipped smirk.

"Why, what a pompous, vac-headed—"

"We don't have to listen to this—"

"You sure better listen." I interrupted Nilod. I launched into the potential monstrous eco-disaster they'd carelessly participated in. "You could face far more serious consequences—"

"Enough," Dr. Morbe said forcefully. "We never requested your presence in the first place. Dr. Emmel did, and she was never a proper team player. It's time to finish this absurd matter, by sending you back to your school."

That caught me completely offguard. "What? No arrest or charges?"

"I think that could become too messy, painful, and time-consuming for everyone concerned," the BGB said, with obvious satisfaction. And you'd lose, I thought bitterly, as he continued. "Moreover, taking you to court, for slander, an unprovoked attack and false imprisonment of one of my employees is simply unnecessary. You're here on a work visa. We've revoked it, and booked you on the next return flight, a week from now."

"What about now?"

"There's nowhere on this planet you can hide. Otherwise, we'd let you!" Nil cackled.

"You can stay here, safe from all the Enchanted Forests," Morbid said, and they both laughed. They turned to leave, sealing their raincoats.

"Wait a micro!" I yelled desperately after them. "What about *habeas corpus* and all that?" My FIL law classes had bored me to death, but this didn't sound at all right.

Morbe turned in front of the opening door. "We're a bit slow out here in the provinces. The police allow us time to work out our problems, before troubling to come out here." He and Nilod lurched out into the rainy night, and the door slid shut again.

Ness had acted absorbed over comwork, but her ears had nearly twitched like a Tliesjian's during the visit. She stood up, dragged my backpack over, and she opened the cell door with her wristcom. She turned the pack over to me.

"Aren't you going to search it first?" I said, before I could stifle my surprise.

"That really didn't sound legal to me," she muttered. "No, why? Is there anything in your pack I should know about?" She looked straight into my eyes.

I thought about it. Davin had my stunner. My old pocket knife? I was going to threaten to stab Ness to escape? Not in an absurd eon. "No."

"Fine. You'll need your stuff, if you're staying in here for a week. I don't want to have to smell you in those clothes the whole time. That reminds me. Do you want to shower before I lock up and leave? You've got your own toilet and sink. The employee locker room has the rest."

"Uh. Sure. Thanks. I'll be quick." I dug through my pack to find clean clothes. I froze for a micro, as I palpated my stunner. I continued as if nothing had happened, and carried my fresh clothes to the door Ness pointed me to, to the left of the snack counter.

I wouldn't do anything hasty. I was in enough trouble. I entered the locker room and I set my clean clothes down on a bench, between banks of lockers, and sat down to undress. Then I stood and stared—there was a back door. The unlocked door slid open for me, letting the rain slash in. Naked, I became obliviously goose-bumped and soaked, as I gazed at the black starless sky. Had Ness forgotten about the door, or wanted to let me have a chance to run away? But what could I do without my pack? I turned towards the shower and the door slid shut.

My brain churned as I roasted myself in the steamy shower. Not only did I wonder about the back door, what about my stunner? Had Davin replaced it for secret support? Or to incriminate me, when my belongings were searched? Or to avoid getting caught with a weapon used in a crime, a weapon he didn't hold the license for?

For that matter, were Morbe and Nilod as vac-brained as they acted, or maliciously obstructing me? Did Gnaf slant her story? Did Temm hate me now? Who was friend or foe? I didn't know how to proceed, until I commed some of this. At least I still had one week left to com what to do. Ah, the power of Giem's positive thinking. I missed her support.

When I finished, and limped into the main room with my dirty clothes in my arms, I found Ness bent over her deskcom again. "Sorry I took so long," I apologized.

"Huh?" she jumped a bit. "Oh. That's okay! Great Galaxy, who's been beating you?"

Not again! I had changed from trousers and a long-sleeved shirt, for hunting, into shorts and a T-shirt for bed. I glanced down at all my colorful new scrapes and bruises. "No one," I said. "It was an accident." I tried to hide my lameness as I returned to the cell.

"Do you want me to try to find you a lawyer?"

I dumped my dirty clothes on the floor next to my pack, and sighed as I sat down on the cot. "No thanks. Instead, do me the favor of concentrating any extra time you have into reassessing Rash eco-reports, okay? And discuss the problem with anyone else you think might help. Quarantine Station Four can send you a lot of good data. Talk to Dr. Steffin or Giemsan Fane. I think it's urgent, and you're the perfect person to help review our findings."

"I'm far from perfect! Sure, I can do that. I've already begun." Ness stood up and reached for her coat.

I gave her an anxious glance. Space, how I was ever going to get to sleep tonight?

"Ness."

"What?"

"Aren't you going to lock me back up?"

"Oh, just shut the door. It'll automatically lock again."

So she wasn't that generous. I slid the door shut, and heard the lock snick shut. Ness reached down to shut off her comscreen.

"Do you still have the Mek Ikkol story available?" I asked her.

"Yes." She grinned. "I'm hooked. Why?"

"I don't suppose you could loan me the story tonight? It might help me to defuse."

Ness laughed. "It's more likely to keep you up half the night. Sure, no problem."

"Oh, and Ness, I need another pain pill."

"I'm not surprised."

CHAPTER 42

I discovered the Evil Agents of Entropy intent on mutilating and destroying crater pups, color by color. Before I could escape, a cage clanged down on me. I hurtled uselessly at the bars. One of the Agents shot me with a stunner rifle.

"Make her puke," one said, and another opened the cage to give me a huge injection.

"If she hasn't eaten any crater pup she's a spy."

I was terror-stricken, because puking while stunned is perilous, and I hadn't thought to eat any crater pup to protect my cover. What would my instructors think of my lack of preparation? Their poking and prodding became more vigorous—

"Wake up, wake up."

"I can't." I scowled, disgusted with the vacful request, and then managed to open my eyes. Ranger Ness frowned down at me and reached for her comscreen, partly tucked beneath my pillow. "Oh."

"Well, you look like you had no problem sleeping solidly last night," she said. "The story get your mind off your problems?"

"Ohhh."

"Suppose you could set your comscreen for another Mek Ikkol story for me tonight?" I made my usual request at closing time, several nights later. Watching Ness repeatedly interrupt her comwork to set up hunting and harvesting permits, while her more curious applicants enquired into my crimes, had descended me into irritated boredom.

"Hmm." Ness paused in thought. "At this point I'll have to go back a bit. A good story did come out a couple months ago." Ness straightened out her desk, and stood up and stretched. "Are you certain that's wise?"

"I just had an unusually bad night, after that visit from my mentors," I said in answer to her nightly concern. "Speaking of bad times—you put in a lot of hours like this in here?"

Ness grinned. "Not so glamorous, is it? A bunch of us take turns rotating through here." She peeled a comscreen off her desk after coding it, and brought it over to me, opening my cell. "Shower and dinner-ordering time," she said. "Hurry. I've planned a dinner at home for two tonight, to make up for the last date we missed."

"Must be nice," I said, heading for the shower with another change of clothes. I made it a five minute quickie, and ordered a dinner tray with a vegetable and meat pie from the station dispenser. Not crater pup—I'd sworn even their cloned cells off my menu. This time I tried crater smale, to even the score a bit. It was weird, I decided, as I tried a steaming, somewhat sour bite, on my way back to the cell.

"I should tell you," Ness said, shutting my door for me, "I haven't made much progress trying to get investigative help from Port City ecologists. They're rather skeptical, to say the least. We'll need some persistence."

"I know," I said, dumping my clothes on a growing pile next to my pack. I sat down on my cot to eat. At least Ness had joined my cause surprisingly fast. "I can't help overhearing some of your calls, especially when you get put off."

Ness laughed, and as I chewed slowly, I considered asking her for a second dinner selection. She was so obviously eager to be off, and so apologetic in her eagerness, that I couldn't bring myself to do it. As soon as she left, I gulped down the juice on my tray, to rinse the taste from my mouth. I absently nibbled on a bland pastry dessert, as I leaned back with the screen propped on my thighs.

Several hours later, I felt more awake than when I'd started. I was so intensely embroiled in Mek Ikkol's escape from the Interdimensional Fiends, involving as it did the unfortunate maiming of her fabulously handsome partner, Xherd Kenrat, that it was a while before the absurdity of that name hit me. Then I realized it. "That's Drehx Tarnek, turned around. So Mek Ikkol has to be Lokki Kem. Our two pre-ecology field trip leaders! That means the author, Gornathe Merrea, has to be Aerrem Nathegorn! Why didn't I com it sooner? Now everybody gets to read her secret stuff. How hilarious! My old dorm sib, a famous author."

Ness opened the front door, sat down at her desk without a word, and focused intensely on her deskcom. I returned my attention to the story.

"Hello, Taje. Taje? Enchantment to Taje!"

"Wha—" The screen dropped to the floor as I jumped up. "Oh, hi, Giem. Giem! What are you doing here?" I said, with surprise and embarrassment, and looked from her alert expression to Ness, who sat resignedly at her desk, and studiously ignored us. Somehow I got the distinct impression that letting Giem in here was as far as Ness wanted to get involved tonight. Perhaps she had a line she couldn't cross. Or maybe she was just upset about another disrupted date.

Giem moved right up to the bars and talked in a low, private voice. "Nessel contacted me for data, and let me know what happened to you. Neither of us believed they could do this to you without a hearing, but apparently it's all okay by local law."

"Giem, it's great to see you," I interrupted enthusiastically.

"Shhh." Giem never thought me quiet enough. She glanced nervously back towards Ness for a micro. "Just listen to me. I've spent every spare moment reviewing as many station records as I could get access to, not to mention trying to hunt up some legal advice for you. I even got a chance during lunch today to sneak a look at the latest messages on Dr. Steffin's office deskcom. And guess what I found?"

"What?"

"Orders from One, to refuse all discussion of ecological issues with me, and to be sure I'm confined to Four until I'm shipped off, along with you. They're revoking my visa too! And they've told Steffin we're a pair of trouble-making, bleeding-heart, FIL students, making up scare stories to ruin business."

"Obstruction! From the day they found they couldn't stop our externship, and decided to delay us on horses, and split us up on remote stations! That must be what they're doing! Can we still trust anyone?"

"I don't know," Giem said, disgruntled. "I doubt we can trust anyone at Station One, or the local government. I think we need to head straight to top authorities in Port City and march right into their offices. Nessel tells me lower level bureaucrats keep filtering out all her calls."

"So you left your station against orders too?" I asked, putting the holo together, and beginning to tremble. From excitement or fear—probably both.

"Well, Steffin hasn't informed me yet, officially. He had to work through lunch today, and I'm sure he didn't see or avoided the new orders before closing tonight. That is when I left, to keep him out of official trouble, too. He knows how upset I am over this whole business. He's starting to get rather upset too, and if he had more free time, he'd probably make a good ally. Unfortunately, we're running out of time to recruit anyone, besides the two of us, to try to convince authorities of the potential seriousness of this matter."

"The two of us—do you mean it, Giem? You're still free—why don't you head straight for the tube, and Port City?"

"I'm afraid I may no longer find it that simple. I wondered how they'd ever manage to keep me at Four, since I knew Steffin and his husband wouldn't force me to stay. Simple geographic isolation might have done the job. I've made friends with several of our regular hunters, and I started calling around for a ride here. But everyone had excuses."

"So how did you get here?"

"I relented and called Davin."

"He's been nova to take you out!" I smirked.

"Well, not anymore. Turns out there's some sort of local general alert out on both of us; something to the effect of reporting any sightings of troublesome station students. Davin wanted no more part in it. I only convinced him to drop me off at Nessel's house tonight by promising neither of us would ever try to have anything to do with him again."

"I can't decide if that's good news or bad."

"I don't know either," Giem said. "To continue. It wouldn't surprise me if the tube has programming against our wristcoms. That means I don't believe our mission is going to get any easier for the foreseeable future. I want your help, Taje. You made the initial discoveries, so I need you with me."

I felt startled gratitude. "Do you realize what you're saying?" I asked her, very quietly.

"Of course," Giem said impatiently, as she met my intense stare.

"Is Ness in on this?" I whispered.

"No. Do you think she'd help us?" Giem said softly, hopefully.

"I don't know. And even if she's willing, I'm not sure I want to get her into trouble with us."

"Well, I had to beg to get her to leave her ranger friend long enough to walk over here with me for a quick visit. And I've got my stunner." Giem patted a small lump under her dark green cloak, giving her the authentic look of a Bold Rescuer.

"And I've got mine—"

"What? Why haven't you broken out of here?"

"I was trying to be good," I said, annoyed. "I tried to get Ness to help instead." Giem held her finger to her lips, and I lowered my voice again. "They wouldn't have found me here at departure time, if the crater pup situation still wasn't resolved."

"That's being good?" Giem's lips twitched, and I realized she was teasing me. She straightened up. "Where's the cell lock release?"

"Ness has to use her wristcom."

"Okay." Giem drew her stunner and turned back toward the ranger. As Giem strode across the room, I wondered if she thought I was wearing my stunner too. I leaped for my pack.

"Sorry to do this, Nessel. We have to leave," Giem told her. "I need you to open the cell."

I threw clothes out of my pack to find my beat-up, questionable stunner, and lunged against my cell bars in time to see Ness give a startled look. That look quickly turned to anger, and zapped guilt into my heart.

"You both lied to me! Why should I do anything more for you? Now you want to stun me!"

Giem turned around to give me an uncertain, questioning glance, and Ness jumped up from her chair, towards the stun rifles racked on the wall behind her.

I aimed at her and fired desperately, but nothing happened.

"Shoot her, Giem, shoot her!" I yelled. Giem stood frozen for an agonizing moment. We'd had target practice, and we'd stunned each other in class to learn how it felt (I hadn't mentioned I knew). I don't think she'd ever shot anyone else. At last she fired and Ness slumped, knocking a rifle to the floor with her.

CHAPTER 43

"Now what?" Giem said, looking upset and sickened.

"Bring Ness's wristcom over here."

Giem retrieved it for me. If Ness had hidden or alarmed the cell lock release transmission code, we were in deep trouble, but I found and used it easily. Apparently security wasn't a big issue here.

"Wow. Just like a 3D holo thriller," Giem said as my door slid open. "Quick, dress warmly and pack up." Giem returned to Ness and worked to drag her into the cell, while I pulled out some more clothes, and threw my dirty pile into my pack. I apologized to Ness as we locked her in, and dropped her wristcom on her desk. As Giem closed the cell door, I glanced back guiltily, remembering to check Ness's breathing. She looked okay.

Giem had left her pack parked on the front porch, and she heaved it on while I adjusted my straps. We both gasped for breath.

"Come on," Giem said.

"I hope we aren't getting Ness into too much trouble." I tried to calm down as I realized we'd bought ourselves some time. Ness probably wouldn't get any help until her morning customers arrived.

"Nessel can make up any story she wants to about this." Giem saw the guilty look on my face. "She can even claim I forced her to let me in."

"That could get you into more trouble!"

"No more than you're already in," Giem said, amused. "I just copied your way of keeping that maintenance tech out of trouble. Anyway, we've done it. No sense in worrying about it. I think we're committed, like a Big Maxson breakfast." Giem headed down the steps, turned left, around the station, and to the empty street. I followed, baffled.

"What?" Committed, as in nova?

"Don't you remember those two Big Maxson traders in the first restaurant Ziehl took us to?" Giem said. "One of them said it's like quelsh eggs and skitsch sausage. The quelsh is involved, and the skitsch is committed."

I groaned. "I hope that's not a prognosis on our chances."

"Well, I don't know, Taje. You're limping, and no one's hurt you. Or are you holding out on me?"

"It's nothing, Oh Fearless Leader. A minor, self-inflicted injury, during a small disagreement with Davin."

"Is that why he wanted nothing more to do with us? What exactly happened?"

"He didn't tell you? By the way, where are we going?" She turned left, away from the exit switchbacks.

"Down Main Street," Giem said, in a tone expressing shock with my faulty sense of direction.

"I know that," I said, insulted. "I meant, what is our destination?" I saw her triumphant teasing look and I realized she'd zapped me again. "In this Incredible Escape Plan of yours," I finished, very insincerely.

"Oh, there's no Master Plan," Giem freely admitted, with some relish. "It's all purely ad lib."

"That is completely obvious," I said. "I repeat, where should we go next?"

"Well, the tube's still a good bet, especially this late, when no one's likely to be around to recognize us. I refuse to become totally paranoid, until we check it out."

"Sure it even runs this late? Remember, we're out in the boonies of Enchantment."

"Good point. Let's go find out."

Our boots echoed quietly on the pavement, dimly lit by street lights. Soon we turned to confront Station One, crouched with glowing yellow windows randomly lit in a skull-like pattern. It appeared to leer over its decorative plaza, artfully lit up. In the plaza stood the tube translifts, brightly outlined with official blue and red stripes against the midnight-blue sky. The rustling of ornamental trees and fountains was the only other sound as we wound between planters and benches to the lifts.

The lift we chose at random gave us no trouble. Down in the empty tube station, the gate we chose for automatic ticketing flashed a schedule as we approached it. We both stopped and groaned—we'd missed the last ride out for the night by about ten minutes. We'd have to wait nearly ten hours for the earliest morning ride.

"That would still get us out of here before the ranger office opens in the morning," I said, as we tried to decide what to do next.

"Yes, it also allows a lot of time for something to go wrong," Giem said, "and someone in the morning traffic might recognize us."

"So what do you suggest? Rent a car? Some Escape Plan you've commed."

"I told you, I have no plan. And where would we rent a car this late?"

"The Enchanted Inn lobby is open all night," I said. "Think the warning about you has gotten this far? Ness didn't seem to know about you. You could probably go in, rent an aircar, and pick me up."

"That's right." Giem clapped me on the shoulder. "Great idea." We headed back towards the lifts, and abruptly she stopped us before a tourist comscreen.

"What are you doing?" I said, as she played with the map controls.

"I don't want to drive all the way to Port City, nor do I want to pay for it. I'm looking for either a reasonably close all-night tube station, or one with a campsite nearby, so I'll have my itinerary ready for the hotel rental, and I won't have to make something up. Hmm. Looks like a campsite will have to do. Let's get a copy of this."

Giem tried to download it into her wristcom, but the machine didn't give her a map. Giem repeated her order and the screen politely asked her to wait. She squinted her eyes in puzzlement, while the hair on my scalp began to crawl.

"Giem, I don't like this. If the comscreen's malfunctioning, it should just say so. It shouldn't ask you to wait for such a simple request."

"You're right." Giem cancelled her order, and we loped back toward the lifts.

"What will we do?" I wailed.

"How should I know? Get away from here first, before something worse happens!"

We leaped into the nearest open lift, and the door slid shut after Giem voiced our destination. I had just begun to thank the Galaxy public translift rides were free, when an alarm screamed and the lift refused to open for us when it stopped.

"Great. Just wonderful. Trapped before we even leave town!" How humiliating. The alarm hurt my ears. I clapped my hands over them as Giem searched the control panel screen, and pried open a panel below.

"What are you doing?" I watched her strong fingers probe inside the panel. Surely we'd run out of hope. Someone in authority would show up, and take us back into custody—

"Following the emergency power outage instructions for people who get stuck in here—I just need to convince it—"

The lift door popped open, and we tumbled out among blaring alarms into the cool lights of the plaza.

"Look!" We saw the clear front doors of Station One slide open for a security guard. Yellow light gleamed on a uniform and a stunner rifle. Giem grabbed my pointing arm and hauled us around to the back of the bank of lifts, our only immediate cover. From there we wound around buildings in the dark, our packs an irritating burden in our haste to escape unseen.

I was trying to make out a confused and frustrated shout fading behind us when I banged into Giem, halted at a dark corner of a Main Street store.

"Ow. Sorry. How did you—ever get us—out of that lift?" I asked her softly, between panted breaths nearly in sync with hers.

"Whoever programmed—that trap—forgot about—the emergency power supply," Giem whispered. "What's really amazing—is that someone did that kind of programming—at all—against me! We've got a battle on our hands!"

"Sure scans that way." I picked up a foot to adjust my boot seals. They had made me nova. Swimming around in a loose boot while trying to make a getaway didn't ever seem to be a problem for Mek Ikkol. Nor did she have a knee with broken parts. I tried to put the pain out of my mind. "So what's our next move?" I was fresh out of ideas.

"Well, if we can't use our wristcoms, we can't rent a car. The only other transportation faster than our own legs for getting us out of here would be animal mounts."

"Is it important enough?" I found myself asking.

"What?" Giem said.

"To do what I think you're suggesting."

"Don't you think so?" Giem had a delighted look of mischief on her face. "Come on. I've always wanted a good excuse to do something like this!"

CHAPTER 44

"I'm amazed with you," I whispered, as Giem and I snuck between two buildings, to peek down Main Street. "You treated me as if I was fused, and I think you've gone more nova than me."

We both jumped back at the sound of more than one pair of running feet. Had Ness's date decided to check on her? We could have all sorts of people after us.

"Keep your voice down," Giem said. "I just wanted more proof, that's all. I'm not even sure why I was so hard on you, back when Davin drove you to Four. Now I've seen more evidence, I'm willing to be reasonable. Hmm, it looks like we'll have to take the back way."

This is being reasonable? I almost asked, as we had a long, sweaty trek to cross town under our backpacks. We finally followed our noses through the dark to the paddocks and locked barn of Enchanted Inn, at the end of Main. Discreet use of our flashlights revealed no handy mounts allowed outside their stalls this night. Frantic searching turned up a Dutch door with the top half open. We climbed clumsily with our packs over the paddock fence, through mud and other unmentionables, and over the locked lower door.

King almost blocked our entrance in his eagerness to greet us. He nickered as Giem climbed in first, and she happily petted him as she backed him up out of my way. I bruised my crotch painfully on the doorsill, before almost tumbling into King's bedding.

"What luck!" Giem whispered. "He's mine. Go find another for yourself."

That proved easier said than done. I left my pack in the aisle to search from one end of the stable to the other, and found Giem's pack propped next to mine when I returned. Giem was just hauling a saddle and bridle out of a tack room, and she had King in a halter, clipped out in the aisle.

"No luck, Giem. Only one other mount in the house. Some big ugly brute whose species I don't even recognize."

"Well, we haven't much choice, do we?" she said, irritated, as she set down King's tack. "Let's have a look."

Giem knew a lot more about domestic FIL mounts than I. It was one of her childhood hobbies. When she scanned the huge hairless blue-grey warty creature with almost no neck, giant black teeth, and a sloping back, stomping around on flat black-clawed feet and threatening to roar at the slightest provocation, even she looked daunted.

She wrinkled her nose. "They'd track us down by the smell alone! Okay, forget this one. At least King is big. Someone has sure emptied this place out."

I followed her back to King, and impatiently watched her pick his feet and brush out his back and girth area.

"I should have guessed it when I saw how empty the tack room was," Giem said. "The only usable saddle I found is too good to be true. It's probably the manager's. You'd better sort out our most important gear, so we don't completely overload King."

"It'll all have to fit in my pack, if I'm riding double behind you." I opened wide all our pack seals with trembling hands. I hated packing for a trip under pressure, without a meticulous equipment list.

"Right," Giem said. "If you need them, I think I spotted a set of saddlebags in the tack room."

The tent, sleeping bags, first aid kit, and raingear all went into the priority pile. Then more warm clothes. And what about extra underwear and clothes, in case we got wet? And all our leftover food packets—how long would we be stranded from civilization? Maybe it was a good thing we'd bought too much food for our last trip. Better include our water bottles—

"Hurry up, Taje! I hear voices!"

Giem had King ready, and she helped cram my pack ruthlessly. I saw the fatal outcome ahead of us, and ran for the tack room. "Get some supplement for King, too!" Giem called after me.

I swept up an armful of equine packets out of a bin, and almost gave up after a minute's search for the saddlebags. Somehow I thought to flash my beam over the floor on my way out, and scanned the bags under a layer of filth in one corner. I grabbed them up and shook them off as I dashed back out, coughing on dust.

"Here. Put this on." Giem was holding up my pack.

I stuffed King's supplements into the outer pockets, and strapped in. Giem stuffed the saddlebags with almost all of the remainder of my priority pile, mainly our surplus food packets. And left behind mostly our dirty laundry, along with Giem's empty pack.

"That can be our deposit," she joked. She found a way to strap the saddle bags on the front of the large saddle, to my relief. The saddle took up plenty of King's back, but I knew I wasn't going to get to sit in it. At least not on the seat.

Giem unclipped King, mounted, and reached a long arm down to me. "I'll help you up." She removed her boot from the left stirrup.

Suddenly the aisle got a lot brighter, as a door at the end of it slid open.

"What in the Galaxy are you doing with my horse?" the angry manager shouted at us, and King shied just as I was fumbling my left foot into the stirrup. For a micro I thought I'd get dumped like an Earth turtle on my back and trampled to death. My armpit nearly split apart, as Giem hauled me on up by my wrist. Thrown onto the saddle skirts, I locked onto Giem with a death grip, while King almost fell to his knees with surprise.

"Haven't you heard?" Giem yelled back, while somehow all three of us kept from falling over. "There's an emergency down at the tube station! All the alarms have gone nova!" And she whispered "This is great. She's got the door unlocked for us."

With that, Giem urged King straight into a gallop, he gallantly obeyed, and the baffled-looking manager stepped out of our way. Thank the Galaxy, because I doubt King would have willingly run her over. As we flew past Gnaf's wife and on out of the barn, I saw her recover her senses. She came running after us, cursing and swearing.

"Hah! Too late," I said to Giem's back. Quickly Giem and King found the trail leading up out of Crater One, and we lost sight of our pursuer in the dark. Unfortunately, that also meant we'd left behind a hostile witness to our escape.

I could describe a thrilling gallop up the switchbacks of One, a posse on our heels, and a shootout among the rocks at the top, but the reality of it didn't match any of my favorite holo adventure stories. King snorted and heaved as Giem got him to lunge up the dusty trail, bouncing me and my heavy pack on the stiff saddle skirts. Occasionally I banged my tender crotch on the cantle, had to suppress a scream, and wanted to ask her to slow him down.

"Giem, you aren't making poor King gallop up this trail?"

"Of course not." Giem sounded annoyed. "He's just a very fast horse."

"Well, that's good."

"Uh huh."

I fought my swaying pack to keep from dumping me over sideways. And I worked at not dragging Giem out of the saddle with me, as gravity tried to slide me backwards, down King's sweating rump, on the steeper parts of the trail. I didn't want to think about a fall from King's height. So I dug in my increasingly raw knees and managed to cling to my perch, in spite of the jarring to my abused right knee. How Giem kept her seat solid, for both of us, through the entire ride, I'll never know.

I dark-adapted in time to know when we'd reached the top edge of the crater. I had to resist the urge to whoop aloud in victory, as Giem reined King to a halt. She turned him back around, for us to view the scattered lights of One below.

"Wasn't that fun?" Giem cheered.

"Like a Mek Ikkol story," I said.

"Except it wasn't really a chase scene," she said. "I wonder why. Oh, no. Good news and bad news."

"What?"

"Like I said, this saddle must be the manager's. It has all the latest options: a built-in com with a map projector, road signal reader, compass—"

"I assume that's the good news."

"Yes, well, we've dropped the saddlebags."

"What? Where?"

"Where? I don't know where! Somewhere along the trail up out of One."

"And you didn't notice? Giem, they had all our food!"

"Hey, I was busy getting us up that nasty trail in the dark, in case you didn't notice. Anyway, we can do without. It shouldn't be more than a day or two's ride to the tube station I picked out."

"And that's assuming the tube will accept our wristcoms." My stomach growled with unfortunate timing.

"What else can we do?"

I snickered. "Hijack a car."

"More likely we'll ride poor King the rest of the way."

I began to shiver. I slid down off King's big rump, and grabbed his tail to make a gentle landing right behind him, too close for a kick from him to hurt me. King was too nice and too tired to worry me anyway. I limped over to a rock to drop the pack against it. I searched for my coat, yanked it on, and found my hat and gloves.

Giem twisted in the saddle. "What are you doing?"

"I'm cold, and I'm ready for a rest stop. Aren't you?"

"Here? Are you nova, Taje? Just because this isn't a chase scene doesn't mean it won't turn into one soon. And we didn't even warm up poor King for that ride, so we need to keep him moving longer to cool him down. Get back up here."

I sighed, unable to argue with that. I got down on the ground to strap back into the pack, and mostly used my good leg to stand. Giem gave me a stirrup and a hand to haul me up again. I guiltily felt King's hot, heaving flanks under my legs.

Giem urged King to move on at a walk, and used the saddle receiver road signals to keep us out of sight and parallel. We didn't see or hear people or vehicles. I'm not sure that meant much, considering how sleepy we got. Soon I wrapped my arms around Giem's waist, turned my head, leaned against her back, and set my internal alarm to wake me if I tilted to either side. After who knows how many short bouts of sleep, Giem insisted we dismount.

I hoped for a rest stop at last. Instead she gave me a quick and dirty saddle navigation lesson. She took the pack from me, made me get up into the saddle, and she mounted behind me. She leaned against my back, with her arms around me and her head on my shoulder, to doze off.

The compass on the pommel kept pointing the way for me. The saddle beeped. Giem jerked awake.

"Do you see it?"

"See what?" I said. "The sun isn't up yet."

"Devil's Crater," Giem said. "I set our course for it. It's not big, but it should give us cover."

"We get to rest?"

"We have to get out of sight before the sun rises," Giem said.

Giem looked just as wretched as I felt, when I turned in the saddle to face her for a moment. "Who's Bright Idea was this, anyhow?"

"Fortunately, I don't remember," she said.

Giem didn't remember? I doubted it. The grey, cold beginnings of dawn met us at the lip of the small crater, in time to provide just enough light for King to plod his way down into its trailless depths. Dark, towering, creaky old trees, reminiscent of Forest Crater, even thicker, surrounded us with cover, and the moment we stumbled across a relatively flat plot of ground near a stream, we called a halt.

By the time Giem had King watered, unsaddled, fed, and clipped to a tree, I had the tent triggered, and the sleeping bags and our other belongings thrown inside. King whickered forlornly as we ducked into the tent. We pulled our boots off, undressed, and squirmed into our bags immediately. Within minutes of listening to the quiet gurgling of the stream, King's fitful snorting, and a breeze rustling in waves through the podtrees, we were no longer conscious.

CHAPTER 45

I sighed over the Abnormal Ingestion, Digestion, Absorption, and Excretion exam, and made the nova mistake of trying oral electrolytes on a case with ruminal stasis. I reached the end, material we'd covered last in class, so I'd also studied it at the end of a cram session at an hour last night too nova to admit. As our last minutes for the final melted away, I felt both humiliation and guilt. Waves and waves of tremendous guilt and shame.

The guilt and shame of not learning my lessons properly, after all the efforts of my patient, overworked, suffering teachers. Especially amidst the relentless public humiliation of my empathic sending and receiving, without any control. That included my terrified reaction to sickness and deaths from a bioterrorist virus.

I feared losing my best friend, and I had few others. I knew she was in trouble, and I had to stumble through woods again, panic striking me from all directions, looking for her. Sweat poured down my face and mixed with my tears as I panted, fighting the cramp in my side and my weak knee. I made my way up steeper terrain and kept slipping. Until I slammed into a tree trunk and grabbed hold of it to keep from collapsing to the ground.

The electric shock of it turned each exhalation into a strangled sob. I shut my eyes and rested a cheek against the rough cold bark. Abruptly, all the feelings of horror multiplied a hundredfold. Clinging to the rough tree made me feel even worse.

I broke away and made my last run—

And I broke out of the woods, at the edge of the crater. Tears smeared my vision, as I gazed dully over a distant panorama of rolling hills and fog, and the sun rising behind it. How did I get here? I had awakened from a terrible dream—a dream that felt all mixed up with Shandy again, and I must have sleepwalked, which I'd never done before.

Despite utter disorientation, somehow I knew I was no longer alone. Had pursuers tracked us here? Maybe I'd heard a strange voice. I wiped my eyes, looked around, and Giem was nowhere in sight. I'd have to dash back down to camp to warn her, before someone scanned me.

As I began to leap down between the podtrees again, towards their dark shelter, a wave of dizzy nausea almost knocked me off my feet.

The woods! Utter revulsion hit me at the thought of returning to them. I shook my head, and couldn't shake my relentless fear, as I wondered whether I might still be dreaming. The impulse to flee my cover overcame all my good sense. Within minutes I blinked again at the orange, foggy sunrise, visible between the last and youngest of the blue-green trees spilling up out of Devil's Crater.

And I met the gaze of Ranger Ness, stunner rifle in hand, and saw another armed ranger at her side, less than ten meters away.

CHAPTER 46

I slunk back behind the nearest sapling, gripped its repulsively sappy bark, shut my eyes, my head spun, and I uselessly hoped Ness or the copper-scaled Lorratian ranger with her hadn't spotted me. "You can't see me, you can't see me," I whispered in a childish chant, as if shutting my eyes helped.

"I can't see her, anywhere," Ness's slow voice almost startled me out of my odd trance.

"We should have brought hunting rifles, with proper scanners," the male Lorratian said. "How can anyone be so sure those two students will come running out, right here? Even if they are supposed to exit the fastest way out, screaming senselessly, if we're off by one thick stand of trees, we may not see or hear them."

"I don't like it here myself," Ness said uneasily.

No, you don't like it here at all, I thought in vicious retaliation, keeping my eyes clamped shut. If I can't see you, you can't see me. And you hate it here even more than I do. Somehow I had the feeling I'd been maneuvered again into a game I didn't feel like playing.

I felt like a crater pup trying to disappear from a hunter by freezing.

"Let's go back and recheck the field scanner," the Lorratian ranger said.

"Yeah, I'm afraid they could just as easily ambush us here—"

"Ranger Niktreckin, Ranger Niktreckin." Ness's wristcom interrupted her.

"Here!" she snapped. "No luck at these coordinates, so far."

"Well, we've got Fane, and a new reading on King's transmitter. Jesmuhr's reading has faded out. We think she's on the horse, heading up out of the crater a little more to the east."

"Where are you?" the Lorratian said.

"A bit northwest of you." The com voice rattled off coordinates. "We could drive the truck—"

"No, we're so close, let's go after her," Ness replied. "Stay right there with Fane, and don't drop your guard around her."

"Right. And beware of Enchanted Forests!"

"Same to you!"

The two rangers launched in one direction, and I took off after them, just below the crater rim. I stayed among the saplings, and flicked their rough trunks with my sap-sticky fingers, for luck in passing. Defeating the odd story about running up out of here, screaming senselessly, improved my spirits. All I had to do was rescue Giem. I'm not here, you can't find me, you can't see or hear me!

I reached a tributary creek crossing at a run, boulder-hopping without slowing. Until I hit one rock with a surprisingly slick growth, slipped, and I landed with a hard crash in the cold water. I slipped and crawled my way out, shaken, and my knee hurt with fresh vigor. A few meters on, dripping my way between saplings and bushes, I heard voices just above me.

I'm not here, you didn't hear me, you can't find me. I'm invisible!

I kept a light touch on the young tree before me, and I squinted out through the edge of the foliage. The stable manager and what looked like a Station One security guard had stunner rifles trained on Giem, who appeared both confused and upset. The guard and manager wore wristcoms, probably set on scan, and behind them a white Quarantine Station One airtruck was parked but still running, with its doors left carelessly open.

I patted my pants pockets, and with some wonder, recovered my soaked stunner. Well, now or never, I thought.

I leaped out from my cover, roared as I mounted the crater edge, and fired.

Giem caught on fast. She had blocked the guard's rifle and felled the man with a simple fold and leg-sweep, by the time I'd stunned the manager and turned to aim at the guard. He slumped, and Giem turned to me with the same look of surprise that had slowed her captors' responses.

"Your stunner! It's started working again?"

I expected astonishment over my great sneak attack. I stared sheepishly at the battered, dripping weapon in my palm. I'd forgotten its failure in the ranger station.

"Quick, get in the truck! They're coming around," I said, as the manager and the guard groped at the ground for their weapons.

We ran for the airtruck, leaped in, and Giem hit the controls. The doors slid closed as we took off, and within seconds we had sped away. Giem turned to me with a laugh.

"Isn't this great? We get to be really bad. Port City, here we come!"

I gave her a galaxy-spanning grin. "When I suggested hijacking a car last night, I was joking. I can't believe this! They even left some snack packets on the dash." Of course that wasn't saying much, considering we possessed nothing except the clothes on our backs. We tore into the food.

"Giem." My smile grew less self-confident. "What happened back there?"

Giem was programming the truck, so she didn't answer right away. Neither of us had a license to fly aircars, so an autopilot flight might prove safer.

Giem sat back at last, hands off the controls. "What happened? I was hoping you could tell me, Taje. Those woods—"

"Enchanted Forests!" I latched on to it like a dream trying to flee. I still had fragrant sap on my hands, and the haunting odor made me tremble. "It's the trees! It must be! Everyone expected us to come running out, fused and screaming. Every experience we've had among the podtrees has been full of anxiety. Forest Crater, Fallen Moon Lake Crater, they surround Station Three, my brief escape from Davin into a podtree crater, and even parked under a small stand outside of Quarantine Station Four, not to mention this last crater."

"Once again, you've come up with a totally nova idea, Taje. But I can't rule it out. Why was I so hard on you?" Giem thought more. "It's odd there's no official warning. Just the 'Beware of Enchanted Forests' we keep hearing from everyone."

"Not only from Dr. Nilod, when he sent us out here on horses, remember?" Visions of conspiracy—delay and scare tactics—spinning through my head. "Maybe they just take it for granted on this planet—stay away from the mean, telepathic trees, or should I say empathic? Broadcasted, anxiety-inducing fear—what a nice natural defense! No wonder I've never seen a crater pup, or any lifeform bigger than a worm, among those trees. And therefore, no flowering bushes, further evidence for crater pup-flower symbiosis. Have we noticed flowers anywhere in the same crater as podtrees?"

"I suppose it could be just a matter of competition for sunlight," Giem said, and sighed. "I should have realized King and his saddle would have transmitters. What better way to keep track of rental mounts? No wonder they didn't bother to chase after us last night. They made it easy on themselves by just waiting for us to stop. And when they tracked King's signal to that aptly named crater, they must have commed they had us."

"Yeah," I said. "They probably commed a couple rotten hours of sleep would drive us right up into their arms at sunrise!"

"Come to think of it," Giem said, "how did you manage to evade them? And how did you get so wet?"

My heart began to pound. Would she believe this one? Did I even believe it myself? I felt the stunner in my pocket. "Giem, what happened to you down there?" I temporarily evaded her question with another.

"Hmm." She shut her eyes. "Well, I woke up in the tent—at least I thought I woke up—from a series of ghastly nightmares. I discovered you were gone, and an odd fear overwhelmed me. I yanked on my clothes and boots and came running out after you—"

I glanced down at my own clothes and boots, and realized I had no memory of putting them back on— thank the Galaxy I had—

"—convinced, somehow, you were in terrible danger," Giem said. "Believe it or not, I think it had something to do with you falling into a dark pit. I guess I've been reading a little too much Mek Ikkol."

"I think it was Shandy, again." I felt for the power control on the stunner in my pocket, and turned it down to the lowest setting.

"Great Galaxy—awake? Or did I just think I'd awakened?"

"I don't know. I don't even know when I woke up."

"I think you've just filled my head with your stories," Giem said, once again refusing to believe me. "I even caught up with you at some point—you crashed around in the bushes quite a lot—or at least I dreamt I did. I lost you again. Does that make any sense? I got so scared I ran up out of the crater, and once free of the trees, I did at last feel awake. And that's when I realized it was dawn, and two people had stunner rifles aimed at me."

I released the safety on my stunner, took a deep breath, and fired it through my damp pants pocket at my leg. Nothing happened.

"So what happened to you?" Giem said. "I thought they had you pinpointed for sure on their scanner."

"Um, I, uh, believe I had another of those shared dreams with Shandy," I admitted reluctantly. "Those podtrees—if they each put out a weak fear signal, and maybe they amplify each other and the victim's resultant anxiety, in a nasty feedback loop. Well, maybe they picked up the weak signal between Shandy and me, and amplified that too. Warping it into something even more nova. So that you got caught up in it too. And maybe it built up so much that I—gained some power. I think it's possible I temporarily became a projecting empath, and convinced my pursuers they couldn't see me."

"That's not something Shanden ever managed to do, was it?" Giem sounded skeptical.

"No. That's his problem—no control." I took my dripping stunner out of my pocket and under Giem's curious gaze, dialed the power up. Could I really have gained more temporary ability, in one critical morning, than Shandy had in his whole life? "I wonder if spending some careful time here would enhance Shandy's powers, enough for him to gain some control over them?"

"Not if you're right about the fear loop," Giem said. "He'd probably just go completely nova—hey, Taje, what are you doing?"

She tried to grapple with me, too late. I shot myself first. But nothing happened.

"The light's still on," I said of the power indicator, "there's just nothing home inside." It was my attempt at humor. I let my trembling hands release the stunner into Giem's.

A moment of shocked silence followed, and I turned up the airtruck interior heat so I could dry off. I stared through my window, away from Giem, at the speeding blur of scenery.

At last I said quietly, "My stunner still doesn't work. It never did, after that autoserver ran over it. I just forgot, for a couple crucial moments. Giem, I stunned Gnaf and our pursuers because I believed it would work."

Another minute passed, and Giem sighed as she handed my stunner back. "Taje, you do realize there is such a thing as an intermittent failure?"

"Right." I pocketed it, and we both leaned back.

Giem slid her window open part way. "So how did you and your stunner get so soaked?"

"I fell in a creek, on my way to rescue you."

We both chuckled softly. We fought a sleepiness washing over us with the warm air blowing into the truck. Until necessity overcame us, and we foolishly risked drifting off once again.

CHAPTER 47

Alarms and Giem's curses jolted me awake about another hour later—I checked the time meter on the dash, as I tried to make sense of the situation. A brown hunter's airtruck had steered uncomfortably close ahead of us. In automatic response, ours was slowing, despite Giem's attempts to make evasive maneuvers.

"I was afraid of this," Giem said angrily, working the manual controls with intense concentration. "I thought if we drove at top speed, we might at least reach another town and hitch a ride, before getting caught."

"Station trucks must be even easier to track than saddle transmitters."

"Yep. We should have taken their wristcoms with us, so they couldn't call for help."

"The—stun—didn't last, because I didn't believe in it strongly enough," I said. Anyway, it wouldn't have given us much of a head start. Just another theft charge. The two rangers looking for me may still be on foot."

"You're right." Giem swerved sharply. The other truck kept right on us, in a dangerous game of bumper cars, and our truck was still slowing. "So what's next, oh Brilliant Partner in our famous Vet Student Duo?"

"Alas, I am fresh out of ideas." I yawned. "In fact, I'm not feeling very brilliant. And I'm afraid my sensei will kill me anyway, if we ever get out of this mess."

"What do you mean?" Giem swerved our truck off the road and the ride grew bumpier, in spite of also slowing down more.

"First, no anticipation and avoidance of danger, and second, trying to take the law into our own hands. Maybe this serves us right."

"Nonsense!" Giem braked, spun our truck around, got us back on the road, and accelerated in the opposite direction. "Part of the law is supposed to be in our hands!"

"You mean, if we live long enough" I checked the dash. Giem had increased our speed to the maximum this road allowed. "Aren't we going in the wrong direction?" I checked behind us. Giem's trick had bought us a little time. The brown truck was almost on our tail. I wondered how they'd overridden their airtruck's safety inhibitions. Probably an illegal mod, or a ranger's wristcom override permit.

"Whatever," Giem said. "I haven't time to quibble over the finer points of the ethics of trying to save lives! Taje, you realize this is our Car Chase Scene?"

I looked over at Giem, and felt surprise. "You're enjoying this!"

"Of course!"

I sat back, and tried not to grip my harness with white-knuckled fists. "I didn't know you watched any of that old 2D stuff," I said, remembering I'd recommended my favorites. At least my clothes had mostly dried, and we had returned to the smoother road. "In all the excitement, I'd almost forgotten we're trying to save numerous species from almost certain extinction."

"Yes, it's Giemsan Fane and Tajen Jesmuhr to the rescue of innocent crater pups and the wondrous flora of Enchantment!"

"Against the Evil Agents of Entropy," I said. "Who, by the way, seem to be gaining on us again."

"I know," Giem said, disappointed. "Want to try flying?"

"I know even less about atmospheric flight than I do about space travel. And an airtruck smashes up even easier than a shuttle. How about you?"

"I know nothing about either, and I think one semi-controlled crash on Big Maxson was enough for me," Giem said. "I guess we'll have to stay less than a meter off the ground. They're forcing us to stop, and, oh joy, here's a ranger truck heading our way. What do you want to do? Can you blast everyone down with your head again?"

"First of all, there aren't any podtrees here—"

"Yeah, I know. I've actually been looking—"

"Second, Shandy has disappeared from my head, and I don't know how to call him. Third, you could be right about intermittent failure—maybe it's just a loose connection—I doubt it has fixed itself. Fourth—"

"Taje, we're stopping! What do you want to do?"

"I don't know! How about giving up, for once? Might completely throw them off. I'm tired."

Our airtruck gave up the chase, and preserved its shiny white coat by putting itself in park, on the side of the road. A moment later two pairs of faces and stunner rifles showed up at each of our windows. The faces looked rather fused, and one of mine belonged to Ness.

Giem and I exchanged looks. "Well, it was fun while it lasted," Giem said, winking bravely at me.

"Are you giving up?" I asked. No sense in trying any escape move without a team effort.

"I'm too tired to fight," Giem said, as her door was opened from the outside.

Mine slid open. The Lorratian slapped my harness release, his scaled hand sounding like a bag of coins against it. He wrenched me out of my seat and threw me spread-eagled against the truck. Ness let out a satisfied grunt when she found my hand stunner. I gave her a rude look, while a more civilized part of my brain breathed a sigh of relief when she didn't consequently drop in her tracks. Still, I wanted so much to erase her angry, smug-looking expression. Scratchy Lorratian hands held me back, and I couldn't argue with Ness's rifle.

"Alright, hands behind your back," Ness said. She slapped a pair of field cuffs on my wrists, removed my wristcom. Giem was marched around to the front of truck, where she was searched and cuffed, under the stunners of two hunters. When I glanced at their faces, my heart tried to pound its way out of my chest. They were Briegal and Xaffe. They volunteered to turn us into a police station.

"Thanks guys, you've done enough," Ness said, "by responding so rapidly to our call for help. We couldn't have caught up with these two without you."

"No problem," Briegal said. "We just happened to be in the neighborhood."

"As a matter of fact, we had plans to start back towards Port City," the taller pale redhead, Xaffe, said eagerly. "So we can haul them into the police department for you."

How heroic. I wanted to choke.

Ness looked at us a bit dubiously. Did we worry her that much? I found it hard to believe. "Oh, no, that won't be necessary."

"Don't even think about it," Xaffe said. "We have a back seat in our cab, and Briegal can cover them on the way to the police, while I drive. A lot nicer than you having drive so far out of your way. Plus, trust us, we know how to handle our stunners."

Why did I have a bad feeling about this? Could these hunters still hate me so much, for turning them away from Three only one time? Ness agreed to the convenient plan, and in a last humiliating effort, I gave her a pleading, terrified look as she turned away. I didn't think she'd listen to any more arguments at this point.

She either missed my silent effort or ignored it, got into the white truck with her fellow ranger, and drove off. In short order we were loaded into the back seat of the brown truck, harnessed in, uncomfortably leaning against our bound arms. Briegal turned around in the front seat to guard us.

After a long ride, the hunters parked their airtruck and marched us down along a creek into a podtree crater. Frustrated, I couldn't touch any of the trees, and dusk was appropriately turning grey and overcast.

"Many say it's just a fused rumor," Briegal said, as if trying to convince himself. "An absurd, local superstition."

"That's the official view," Xaffe said, leading the way. "So no one can officially complain about this."

"Where are we going?" Briegal asked nervously. "Don't we need to get back to our Crater One hunt?"

"That's why we're going here first," Xaffe said. "We'll stash these two in the Chelner cabin."

"What's to keep them from escaping and telling? And won't they be missed?"

"The cabin has no windows and I brought a lock seal for the door." Xaffe slapped a coat pocket. "We can just tell the rangers we dropped them off with the police or the police that the rangers still have them. Or any delay happened because our truck broke down and needed some repairs. The rangers said these two need to leave town in at least several more days anyway. Quit whining."

I gave Giem an apologetic look.

She gave me a questioning look back.

I shrugged.

We were pushed on down through the podtree forest.

CHAPTER 48

We came upon a savage clearing of hacked, dead tree stumps, surrounding a windowless log cabin. It had just one large, tight-fitting door, that looked scavenged from an airlock. As if the vac-head who had built this cabin from podtree trunks had hoped to physically block out any bad vibes.

Xaffe wrenched open the door, and the two hunters shoved us inside the dark and dusty-smelling room. We heard the lock seal slap into place as soon as the heavy door slammed shut again. At least automatic interior lights came on after a slight delay, while the outside voices rapidly retreated.

"They never even uncuffed us," I said, eyeing the sparsely furnished room, and wishing I could reach my face to wipe away my sweat. I used my shoulder instead.

"Why would Nessel have any reason to give them the release code? We're supposed to end up with the police today, remember?" Giem said.

"Well, I'm not putting up with this." I sat down on the dusty, sour-smelling, faded yellow-green carpet.

"What are you doing?" Giem eyed my subsequent contortions with alarm. I could see her wondering if I'd gone nova.

"Just—working—my legs—back through. Ahh, there, that's better." I had my hands cuffed in front of me—a little more useful.

"I can't do that," Giem said, bitterly. "My joints don't work like that."

"I'm sorry, Giem. What can I say?" I wiped more sweat from my face, my hands chilled. It seemed inordinately difficult to maintain a brave outlook in here.

"Do you feel bad?" Giem eyed me suspiciously.

"Don't you? Although I'm not sure just how much is anticipation. We spent a lot more time in Forest and Fallen Moon Craters, without feeling much more than simple uneasiness."

"And I think those larger craters had more podtrees," Giem said. "Maybe, in theory, we'll just feel a bit paranoid for several days."

"And have nightmares," I said.

"I suppose so. They expected us to flee Devil's Crater. Sleeping must lower the last of the mind's defenses."

"Fortunately, we prepared so well for this ahead of time, with lots of solid, refreshing sleep." I sat down, this time on a sagging old dirty-yellow couch. A cloud of dust arose. I sneezed loudly and promptly stood up again.

We studied our surroundings a little more closely. Most of the middle of the room was taken up by the immense couch, a crude wooden table, and two unmatched chairs. A huge mattress occupied the back left corner, while a sort of closet in the right rear corner contained a large toilet, both obviously for a biped larger than the average human. "We'll have to be careful not to fall in," I said, looking at the toilet. That actually grew a smile on Giem's face.

We turned around. The door was set in the right front wall. In the left front corner was a minimal kitchen setup, mostly consisting of tall counter space, with piped-in water—from the creek?—and a sink at one end. Scattered next to the sink, on the counter, sat some very dusty large glasses and filthy platters. Along with half a dozen antique-looking camping food packets, with faded garish Chelner-style quisine illustrations.

"Feeling hungry?" I asked, as I showed Giem a packet lavishly illustrated with writhing tentacles. "Sort of reminds me of krazzle claws." There was really little resemblance, but I was teasing her. She hates krazzle claws and I love them. "Want some?"

"I'm not that desperate." Giem wrinkled her nose.

I *was* hungry. I tore into the packet. I scooped up and gnawed on stale tentacles.

Giem gave me a disgusted look. "I'm thirsty."

"So am I," I said, after swallowing with effort.

I stuck my hands under the faucet, and it responded with loud sputtering, followed by a squirt of hideous sludge. I jerked back out of the flow, my hands slimed and stinking.

"Yuck! Giem, we may die of simple thirst in here."

"Stick your hands back in."

"Are you nova?"

"Come on. I can't do it, and the pipe may clear if you give it a chance."

I reluctantly obeyed, mainly because I didn't want to wipe my filthy hands off on my pants. The flow did gradually come clean. I waited a long time before I washed my hands and rinsed out a large glass, filled it, and drank it down.

I hadn't had a drink of water since the night before. Giem grew impatient, and I rinsed, filled a glass for her, and helped her with it. We took turns tanking up.

"Well, I don't think I'll be very hungry anyway, and at least we won't suffer from dehydration,"—my version of optimism.

"That doesn't help me much." Giem began searching the yellow and reddish log walls of the cabin. Her footsteps were dulled on the musty carpet. No doubt under it lay more log slabs. "I always get hungry when I'm nervous."

"Are you feeling it?" I asked again, out of clinical curiosity. I sat down very slowly at one end of the couch, so as not to raise more dust, and watched Giem pace around the room. The couch was so big I could barely reach the floor with my feet. So I popped my boots off, drew my legs up, and used the armrest as a backrest.

"Like you, I'm not sure," Giem said. "I'm not resigned to staying in here."

"I haven't given up."

"So what are you doing?" Giem asked. She was poking her nose at some controls on a small panel, in the wall alongside the mattress.

"Resting. Thinking. What are you doing?"

"Trying to turn on an incredibly complex air filtration system. Come on over here and get this going, please. I don't want you to suffocate while you're thinking."

I got up again and checked it out. She wasn't exaggerating. She'd gotten the control panel to give a status report, and it wasn't comforting.

"Great Galaxy, Giem, how did you manage to get this far? It's hard enough working this with my hands cuffed in front of me."

"Incredibly fantastic coordination."

"I guess."

"You see what it says?"

"Oh yes!" I sighed. Currently, the cabin was maintaining a complete seal, with a positive pressure differential, and we both breathed a sigh of relief when I got the filtered airflow going. "Great Galaxy! How nova! Do you think this could really help?"

"I have no idea." Giem continued on around the room. "Maybe we'll feel fine soon. I doubt trees can 'broadcast.' Maybe they put out fear pheromones or toxic pollen." She reached the door, leaned her shoulder against the emergency handle, and threw her weight into a hopeless effort to wrench it back open.

"Giem, as you've said sometime, pheromones are highly receptor-specific biochemical signals, that would hardly ever affect alien visitors. Including pollen."

Another more forceful attempt on the door ended in a moan of pain. "Taje, instead of sitting there arguing with me, why don't you come over here and try to help?"

"Who's arguing?" Though I wanted to—how could we possibly break a lock seal barehanded? Unless Xaffe had applied it too hastily. Another look from Giem got me to join her in several semi-coordinated, clearly useless, bruising attempts. We both returned to the couch, and leaned against opposite armrests. There was plenty of room.

"Now what?" Giem said.

"I don't know," I said. "What would Mek Ikkol do?"

"She'd find some very ingenious escape at the last minute."

"Well, perhaps it's not the last minute yet," I said.

"Or handsome Kenrat would struggle through incredible odds to come to her rescue."

"That obviously won't help us." I sighed, jealous over the fictional character's sex life. "Davin was our last hope."

Giem grimaced.

"How about the air filter? Maybe if I lift off the cover and pull out the filtration unit, I could squeeze through and get out."

"Don't you dare try it, Taje. If you break it we're completely fused."

"Okay, there's always ten-count breathing," I said, in an effort to cheer Giem's flagging spirits. I sat up, crossed my legs, and began to slowly inhale through my nose, and exhale through my mouth.

Giem reluctantly joined in for a minute or two, and then sat back again, with defeat on her face. "I can't do ten-count breathing for three days."

I yawned, and slumped back, my slowed heart rate starting to accelerate again. "Nor can I do without sleep for seventy-two hours," I said.

"Sleep! Don't even talk about it." Giem shut her eyes. "The sleep I've gotten lately wouldn't rest a sucker thread."

Sleep. Unavoidable and disastrous.

CHAPTER 49

"Have you ever noticed," Giem remarked from where we lay, some desperate hours later, on the odd-smelling mattress, "story heroines are boringly beautiful, ridiculously talented, and totally fearless?"

"And completely physically fit?" I stared up with her at the high, log-beamed ceiling. I clenched my teeth to keep them from chattering. The cabin's controlled environment wasn't cold, but peripheral vasoconstriction had frozen my hands and feet. My circulation had vacated nonessential areas. My pupils had probably also dilated at least as much as Giem's. Flight or fight.

"It does follow a rather monotonous pattern," I said, "and it's not very good for identifying with. I mean, when is an author ever going to portray someone like me—not particularly talented or beautiful, almost as skinny as a skeleton, and cowardly too?" I wished my heart would quit pounding in my throat, and stay where it belonged, in my chest.

"You don't look like a skeleton," Giem said. "And you're not a coward when it counts."

"No, then I'm a rash, thoughtless fool."

"Now who's being too hard on themselves? At least you're not big and ugly, like me." Giem turned her fear-filled face away from me.

"You're not ugly," I said angrily. "Don't you dare talk about my vet school roomie that way. I'm the one who looks like a pale skinny dwarf, next to you. Plus you've got the greatest sense of humor. Not to mention that fantastic brain of yours."

"That's just it—a lot of people don't necessarily like very intelligent friends or mates. They become envious and intimidated. And I don't get to enjoy feeling smart, not even in vet school. Every quarter makes me feel more and more vac-brained."

"I know what you mean," I said, dismally. A black pit opened up in my stomach, at the thought of facing Senior Year, Graduation, and the Real Worlds. How could I possibly learn enough to feel ready for the FIL board exam, much less real practice? "Giem, I don't want to do it alone!" My eyes began to fill with tears.

"What do you mean?" she muttered almost inaudibly, having turned over so her back faced me.

"Senior clinics—they'll split us up—and after graduation, getting experience aboard a FIL SEAR Ship. Are you really going back to Ballophon, instead?"

Giem's breathing was ragged and sniffly, and she didn't answer.

My cheeks were streaking with long, slow tears. "Giem, I can't do it alone! Don't let me fall asleep! I'll get all mixed up with him again, and it hurts too much."

I fell asleep, blast it all. More nightmares on Shielvelle, and vomiting my dinner on the expensive Istrannian embassy carpet and in the voluminous toilet here.

Great Galaxy. Each slimy rehydrated tentacle shot up my throat, out my mouth, and into the toilet, along with all the water I had drunk. Lovely. Evilly, I left them in the toilet for Giem to see. I had to fumble to the kitchen sink to rinse the taste out of my mouth before I could return to bed. There I tossed and turned until Giem got up. I heard a shriek and grinned.

CHAPTER 50

Giem returned to bed and sleep, awoke with a start, and eyed me fearfully as I lay there, shivering convulsively.

"What's wrong?"

"I—don't know." It was too difficult to try to explain, and I had tired of her not believing me. "I'm scared."

"So am I! And I'm beat by it," Giem got up, and returned to the front door. She wrestled with it again, in vain. "We have to get out of here! We're in danger—how could they do this to us?" She kicked the door, and as my eyelids grew unbearably heavy, she began restlessly circling the room once more.

I listed a grim differential diagnosis for my endless vomiting in the Istrannian embassy, and somehow I made my way through many sad deaths of family and friends to the giant cabin toilet.

Where was all this fluid coming from? I lost too much, followed at last even more alarmingly by several cc's of fresh red blood. I staggered back to bed. Drenched in sweat, I shivered in large, horrible jerks. I stared back at Giem's alarmed expression. I must have awakened her again. All I could think about was the dryness of my throat, my critical loss of fluids, and I kept wondering why my parents hadn't shown up to rescue me.

"Taje, I've been having the most terrible dreams— Taje! Are you alright?"

I stared at her, confused between a vision of a familiar friend, alternating in flashes with an impersonal FIL emergency paramedic. I had trouble believing either. I felt too feverish to trust anyone was ever going to help me. My face felt like it was burning, in contrast with my icy hands and feet.

"Taje! If you think it's Shandy again," someone shook me, "why don't you try to blast down the door, or at least call someone for help?"

"Too much power. Don't want to blast anything down. Never did like the responsibility. I should never have studied to become a vet! It hurts too much." Especially my searing throat. I quit trying to explain, and vaguely later I heard someone beating on the door hard enough to break a chair, while the yelling of other patients began to hurt my ears.

I managed to stand up and make my way towards the kitchen nook. I just wanted a tiny sip of water. After getting it, I had to change course for the bathroom again. Even more fluid lost? Was it possible? I stumbled out, and felt someone's strong arms and waves of fear as I was helped back to bed.

"Taje, tell me how I can help you."

I couldn't even focus on her, much less unscramble myself enough to make any sense. At last I arrived at an answer in my head.

"We need—we need—" I gasped. It was so important, and so frustrating.

"What? What! Tell me."

"We need—Mek Ikkol." I thought I heard someone crying. Then it blended into more fevered nightmares, and I was no longer certain of anything.

CHAPTER 51

Endless escapes and captures, endless travel to nowhere I wanted to go, and someone beating on the door again, this time from the outside. Shouts and surprise as it crashed open, after the faint, distinctive hiss of an emergency torch.

I couldn't even sit up to greet our rescuer. If I'd been an Earth dog with my symptoms, I'd have put myself on heavy-duty IV meds and fluids. I had to be carried out by two people. I tried to object to the spinning scenery—I knew the trees were angry with us—and my struggles were ineffective. And after a jolt in time, I left behind the last vestiges of my nightmares.

I found myself lying on the back seat of a moving aircar. My cuffs—and I learned Giem's—were gone. While the driver kept her face towards the road, she told Giem to retrieve a fluid pack from a first aid kit. Giem reached around to exchange the fluid pack with an empty pack slotted into an injector on my arm.

"How is she?" the driver said anxiously.

"Much better, thanks," I said hoarsely. "Is that you, Nessel? I'm sorry we had to stun you, back at—"

Giem goggled as she held a first aid scanner over me. "Taje's temp is back down to normal."

"Never heard of an Enchantment forest making anyone physically ill before," Ness said, glancing back at me briefly. "I did always feel it was rather rash, ignoring all the scare stories."

Ha, ha. A good pun. I was too weak to laugh, but a smile twitched at my lips.

"Seems to me," Giem said, as she frowned over me, "the whole ecological report on this planet—I consider it highly suspect, after experiencing only a portion of the Rash—was sloppy. How can you possibly ignore a lifeform that projects fear even into nonnatives?"

"Podtrees don't affect everyone." Ness's defensive tone didn't surprise me. "And for those who do claim to feel it, it's usually no more than a general sense of uneasiness."

"What about nightmares?" Giem insisted.

"Okay, nightmares," Ness admitted, "in the rare few stubborn or resistant enough to try to sleep in a forested crater. The stories make rather powerful suggestions, without any objective proof, and it might get bad for tourism if we supported them. It also fits nicely into typical hunter tall tales of strange haunts, and sly harvester warn-offs from valuable finds."

"Is that what you think Taje and I just did—make up stories to scare ourselves silly?" Giem said. "I suppose an intense review of all my worst paranoid fears was just a coincidence, and only Taje became so ill from the water we both drank?"

"Of course—"

"Maybe you never bothered to notice," Giem continued heedlessly, "there's nothing valuable about wooded land for hunters or harvesters—all the native wildlife is scared off, too. And without any crater pups around, you don't get flowering bushes, either. I'm sorry," Giem said very unsorrowfully, "I forgot. If planetary ecology surveyors never properly investigated crater pup-flower symbiosis, we could hardly expect a ranger to take note of it."

"If you think I'm arguing, I'm not." Ness barely controlled her own anger. "Can't you com I just rescued you, from two more nights surrounded by a podtree forest? And I did it despite your clearly demonstrated, callous distrust of me! How many rules do you think I'd broken, letting you in after hours to see Taje after receiving a warning about you, as well?"

"You got the warning too?" Giem said. "You never said anything."

"To incriminate myself further? Of course not. I'm not a complete vac-head, much as you'd like to think it, Giemsan. Otherwise, I wouldn't have bothered to double-check on your safe delivery to the police."

"Oh, is that where you're taking us?" Giem said. "Is that why you 'rescued' us?"

"No."

"So why?"

"Because locking you in that cabin was inhumane."

"So you admit there's a problem."

"Why do you keep trying to pick a fight with me?" Ness said, no longer hiding her anger. *"I'm on your side.*

And you need me. One of Taje's friends tipped me off she was in danger, so I called the police. The police said they heard I still had you in my custody. Next I had to wring it out of those hunters what they'd done with you, and brave the forest myself to break you out. I'm taking you directly to Port City, to try to make sure someone important hears your suspicions before they ship you offworld! Isn't that good enough?"

Giem fell silent. At last she said "I'm sorry," with a record amount of sincerity. "I doubt you'll ever know quite how bad it was for us last night. That's no excuse for taking it out on you. I think you may have saved Taje's life. And my sanity."

I shut my eyes. Giem was changing out my fluid cartridge again.

"Hey," I said, "any more and I'll need a pit stop soon."

"Good," Giem said, checking the first aid scanner again.

"You're friends," Ness said in a quiet voice, with a touch of bitterness.

I almost said "I guess." I was very tired of disbelief.

Giem said, "Sure."

"It's something to envy, for those of us without. What I still don't understand is how someone who only just started reading Mek Ikkol stories, could be such good friends with Gornathe Merrea that the famous author knew to make a paraspace call from some distant FIL Interstellar Scout Ship—to Enchantment—to warn me Taje is in danger!"

"What!" Giem and I both exclaimed, and I sat up dizzily.

Giem and I stared at each other, and Giem smiled and shook her head. "Taje, you lead a charmed life. Even with all the wild classmate friends I know you have flying around for FIL planetary ecology surveys, you manage to get Mek Ikkol on your side, too! It's positively frightful, trying to imagine what you might do next."

"Please." I groaned, my hands over my face. "I'd rather not. And Mek Ikkol's not even real! I'm never going near another Enchantment podtree as long as I live."

"Never is a long time—"

"Hey, it was Merrea, not Ikkol," Ness interrupted, and frowned at us fiercely. We both grinned back at her. "I can see neither of you believe me—"

"I had—a nova dream, about calling Mek Ikkol for help," I simplified it for her. "I seem to be able, uh, to project, with the help of a powerful friend. Maybe the trees concentrated, distorted, and beamed my call to her."

"It was Merrea, and her comcall was real. If you telepathed a call out to anyone, it was to Mek Ikkol's author. I saved her message, I was so surprised. Here. Watch this." Ness set the controls on her wristcom and handed it back to me.

I watched, mesmerized, as an old friend appeared with her warning on the tiny screen. "Aerrem," I whispered. Of course. My brain understood, subliminally. Giem snatched the wristcom from me.

Giem's jaw dropped, and I put my finger to my lips. I could see her smart brain putting two and two together almost instantly.

"It must have cost Merrea a fortune to send this over such a distance, through paraspace, so fast! That's another reason why I believe it's really from her," Ness said. "Only a rich, best-selling author could have afforded this call."

I decided I'd better make one more connection for Giem. "Giem, Ness is also an old classmate of mine from pre-ecology."

Giem's jaw dropped again.

"Nessel Niktreckin, current Enchantment Outpost Ranger, and former FIL Interstellar Scout Ship Planetary Ecology Surveyor, at your service." Ness held out her golden hand to Giem while she kept her eyes on the road. Giem shook hands with Ness in a daze and muttered an even more sincere apology—a historical event I observed with some evil amusement. "And yes, Giem," Ness said, "we probably were in too big of a hurry when we surveyed this planet. We even missed the parasitic lake suckers you reported. If you had our backlog and lack of adequate personnel, you'd have trouble doing a perfect job too."

Giem turned her pained expression on me, and transformed it into outrage. "How come you didn't properly introduce us at the beginning?"

My grin melted into innocent apology. "At Emperor Crater? I didn't recognize her there. We got— reacquainted—later, at the ranger station. And ever since you rescued me, we've experienced too much excitement to even think of mentioning it."

"Excitement. That's one way of putting it." Giem leaned back with a sigh.

"Well, isn't that what you wanted this summer? Some more Adventure?" I teased her.

"Is that what we've been doing? I thought it was mostly escapism until we failed."

"Adventures aren't planned vacations," I said. "And they aren't Adventures without Things Going Wrong. Or, as Garth Riddock would say, 'Everyone has runs of bad luck, even with the best of intentions.' I'd say we did very well for ourselves."

"You two get into these messes all the time?" Ness said, in a surprisingly serious voice.

"Oh, all the time," I replied immediately.

"As a matter of course," Giem added, before whispering to me: "I think it's time to take that injector off. You're feeling too good."

"Well then, why are two such experienced Adventurers talking as if it's all over?" Ness said.

"Huh?" I said.

"What do you mean?" Giem said.

"You haven't even begun to confront the bureaucracy of Enchantment's Ecology Protection Department. Do you truly feel ready for such a big challenge?"

CHAPTER 52

In short order, Ness drove us through lush green and purple ranches and farmland, prelude to a town with a tube station. Strong yellow sunlight angled under heavy, dark blue clouds, lighting up the land strikingly, brighter than the sky. The view impressed me, until civilization crowded out the fields, and the clouds released a heavy downpour.

It felt like such a let-down to return in this fashion, and I bet I'd never see the Rash again. When Ness pulled up and parked in front of a clothing store in the middle of the quiet town, Giem and I didn't even bother to ask her why.

"Stay here. I'll return in a few minutes," Ness said.

We sat listening to the rain spattering on the truck and the pavement, and I glanced at Giem, who seemed unusually pensive. At last I felt good enough to wonder how much she'd suffered.

She noticed my concern and smiled. "How are you doing, Taje?"

"Better. Good enough to take this off." I released the injector, with its last empty cartridge, and thumbed the injection site on my arm to stop bleeding. "How are you doing?"

"Better. My nightmares have faded."

I knew sooner or later she'd talk about it in great detail. She was always more open about personal experiences than I was. Right now she looked too tired. Neither of us said anything more, until Ness hurried back with her purchases, three large waterproof ponchos with hoods.

"I got them to keep us dry, and to cover us up," she said. "I don't think bulletins on you two have reached this far, but I'd rather not take any chances." Ness handed the ponchos to Giem while she buckled back into the driver's seat.

I admit a little disappointment Ness hadn't also bought us a change of clothes. She'd probably felt too rushed, and I tried for a light-hearted response. "Trench coats would have been a smooth finishing touch."

"Hush, Taje." Giem sifted through the three brown ponchos, threw the smallest one at me, picked out the tallest for herself, and gave the last one back to Ness. "They're matching, Ness. Won't that draw more attention?"

I pulled mine on, while Giem did the same. To my disappointment, they just looked like cheap rain gear. Then I noticed a lump weighing down one of my pockets. Ness had returned my stunner.

"They're what nearly everyone around here buys to muck around in," Ness said. "They hide mud. And here are your wristcoms. You'd look strange without them. Just don't risk turning them on. You'd be located in a micro." She drove us around to Long Term Parking, near the translifts for the local tube station. She pulled on her poncho. "Pull your hoods up, and try not to show your faces. I'd prefer to avoid creating any scenes here."

"Maybe they'll also cover up our stink," I whispered to Giem as we got out of the car. We followed Ness's rapid stride to the bank of lifts. "I sure could use a shower, and a change of clothes."

Giem shrugged, while I tried not to bump into other people. I wondered what would become of our other belongings on Enchantment. I was amazed we'd gotten most of our baggage back from Big Maxson's Planet the summer before last. I supposed we couldn't hope for that kind of luck twice. I gave Giem a brief glimpse of my stunner. "I doubt she knows it doesn't work," I whispered as I nodded at Ness's back. "But maybe it'll make her feel braver."

"I wish I did," Giem said softly.

We joined a light crowd in one of the lifts, and I backed into a corner, as much for the support of a rail as to avoid other people. I still felt a bit lightheaded, and a dull ache in my knee refused to go away. I noticed a time meter set into one wall, and tried to orient myself to today's time frame: late morning.

I couldn't shake the feeling we had nearly reached the end of our visit on this planet, and not just because of the reaction we'd probably get from Port City authorities. I also suspected it was because my whole state of mind and body so closely resembled how I'd felt on my arrival here—drained and disoriented—and I'd made the connection, whether logical or not.

The lift released us into the underground station, and Ness glanced with worry at me as we hustled for a ticket gate. "You okay, Taje? There's a clinic in town. Or we could go back for the injector."

"No, I'm alright. And we might attract too much attention. I'll be fine, as soon as I can sit down again."

The line ahead of us passed through, and as Ness hesitated at the ticket gate, people gathering behind us grew impatient. Ness sighed, showed the gate her wristcom, made her selection, and the gate let us through.

It wasn't until she headed away from the regular passenger cars, and led us to one with compartments, that we realized the reason for her hesitation. Her choice made sense, yet also extravagant. I beamed as we sat down in our own little four-seat compartment, and sealed the door. "Thanks, Ness. This is great!" I wouldn't have to feign normality for the whole ride to Port City. I sat lengthwise across the bench seat facing Ness and Giem, backwards to the tube's direction.

"Yes, thank you, Nessel," Giem said. "I'm glad I don't have to wear this poncho the whole way. I had begun to wonder what people would think of me keeping my hood on through the entire trip." Giem shucked her poncho, while I just unsealed mine and pulled the hood back.

"They'd only think you have different habits." Ness frowned at the credit readout on her wristcom. "There aren't any adult natives here." She emerged from her poncho as the tube almost imperceptibly picked up speed.

"Hey, Ness, we'll pay you back for all this," I said, "just as soon as we can turn our wristcoms back on. And if you find any of our other stuff, we'll pay for shipping."

"Speak for yourself, Taje," Giem said sourly. "That's about as likely as passing our externship. How can you expect anyone to return to Devil's crater for us, and who's going to argue with the Enchanted Inn after what we did?"

"And by the time you're ready to pay me, you may have trouble even finding me," Ness said.

"What do you mean?" Giem said.

"If I'm not in jail for aiding and abetting criminals, I'll at least be job-hunting. I might even have to rejoin a PES team, on another FIL Ship."

"What's that?" Giem said.

"A Planetary Ecology Survey team. Ness, I wish you wouldn't talk about FIL Ship work that way," I said, and then felt guilty. "Why not go home, try to save your reputation and your job here, and leave the rest of this to us?"

"Because if we made a mistake here, I am partly responsible, and I know the system for fixing it better than you. This may even explain part of the reason I stayed on here—a suspicion we missed something. Don't try arguing anymore with me about it—I'm committed to seeing this through."

Giem and I looked with amusement at each other, but neither of us had the bad taste to repeat aloud the Big Maxson expression about commitment. Ness didn't need to hear it.

CHAPTER 53

I napped fitfully until we reached a central station in Port City. We debarked, again in our ponchos, hoods pulled low over our faces. Ness took a look at both of us, and walked over to a tourcom screen, and asked for a listing of hotels.

"What are you doing, Nessel?" Giem said, as I checked the comscreen time meter. It was only mid-afternoon. I hated not having my wristcom turned on.

"Checking out the local hotels," Ness said. "Planetary Administration isn't very far from here. I need time to set up appointments, and you two don't look ready for anything besides laundry, showering, and sleep."

"I'd take that as an insult, if I didn't have to admit you got it all covered except for food," Giem said.

"No need." Ness gave the comscreen a frustrated look. "The only hotels near Admin with any vacancies this last micro are so pricey their rooms have it all. We might as well go to the closest one."

"Poor Ness." I eyed her wristcom meaningfully. "We will pay you back." I yawned. I didn't know if the wretched look on Giem's face meant she was exhausted or she couldn't afford it, but I could.

One of the station translifts delivered us into the vast, plush, cream-colored, quiet lobby of the hotel Ness had selected. Giem and I tried to hide in a far corner while Ness argued with a real, dour-faced person in a uniform, behind the front desk. I wanted very badly to collapse into one of the fluffy armchairs or soft couches scattered about, but didn't dare expose any of the expensive furniture to my filthy clothes. At last Ness returned for us.

"They're out of three-bed rooms. I had to get a separate room for myself." Again her wristcom received a nasty look. "I suppose it's just as well. You two can sleep while I'm making calls."

One last lift ride took us to the hall with our adjacent rooms, and Ness unlocked our door with her wristcom.

"You get the Sunflower Suite. You'll find all the luxuries of home in there," Ness said. "And I don't think you'll want to join me for a night on the town, am I right?"

"Right," we both said at once.

"Good. That'll help my budget. Stay here, and I won't see you until morning, unless an emergency arises. Don't attempt to leave or call me."

"Understood," Giem said.

"Goodnight," I said, in only a mildly mixed-up way. Although it was not evening, Giem and I entered the room with nothing more than a complete night's rest on our minds. I was ready to fight with my last bit of strength for the place in the shower, until we discovered with delight the luxury room had two ridiculously well-eqipped bathrooms with bright yellow toilets.

We stripped, and threw our disgusting clothes into the laundry slot on triple cycle. We spent more time scrubbing away filth and sweat, than we did on dinner selection and consumption afterwards. We took our food trays into our large, soft, cozy beds with us. Our puffy comforters were covered with yellow flowers. More happy flowers marched across the walls. I don't know what Giem chose. I was starved. So I ordered roasted, barbecued vat-grown chicken, and the generous sauce flooded the platter, making the mashed potatoes taste great. I'd selected a native vegetable because I liked its magenta color. It came in centimeter chunks, roasted, fibrous, tender, with a flavor—blending well with the barbecue sauce—sweet and sour. The orange hue and taste of the latter mixed so delightfully with everything, I happily ate all my food and licked my platter clean. I gulped down a large dilute fruit drink to quench my thirst.

We were watching a mindless ancient Western on the comscreen on the opposite wall. I had argued 3D holo movies gave me headaches, and Giem said she'd had enough of car chases so we went further back in time.

"This is great," I said, as I tackled my dessert, two triangular, large, flaky pastries. Their buttery crusts enveloped crunchy dark chocolate shells surrounding a ground-up sweet nut filling. I licked my fingers while I watched someone get shot from their horse and actually bleed, set my empty tray aside, and slipped deeper under my warm duvet. "Aren't you glad we didn't live then?"

"Did he just—"

"He's dead, Giem," I mostly quoted another favorite, old 2D show I didn't expect her to recognize.

"I don't think I want to watch this anymore."

"But it's got very beautiful, fast horses."

"True," Giem said.

"It's just fiction, anyway."

"I don't think Mek Ikkol kills anyone."

I didn't have to think about it very long. "True."

"So your friend doesn't think killing is necessary for adventure stories. I wonder what this is costing us?"

"Giem, I don't care what any of this costs."

"I didn't agree to that."

"You're enjoying all of this room's features. Admit it, Giem."

"Hmm," Giem said, finished with her tray, and sounding sleepier by the micro. "Funny how a little externship can make me appreciate a good dinner and bed."

CHAPTER 54

I awoke to the sound of a com buzzer. It must have been buzzing for a while, because Giem had gotten out of bed to answer.

"Good morning, Giemsan," Ness said, sounding falsely cheerful, with a matching smile, on our screen.

"Good morning, Nessel," Giem said wearily, sounding just as unready as I felt to face the new day. "What's up?"

"Appointment in one hour with a real VIP, in the Enchantment Ecology Protection Department. Grab a bite, and get dressed."

"Already?"

"It helps to have some contacts. And, I admit, a somewhat slanted story, about needing help with evidence of a powerful new poaching outfit. I'm surprised I got through so fast. So let's not spoil it by arriving late."

Giem and I gazed at each other, not too happily. I got out of bed, and we retrieved and pulled on our clean camping clothes. Not exactly dressing up. It would have to do. We ordered juice and rolls, and Giem commented on my miraculously renewed appetite.

"Making up for lost calories," I said, "and I don't think that—illness—was completely real."

"How'd you sleep last night?" she asked.

"Not terrible. No invading dreams. Not great, either. How about you?"

"About the same. I think I've forgotten how to sleep in a decent bed. I'm surprised I didn't sleep more soundly."

"So am I."

At this point our door opened. We grabbed our ponchos and walked with Ness to the lift.

"So did you have to tell them exactly who they're seeing?" I asked her, on our ride down to the lobby.

"No. You're secret witnesses." Ness grinned.

"Well, at least we have no more lies to keep track of," Giem said.

From the lobby, we stepped onto a busy street of Port City for the first time. All the traffic, pedestrian and mechanical, and towering buildings made us irritable on our five block journey, to the immense monolith housing Planetary Admin.

I wondered why people never learn, and start building underground, so they won't be forced there later, after using up the land above?

My knee succeeded in making me especially unhappy. We had to study a building map on a comscreen in the nova massive lobby. We still got lost a couple times, before we found the Planetary Ecology Protection Department. We had to get directions in its noisy main office, for the particular PEPD VIP we had an appointment with.

"I see why you had us leave so early," I said in a hushed voice, after we entered a small, sterile, grey and green waiting room. According to a time meter on the secretary that Ness showed her wristcom to, we had arrived only a few minutes early. The secretary asked us to wait, so we sat down together, on a shiny black couch along one wall. Exotic holos set into the opposite wall tried to entertain us, with moving visions of the various ecosystems of Enchantment. Of course one of them showed a cute crater pup family, grazing within a gorgeous flowering bush. I nearly gagged.

Ness sat beside me. I felt like I was running out of time. "You know, you could leave us," I told Ness. Giem and I were probably doomed. Why drag her down with us?

"Maybe I should," Ness said reluctantly, "How can I? Where will you stay tonight?"

"Probably in a cell," Giem said. "They'll soon know who we are, and you too, if you stay."

"I'm in this too deeply. Where will I go next? I'm sure my supervisor will want an explanation—"

"Please step into the office," the desksec interrupted Ness with its announcement. A door to the right of it slid open.

Suddenly I got a very bad feeling. For the amount of trouble we'd gone through, this seemed too smooth.

As we all stood up, I turned on Ness. "Leave," I said, pulling my beat-up stunner on her. "You've done more than your share. When you get back, you can tell the same story of duress everyone else is using. If no one acts on our suspicions, you'll be free to carry on the fight."

"But—" Ness's eyes widened. "Not again—I trusted you!" Outraged, Ness grabbed my wrist.

"Don't make me shoot you again." I broke her hold. I didn't believe my stunner would work but I acted like it would.

Ness gave me a look of mixed anger and shame, spun around and stomped out. I pocketed my stunner and turned back to Giem, who looked shocked, although she hadn't interceded.

"I hate this planet," I told her as I limped beside her through the office door. "We can't even treat our friends here right. Maybe I won't care what happens in there."

Inside we confronted a stern woman behind a huge yellow-red wood desk, flanked by two uniformed police officers.

"I'm glad you feel that way," Giem whispered.

"Please. Take a seat." The middle-aged, gaunt woman, in an expensive bureaucratic suit, motioned to two matching wood chairs in front of her scary podtree desk. We couldn't bring ourselves to sit in or even touch the chairs, while she studied us with an only partly disguised expression of disgust. "We have a few minutes to talk, before you're taken to the spaceport. Tajen Jesmuhr and Giemsan Fane, I presume? Where's our wayward ranger, Nessel Niktreckin?"

"We let her go," I said, without further elaboration. We both waited in stony silence, wondering how much the VIP knew, until our mute stance forced the woman to speak.

"Various authorities decided to compromise and let me hear you out before you leave. On the slim chance you might have even a minor, legitimate ecological complaint."

"How nice," I tried to say sarcastically, and almost choked on it.

"If you know that much, I suspect you've heard about our concerns," Giem said in an impatient manner good at putting other people in their place. Although I hoped only I could hear the quiver in her voice. "All you need to do next is check them out, before it's too late to intervene."

"Where is your data?" the woman said, in a manner that proved Giem right. "We have to have some basis to go on."

"Check the recordings we made in our deskcoms, back at the quarantine stations we worked in," I said. "It's all there—suspected crater pup species differences, our observations and calculations, and our preliminary ideas about crater pup-flowering bush symbiosis."

"We did. You don't have any such recordings. We can only conclude you never carried out any serious studies to back your slanderous claims!"

"And not that someone with a lot to lose erased all our data?" Giem leaned forward, anger flashing in her hazel eyes. The police officers shifted a little more attention in her direction, and I don't think she even noticed, but I did.

"I hardly believe Dr. Nilod would allow such a disreputable action, and only he'd have the authority—"

I snorted. "Go ahead and send us back to school. You're not really interested in anything we have to say."

The official's expression didn't change, and she sat back. Was she someone who enjoyed using her power for mean arguments? Or was she under hidden pressures of her own? She returned her attention to Giem. "Do you agree with that?"

"I'm afraid so," Giem said very calmly, straightening up, causing both officers to shift more toward her, and I used the moment to reach into my poncho pocket again. "Send us back to school, please."

"Very well. In fact, very gladly. Officers, they're all yours."

My time was running out. I snatched my stunner out of my pocket. They'd find my weapon and take it away from me quite soon anyway, and it didn't look very useful. Even the power light had gone out. I'd never gotten around to any maintenance on it, since my fall in the creek, and the first accident with the autoserver must have broken its seals.

I heard gasps. I hammered my stunner down on the podtree desk, and I left a beautiful splintered dent in the expensive surface. My stunner leaked yellow, sick-looking fluid, causing a chemical reaction with the finish. It steamed, bubbled, and a satisfying large defect spread through the finish. Looking alarmed, the bureaucrat jerked her chair back.

"I'm turning this in just so you won't worry about us anymore," I said. I leaned over her desk and gave her my most evil grin. "Don't you think you ought to consider getting a different desk? Beware of Enchanted Forests!"

CHAPTER 55

The police searched us anyway, cuffed our hands behind our backs, and unceremoniously dragged us out of the office. In the nearest lift, Giem burst into laughter, shocking our guards.

"I didn't notice it at first," she said, when she could stop laughing long enough. "The poor woman's got an expensive desk made of podtree wood. It's going to take a lot more than two vet students to straighten out this planet!"

The officers gave us bewildered looks, and resigned themselves to escorting two nova students out through the crowded lobby. We didn't give them any trouble—what would be the point?—and we grew quite embarrassed by the hundreds of stares that followed us to their waiting aircar.

I dreaded the spaceport audience even more, but we came through a private port entrance into a lounge apparently reserved just for miscreants like us. It turned out we still had one more night to spend on Enchantment.

Ever spent more than a day in a spaceport? It was okay for our guards, who rotated in shifts of six hours each. However, the lights never went out, there weren't any beds, and the bathroom had no showers or laundry facilities.

"This must be your fault," Giem said, as she paced around the lounge, unable to sleep.

I'd kicked some chairs together, and managed to bunch my poncho into a pillow. "My fault?" I said, hurt.

"Whenever I do something with you, I end up in cuffs in custody."

Making our final public walk the next afternoon, once again under guard and in cuffs, extra excruciating.

Humiliation gave way to surprise, as our security guards removed our cuffs so we could turn on our wristcoms and confirm our flights and baggage routing, at the departure gate.

"We have baggage?" Giem said, startled.

"Your belongings came in about an hour ago, on the tube. Just in time. The word is some ranger collected it all for you," one of our guards said.

I gazed vacfully at the nonchalant officer, and almost broke into tears. I guess I'd gotten more tired than I thought.

"All passengers with special challenges please begin pre-boarding for shuttle flight 115 at gate 237," a com voice announced. The officers promptly cuffed us again and marched us through a long jetway, in front of a Telmid family with an infant, and behind some paramedics pushing a stretcher with someone lying very still on it. We weren't uncuffed until after the quick shuttle flight, another march through the local orbital station, immediate transfer to our paraship, and a walk straight to the microfloral conversion tanks.

"Get them to do regeneration," Giem told me, after the officers released us, and we began stripping down for first tank rotation. Our guards hadn't left.

"What?" I stunk, I was shivering, my knee was throbbing, and I didn't like our audience.

"Your knee," Giem said impatiently, looking quite uncomfortable herself. "You're still limping. Have them remove those stupid synthetic parts, and grow you new real ones while you're out. It's a perfect time to get it done."

"You don't think there'll be plenty of time for synthetic joint repairs, during the rest of our summer break on Olecranon?" The idea of returning to school, and Dr. Hako's office, made me feel extra sick. Not to mention the nova vision of the extraction of various artificial parts, and regrowing ligaments, cartilage, and pieces of bone, on top of another microfloral conversion. I'd probably have to spend the rest of our flight in rehab, fighting nausea and simultaneously learning how to use new tissues just to walk.

Even so I couldn't escape Giem's logic or my knee pain, and I contracted for the work while the techs attached our sensors.

"We can't repair your knee at the same time as microfloral conversion," a tech explained as she held a screen for me to sign. "It might contaminate your joint fluid. And we can't just regrow parts. We'll have to amputate above your knee and regrow your leg. So we'll have to keep you asleep considerably longer, if you don't want to be awake for any of it. Do you still want to do this?"

"Lovely." I contemplated my irrational fear of the uncomfortable, ugly process I'd put off for so long, along with the almost certain risk of more nightmares. Versus the real pain in my knee, and the possibility of lifelong, inopportune mechanical breakdowns. I decided I'd rather face Shandy's nightmares with him than struggle alone with more knee problems. So I signed for regeneration, under general anesthesia. I definitely didn't want to watch my leg regrow. "No guts, no glory," I told the tech as I handed the screen back to her.

CHAPTER 56

Despite the long duration of my treatment under anesthesia, I wasn't haunted by dreams this time. When awake, I learned how to walk with a leg brace, that gradually let my leg do more work. I was released from sickbay well after Giem had left the conversion tanks.

After dressing in my cleaned, shabby clothes, I received our cabin number and directions. I walked slowly and carefully through narrow ship passageways to a translift. I was still weak, a not uncommon side-effect of both of my procedures. And my new leg pain didn't feel like much of an improvement, although medics promised it would get better.

It was evening by ship time, and the nurse who had reviewed rehab instructions with me had also informed me that our exit from paraspace, for docking at Olecranon Orbital Station One, would occur the following morning. I was so worried over how little time Giem and I had left to agree on a report that I almost missed our door. I used my wristcom and entered without buzzing.

I found Giem relaxed on her upper bunk, reading a comscreen. "Oh, hi, Taje. How's the new knee?"

"Oh, okay. They regrew most of my leg, and they say it'll feel normal within a month, with proper exercise."

"Your sensei will see to that."

"No doubt. It took so long to fix! How will we finish our report in time? How much have you done already, without me?"

"Our report?" Giem looked surprised. "What report? All our data was erased."

"I know that. You have such a great memory, I thought you'd at least put together a rough outline for Dr. Hako. How else will we defend ourselves and pass our externship? Who knows what kinds of evaluations the station vets sent?"

"Taje, why don't you sit down a moment and relax? I met some nice folks onboard while you were gone so long."

"Giem, didn't you at least record any of the data you could remember?" I couldn't believe she'd procrastinated this long.

"Of course." Giem peered down at me and looked insulted. "I commed it'd be more accurate if we both worked on it together."

"That leaves us all of one night!"

"Taje—"

"How can we possibly organize all our material—"

"Taje!"

"What?" I was distracted by the luggage waiting on my bunk. I shook my head. "I still can't believe it. Ness must have gone down into Devil's Crater for us."

"And demanded the return of our deposit from the stable manager," Giem said, as I opened my bags, and decided to change my clothes. "Lucky for us, Nessel sure didn't hold a grudge against you for long."

Giem was right—all my sundries and clothes were packed, very neatly. "They're even cleaned." I changed into fresh clothes with delight.

"Had to be disinfected, for interplanetary flight." Giem switched her comscreen to a fresh view, and climbed down to join me on the lower bunk. "Ready? What do you want to say?"

"Let's try to make a formal report."

"It won't have any data tables," Giem said. "Won't a summary do?"

"I think between the two of us, we can remember a fair amount. We can't help the gaps and imprecision. Dr. Hako will understand."

"Will he?" Giem rolled her eyes. "I can't wait for this. Okay, let's start."

The more we recorded, the sillier it sounded, without all the hard data we couldn't remember. And the more vac-headed it sounded, the more we worked at it, and the wearier we became. And the more tired we got, the more vacful it sounded.

We circled in this vicious cycle until far too late that night, when we agreed to delete all of it. We'd get at least a little sleep, and try again later. We hoped to get a little more time to work on our report, within the next day or two, before Hako could set up our debriefing appointment.

CHAPTER 57

"Giemsan Fane and Tajen Jesmuhr, please come to a courtesy comscreen."

I hustled, with all my luggage, to keep up with Giem amidst throngs of students, professors, and techs in the terminal of the Central Olecranon Orbital Station. "Wonder what that's for? Don't they usually use announcements like that to trap criminals in 3D thrillers?"

"We're not on Enchantment, anymore" Giem said distractedly, taking me seriously. "We should try to find one soon. It sounds serious, and we're about to miss the first shuttle flight down."

Normally, four daily scheduled flights provided transfer between here and the planet-based University tube station, on top of other shuttle flights between the Orbital Station and local teaching, research, and residential stations orbiting Olecranon. I was always curious about any paraflights coming and going, so, as usual, I glanced at an interstellar flight board. It listed no others, besides ours, scheduled to leave tonight, none in the last week, and none until the next week. Boring.

Mid-summer quarter, it wasn't too surprising. At any rate, if we missed the first shuttle down, we could work on our report here, in the central lounge, while we waited for the next shuttle. The lounge should be quieter this time of year, and not too distracting.

"Giem, we can always just reschedule for the next shuttle flight."

"Hush—I think I can hear—"

"Giemsan Fane and Tajen Jesmuhr," the com voice tried again, "please come to a courtesy comscreen."

Giem found one then, and there we received a curt written order for us to meet with Dr. Hako in his office, as soon as we arrived back at school.

"Not wasting any time, is he?" Giem said, sounding unhappy. "Maybe we'll get lucky and meet with Hako before he receives reports from Nilod or Morbe."

"It's probably too late."

Under too much pressure before the next flight down, we couldn't produce a report. It felt like the end of a marathon by the time we'd landed, taken the tube to campus, dumped our stuff in our dorm room, and walked on over to the office of the Dean of Student Welfare. The door was open and we could hear voices, and one asked us to enter.

"Hello, Dr. Hako," Giem said, with a nervous smile, as we stepped into the cluttered little room.

"Hello, Dr. Hako," I echoed, equally anxiously. I scanned Giem's puzzled, pleased look, towards the other person sitting in front of Hako's desk. "Krome? What are you doing here?"

Not the politest of greetings for a friend not seen in over a planetary year. Krome took it in good humor. "I got free of a certain little quarantine, long enough to attend an Olecranon ranch management seminar. That is always a good excuse for visiting my favorite uncle," said the blue-skinned, younger-looking, female version of our student dean.

Someday I'd have to find a polite way to ask where they'd both come from. Or com how to look it up. Krome smiled human-style at both of us as she stood up. "I could ask what you're doing here, since I've heard this is still midseason for vet student externships. Somehow, I suspect I shouldn't." The Big Maxson rancher turned briefly towards Hako. "I'll see you again tomorrow. Okay, Laki?"

"Fine." Dr. Hako raised two fingers, and Krome rapidly departed. That seemed rather inauspicious. She had left behind only one seat cleared of jumbled stacks of equipment. Rather than fight over it, or do any further rearranging under Hako's intense scrutiny, Giem and I both remained standing in front of his desk. I suspected we were in for it.

"So. What do you have to say for yourselves?" Dr. Hako said in a horribly calm, quiet voice.

"Uh—" All excuses abruptly vanished from my poor brain. "Actually, not a whole lot."

"Were you both listening during our last meeting, or just pretending?"

Giem and I looked at each other to no avail. We both felt completely baffled.

"Uh, maybe you could remind us?" Giem said, after a long, terrible silence.

"I did try to get you to understand you should not automatically assume people who disagree with you are your enemies."

This was bad, truly fused, no doubt about it. "Uh, I did—I mean, I do remember," I said with a desert-dry throat.

"I've read ship mail reports on both of you," Hako said, while my heartbeat grew more difficult to ignore. "From Drs. Morbe and Steffin—" Giem had all the luck—"plus comments from Dr. Nilod." Oh well. "They're not proper evaluations—nearly everyone will have to resubmit correct forms before I can file them—but apparently you flunked, Tajen."

I wanted to sink below the crust of Olecranon. When you have a nickname in common use, and an authority figure uses your formal name anyway, you know you are swimming in deep piss.

"And both of you have Incompletes. Not to mention the obvious lack of recorded student reports, to be submitted to me along with supervisor evaluations. Just what did you spend your time doing on Enchantment? Besides getting into so much legal trouble you were lucky to stay out of the court system, much less maintain the slightest credibility for any problems you might have uncovered."

"Then—you heard about our suspicions?" Giem said hesitantly, since I was struck dumb.

"Oh yes, the possible speciation, by color pattern, of the crater pups, and other potential ecological problems, from Enchantment hunting and harvesting quotas. Dr. Steffin made some mention of that. Although such transient businesses rarely cause any significant species depletion.

"Incidentally, we have a few crater pups of our own to work with. I'm having them sent over to the Olecranon School of Genetics, although one of their professors pointed out crater pups would have to match their mother's color scheme, to survive to maturity, so it may just be a maternally linked color inheritance pattern."

"They could even be behaviorally separated species. And—the geneticists—they haven't started working on it?" I grasped at tiny shreds of remaining hope. I couldn't bear to think we'd stolen, stunned, locked people up, fought, hijacked, ruined a bureaucrat's desk, and littered Enchantment even temporarily with our belongings, for a misdiagnosis of the whole situation.

"We'll discuss the final results when they come in," Dr. Hako said impatiently, "As you seem to have no formal reports detailing what you did, how about a concise oral summary?"

He said not another word, while we took turns outlining our Enchantment station efforts, results, ideas, and the obstructions thrown in our paths. We sounded weaker and weaker, as we silently regretted our aborted report efforts the night before. Somehow we decided on a course of fairly complete honesty, as our best defense. So it was with mixed horror and relief I described, in detail, our last scene in the Enchantment Ecology office.

Our story sort of dribbled out at the end, like my stunner on the Ecology official's desk.

Another long ghastly pause ensued, before Dr. Hako carefully eyed us both, and spoke again. "You've left me with a lot of comcrap to deal with, and not a lot of solid evidence to back you up. It'll take time to determine the consequences of your actions," he said ominously.

"I've decided to ship you up to the OOVTH—the Olecranon Orbital Veterinary Teaching Hospital—to finish your summer break. You'll get a taste of senior year a lot earlier than most, I fear. I hope you at least got plenty of sleep during your externship, because you won't get much working up there."

We stood there a few more minutes, trying not to visibly quake, before we realized that was probably his dismissal. As we turned to leave, Dr. Hako coughed.

"Uh, just one moment."

We turned back.

Dr. Hako aimed his beady blue gaze at me. "Aren't you forgetting something?"

I gaped back at him, totally lost. I probably couldn't have made my way through a simple Bioscience One quiz at this point.

Dr. Hako suddenly reached down towards his ankle, and plunked Jet on his desk top. "Jet keeps trying to climb up my legs into my lap. You forgot to supply me with a pool, so I've had to feed her in our lounge sink. Please take her back."

"She's grown!" I cried excitedly, snatching Jet by her olive and pink shell, closer now to Hako's hand size than my own. I held her up to my face, and her miraculously tiny green eyes gazed calmly back at me. I wondered how she recognized me, with a brain the size of a pea at best, but I was sure she did, she was so relaxed in my grip. For a brief time I enjoyed the reunion, before Dr. Hako hauled me back to reality.

"You didn't forget your poor abandoned pet, did you?"

"Uh, no, never, of course not."

"Good. Don't forget to check your com messages. I had to route three of them to your room; two directly from my office, and a third from the main vet school office."

"Didn't I get any?" Giem said forlornly.

"One's for both of you, from Krome. If you received any others, Giemsan, I didn't have to route them."

"Who sent my other two messages?" I said impatiently.

"I don't know about the third. The second was recorded by a young man who stopped by my office a couple days ago. What was his name? Pale, thin, and to be honest, not too healthy."

"Shanden Fehrokc?" I almost dropped Jet in my shock.

"Yes, that sounds right." Hako studied me carefully. "An empath who's been haunting your sleep, or so he said. Sounds like you two should get a few problems straightened out."

"Hey," I remembered suddenly, "he didn't bother me in my last tanking, and there was plenty of time. What else did he tell you?"

"Not much. He didn't seem very comfortable in my office. He just wanted to know where you were."

"And you told him—"

"We were expecting you back in a few days."

"Is he still here?"

"I don't know. He used my com to send yours a message, and then he left my office."

I sank back into utter gloom, while Jet finally became impatient with my hold midair, and fought my grip with her claws.

"Is that all?" Giem said, not sounding terribly cheery herself.

"Have you made a decision?"

"A decision?" Giem frowned. "About what?"

"Will you put in an application for a Ballophonian internship next year?"

"That depends."

"On what?" Hako pressed her.

"Whether I pass this year. Come on, Taje, I think we're done here."

"Very well," Dr. Hako said. "Contemplate your errors as you repack today. You have reserved seating on the last shuttle flight back up, late tonight."

CHAPTER 58

Giem and I didn't speak to each other as we made our way back with the chill, dreary wind of Olecranon, to the vet student dorm barracks. We entered our small room for what we commed was the last time. I pulled Jet from a coat pocket, settled her back into her pond, and turned her filtration system on. Giem had immediately taken the seat at her desk, and I reluctantly sat down, and contemplated my own deskcom.

Giem received regular ship mail from her parents, on just about every flight from Ballophon with a connection here, so she no doubt had a whole collection saved up to review. I hadn't touched my deskcom by the time I found her standing over me. Instead, I had my head in my arms on my desk.

"What's wrong?"

"I can't do it, Giem. I'm out of courage."

"Here, I'll do it for you." Giem reached over me to work the controls.

"Hey, wait a micro." I tried to fight off her hands.

"We'll start with Krome's message. It's for both of us, and I want to see it."

She had a point, so I desisted, and Krome's merry pale blue holo face appeared on my screen.

"Hello, Giemsan and Taje! I'll be in class by the time you get this, and I just wanted to make sure you pack up quickly so you can allow time for dinner on me, at the University Shuttle Port. I know it's the only location on this forsaken continent with decent restaurants—forget the campus cafeteria—and it'll give us more time together, before your shuttle flight. Laki has told me how to find your room, so I'll meet you there tonight and we can ride the tube together to the Port. See you later!"

"I suspect Hako told her a lot more than our room number," I said, bitterly. "I bet Krome knows the whole story."

"If she does, at least she doesn't sound too worried about us," Giem said. "Come on, let's see the next entry. Shall we try the mystery message, since I bet it's Shandy's message you're really putting off?"

I held my face in my hands. "Sure. Why not." Giem took my hands away, to watch a short paraspace message:

"Dear Taje, I hope you are now safe and sound, and no longer in need of the services of a certain mutual, fictitious friend? Unlike that physical impossibility (at least in this galaxy), we should get together sometime, and com how to straighten out Shandy's head.

"Your friend in collective compulsory empathic confusions, Aerrem Nathegorn, PES, FIL IS Ship Irreni; aka Gornathe Merrea, moonlighting SF writer."

"She did publish!"

"I take it this also explains how we got rescued by 'Mek Ikkol'" Giem said. "Taje, you have the weirdest friends."

"Ha ha!" I laughed. "She never would let any of her friends read her stuff. So she gets published, and becomes a best-selling author—serves her right!"

Giem gave me a curious look, patted me tolerantly on the shoulder, and kicked in the last message before I could recover my wits. It too was short, and it changed my demented mood:

"Dear Taje, sorry about the nightmares. It took me a while to realize I was involving you. I didn't mean to hurt you. Tank dreams shouldn't happen, but as we know, I'm different. I've been traveling a fair amount lately, and I must have transmitted somehow, through paraspace. Which, as we know, has different physical laws. I traced your transfer record from *Onnarius*, and dropped by here to explain.

"I'm on my way to my first FIL job, as a Planetary Ecology Surveyor. FIL has agreed to find me solo research jobs, on uninhabited planets. So my space travels will soon become a lot less frequent, and my life a lot easier. And I gave your local medical teaching hospital a try, and they've designed a drug they think will stop my REM sleep in paraspace.

"Please take care. Love, Shanden Fehrokc."

I turned the com off, fought tears, and tasted hot salt water in my mouth.

Giem sighed behind me. "Sounds like a lonely life," she said.

"Why—why couldn't he have waited, just a couple more days, to talk to me himself?"

"Too ashamed? Or embarrassed?" Giem said.

"He should know he could trust me for sympathy." Tears ran down my face. "I thought we settled that on *Onnarius*. We may never get to see each other again."

"Maybe he had to make a certain flight departure for his first assignment."

Our door buzzed at that point, and Giem reset my deskcom. "Who's there?"

"Central Supply. I've got your packing crates, as ordered by the vet school Dean of Student Welfare."

"Relentless," Giem muttered. "Come in."

The student University employee agreed to loan us the cart with two battered, standard issue student lockers, deliberately limiting the amount of junk we could haul into space with us. I wiped tears from my eyes as I silently studied my crate and all of Jet's pond paraphernalia, not to mention my belongings, mainly clothes and backpacking gear. Maybe Ness's luggage rescue efforts had been in vain, after all.

"Okay, we'll see if there's room for any of Jet's stuff in my trunk too," Giem said resignedly, after noticing my dismay.

"Are you sure? That would be great."

"I said, I'll see. Let me pack first, and I'll com how much space I can spare you."

I put Jet's filter system on drainage mode, and joined Giem in unpacking our Enchantment baggage. It felt very strange to be leaving this room after so long, especially under such depressing circumstances. I'd heard the OOVTH dorms were even more cramped, and the wonder of it was Giem wasn't even complaining about bringing along Jet's swimming pool.

I had begun to hate travel. All it did was separate people. If only I could get a berth on Krome's flight back to Big Maxson's Planet, whenever it was, and stay in one place for a change.

"Wait a micro," I said, pausing.

"What?" Giem said, stuffing a load of clothes into her crate.

"Shandy can't have left. There weren't any paraflights out in the last week, the next flight out is the one we came in on, and it doesn't leave until late tonight." I grabbed my coat and hat off my bed and headed for the door.

"Wait a micro, Taje. Are you fused? Where will you look for him?"

"The only public hotels are back around the campus shuttle port tube station."

"Wait just a micro, will you? Let me find my cloak. I'm coming with you."

CHAPTER 59

We didn't say much more until near the end of the tube ride. At last I found the courage to ask Giem why she'd come along. "This is taking time away from your packing."

"I don't need all day," Giem said. "Well, I guess I was hoping to buy enough time with you, to talk you out of doing this."

"Why?"

"Because I don't think Shandy wants to see you."

"Trying to protect him, or me?"

"Maybe a little of both. Mostly the latter. Whatever our differences, we're still a team, remember?"

"Thanks, Giem. I don't think it matters anymore, whether he wants to see me. I need to see him. I need some resolution."

"Relax. I commed that on this ride, and gave up on trying to stop you. I commed it was hopeless. You're just as stubborn as ever."

When we got to the campus tube station, Giem took a tube back to our dorms while I checked all three campus shuttle port hotels uselessly, and even madly took a flight up to the orbital station, paid for a holo page, jogged the station gate loop, gave up and then I returned to the surface of Olecranon with a nova headache. Where was he?

I commed I ought to head back to my dorm and take something more for pain, beyond what I'd gotten at the orbital station. I put off admitting defeat to Giem, and detoured to the cemetery, with my head pounding again, maybe because I'd missed lunch. Gee, it had nothing to do with feeling ridiculous and stressed. Right. Maybe Shandy didn't want to see me.I could use a few minutes to mope by myself.

It took me rather a lot of effort, however, for those minutes. Coils of fog rolled in, and by the time I got to the cemetery entrance, I could barely see through the thick white mist. I felt chilled down to the bones in my face, making my headache fiercer than ever.

I went almost blind, as much from the throbbing pain as from the nasty fog. My breath became shallow with the cold air, and it blew out in double streams like dragon breath from my nostrils, as I groped along a row of grave markers. I would just walk to the end of the row, loop back around, and leave. This had become too difficult—

Then I caught sight of a pale, skeletal form, sitting crosslegged on one of the few officer tombstones, and I nearly fell over from fright—

And the ghostly figure screamed—

I'd found him at last. And probably scared him, with my own fear. I stumbled towards him. "Shandy, it's me, Taje—"

"I know. Don't touch me!" he shrieked, and he turned his face away as I got close.

I stood before the gravestone and dropped my hands to my sides, dumbfounded. I could see how ragged Shandy's breath was by the way it came out in choppy streams, and when he turned to face me, his brown eyes stayed focused on the ground.

He had never seemed this bad off before. "Shandy, what's wrong? Is it—my headache?"

He shook his blond head, and briefly touched the mustache I'd felt only in dreams. "It—I—when I got older, I changed even more," he stuttered. "I'm told it's from hormones. Late puberty. I had hoped, maybe around an old friend, I would feel—a little more at ease. But it's—intolerable!"

The last, again, almost came out as a scream, and when he rubbed his eyes, my breath caught at how thin his hands and face looked. "I came out to an abandoned graveyard, to escape everyone's emotions for a bit of peace, and I end up calling you out here! Even though, from the moment you landed, I knew I'd never be able to touch you!"

"You didn't call me. I just came," I said, although I wasn't sure. I had nothing I could do, say, or think. Although his agony cut me deeply, I couldn't touch him in any way. He might as well have been a spirit, haunting the old cemetery. In truth, considering his appearance, I wondered if he'd even live long enough to see his first solo job.

"I hate them," he seethed, still not looking at me. "They both deserved to die! Look what they did to me!"

"Your parents?" I felt stunned, after the sad memories I'd shared with him at our FIL Orphan Center. "Don't you get any pleasure from life? Without their love, you wouldn't exist!"

"Their selfishness made me a freak!"

"You wouldn't be you, without your mother's transplanted genes, besides you're practically a clone of your father—"

"What do you know of parental love? Yours abandoned you too long ago to even remember whether you might be a clone! How does that feel?"

He'd never said anything like that to me before, and it felt like the waves of pain in my head could hardly get any worse. I struggled against it all to say what I had to, or regret the lost opportunity, perhaps forever.

"Shandy, I feel loved by others now. And I just wanted to tell you—I love you." Why was that last sentence so difficult for me to speak aloud, for the first time? "And I care about you very much, no matter what happens, or— what you become. Don't worry about the dreams, and don't drug them away, if you need them, or me. I think I'll be stronger. And Aerrem can help us both, if we need her." There. I'd said it. Maybe the pain was just a little less. Maybe.

Shandy finally looked straight into my eyes, as his tears mixed with the sweat on his face. "I know," he said quietly. "You must thank Aerrem for me, if you see her again. I—love you too, Taje. I always have. That's why you must leave me now. Before I hurt you with my pain anymore. My connection with you is too strong."

My headache had reached the point of nausea, and it was all I could do to peer through my own swimming vision, and say goodbye to him without retching.

I ran back down an aisle between markers to the fog-shrouded gate, and returned to the campus grounds and rows of dorm barracks. There I fumbled through the silent, white, opaque air, hardly able to tell one dorm from the next. Somehow every turn I tried took me farther from my own room.

I gave up on my pride, sat down a bench, turned on my wristcom, and called Giem.

"Where are you, Taje? You sound awful!"

"I'm lost, Giem." I suppose I hoped Giem would come for me and lead me back.

She just snickered. "So you think you're lost again? According to my wristcom, you're just three dorms away from our room. Turn right."

Before I stood back up, I used my upset to try to right one little wrong. I used my wristcom for some difficult research and a bunch of calculations, and my head hurt so bad I just had to trust my results. So I sent Ranger Ness the credits I commed I promised her. I just wanted to get this done without Giem looking over my shoulder.

I groped my way back, and as soon as I returned, I took some more pain meds.

Giem watched me. "You did it, didn't you? You found him. Are you sorry?"

"No." I didn't feel like talking about it. I shed my clothes, and slipped into the shower to warm up and wash it all away.

CHAPTER 59

"Should I come back a little later?" Krome caught me dressing.

"No, we need to get going," I said. "Oops, I haven't finished packing!"

"Relax." Giem looked irritated. "I took care of it. Luckily you're putting your good clothes on. Krome's made dinner reservations at some fancy restaurant at the shuttle port."

"All of Jet's stuff fit?"

"Just barely. Come on."

By the time I had my coat and hat on, they had loaded our trunks on the aircart. I sealed Jet in one of my large coat pockets, and checked our room for any stray belongings, while my alien pet tried to dig out a nest against my ribcage. Giem had been thorough. Our room looked as bare and impersonal as the day we moved in. I'd done so much suffering over homework here, I was surprised to feel a trace of nostalgia creep over me. "Okay, I'm ready. Let's go."

Outside the fog had vanished, and the sunlight was dying. Campus lights turned on, amongst drab buildings, as we made our way across the weedy ground to the tube station. Nothing about this ugly campus had ever attracted me. Yet I felt like I was somehow tearing myself away, and leaving bits of myself behind in the process.

Neither Giem nor I spoke much all the way to our seats on the tube, and Krome's look of concern grew, from the seat she took opposite of us. I sat next to the window, and turned my face towards it, to hide tears streaming again down my face. I couldn't help mourning Shandy's helpless suffering, and my own.

"Is she all right?" I heard Krome whisper to Giem.

"She's fine. She just had a bad day, that's all," Giem said, grimly. "Even worse than mine."

"How did it go with the old man this morning?" Krome said, as the tube picked up speed.

I wiped my face with my knuckles, and sniffled.

"He was totally fused!" Giem said. "I have a nova headache, just thinking about it."

I made an effort to concentrate on the cruel reality of our immediate future. If we had one to speak of. "He must have told you, what we did," I spoke at last, a little hoarsely at first. "I'm surprised you're still willing to take us out to dinner."

"I'm a friend, remember? From Big Maxson's Planet?"

"Didn't Dr. Hako tell you all about our numerous crimes and indiscretions on Enchantment?" Giem asked.

"And didn't I hear that zap from you this morning, about that quarantine Giem and I had a little something to do with?" I said, bitterly.

"Yes—"

"Where's Ziehl?" Giem interrupted. "I could use a good cry on her shoulder, right now."

"Someone had to take charge of both of our ranches while I was away. She sends her greetings, as does Grek—"

I groaned. "Him too?" My alien heart-throb. How did I manage to find such impossible relationships? "Can't anyone do better than nice messages?"

"Yes. I can." Krome grew serious. "I am! What happened in Laki's office this morning?"

I sat back and half closed my eyes. "Hako didn't say? You tell her, Giem."

"Why do I have to tell her? My head hurts. You tell her."

Krome gazed back and forth between us, and she appeared even more baffled.

"Uh, we were rather bad," I relented and began. And faltered at what to say next. It all felt so overwhelming.

Krome coughed. "Well, Laki said he was going throw a little scare into the two of you. He said you were both coming along nicely, except for a regrettable but probably curable tendency towards rashly launching in a bit over your heads—"

"That's not what he told us," Giem said.

"Yeah. We're supposed to feel guilty about our many transgressions, and lack of any solid evidence for our concerns," I said.

"Not to mention we'll probably both flunk, when he gets proper evaluations," Giem said. "We'll have loads of fun, going off to a make-up externship, after everyone else in our class graduates and gets to ship out as real vets. That is, if the vet school lets us do a make-up externship. I've never even heard of anyone flunking one before."

"Is that exactly what he told you?" Krome said, surprised.

"No, it's what he implied!" I said. "It's simply more cruel, sending us up to the OOVTH to slave away, while we worry indefinitely about our status."

Krome began laughing, making us both angry, and apparently we only added to her amusement. "Poor Laki! How did you ever frighten him into overestimating you so much?"

"What do you mean?" Giem said.

"I'm not supposed to tell you any of this. Well, have either of you thoroughly reviewed your wristcom contents, since your visit to my planet?"

I shook my head, baffled.

"Why?" Giem said.

"Because maybe you'll believe the rest of what I say, if you find those Public Health Commendations you weren't supposed to get, from your work on Big Maxson, buried in your student data. Laki likes saving unique missions for his two favorite students."

I doubt either of us looked at all convinced.

"Listen," Krome became impatient. "Your Dean of Student Welfare will keep finding flaws and faults with Morbe's and Nilod's evaluations until it's too late to stop your graduations. With the infrequent ship mail deliveries between here and Enchantment, Laki shouldn't have to resubmit your reports for corrections and clarifications too often, before the vet school will have to graduate you by default."

"Why?" I said, with wonder, trying not to feel too much better too fast. A reprieve at this point seemed so unlikely.

"Because for years he's tried to find a way to get at Dr. Morbe and Dr. Nilod," Krome said. "They were members of his graduating class. Did you know that? You could have looked it up in public records. And since the beginning it's been clear they joined your profession only for personal greed. They haven't tried to keep medically current, they never bother with veterinary bioscanners when they can get away with cheaper tests, and all their commercial projects show a plain lack of concern for nonintelligent lifeforms.

"Dr. Emmel was one of Laki's favorite students. FIL jobs happened to be scarce, the year she graduated. After she unwillingly accepted her quarantine job, she sent Laki a message complaining about her bosses, and together they created your summer externship.

"Laki didn't tell you any of this? He'll boil me in hot oil! Anyway, he was hoping that, left to your own devices, you could stir up a little trouble for his old classmates. At least catch them in some shoddy veterinary work. And instead, you became their worst nightmare! Laki doubts they ever planned to breach eco-protection laws— normally it's tough to deplete any species, before this sort of business fuses. Simply ignoring the possibility could get them into much deeper trouble with FIL.

"And, believe it or not, whether or not your particular theories and concerns are correct, you did force the start of some badly needed re-evaluations on Enchantment. As well as uncovering a lot of sheer incompetency."

"How do you know all that?" I said. "How could anyone? All our work, all our hard data, was erased."

"Not before a veterinarian at one of your satellite stations got concerned enough to obtain copies of your comwork, partly by enlisting the help of a couple techs at another station. He didn't take time to sort it all out—he just sent everything you two recorded—in your ship mail. So it arrived with your evaluations.

"As a consequence of all your data, all hunting and harvesting has been stopped until the U of O completes some thorough research. That will take too long for Morbe and Nilod to stay in business. Their licenses to practice have also been suspended during a serious FIL interplanetary veterinary board re-evaluation. That may require your testimony by com. And the Enchantment eco-surveys will be completely redone."

"That's wonderful!"

"Why, that blue-eyed—"

"Taje!" Giem cut short my outburst just in time, while Krome sat blinking her innocent, brilliant blue eyes at us.

"Hako lied to us."

"He merely complained he didn't get formal reports from us. Like we recorded for Dr. Bioh, our first summer. What he must have seen was our raw data, our calculations, notes and theories, and, uh—"

"And what?" I demanded.

"My recordings. Of all our com conversations."

"What? You recorded all of our talks? Giem, that was private."

"I was lonely. We didn't get to talk much. Yes, I recorded all of it. I didn't plan to share it."

"Ohh." I groaned. "That's too humiliating. All our personal talks, and my private journal—"

"Your journal! What journal?"

"The one I always write on summer break."

"I didn't know you had enough time to keep that up."

"It's an addiction. What can I say? I made the time."

"Excuse me," Krome said firmly, as she stood up. "The tube has stopped. Care to get out and join me for dinner?"

CHAPTER 60

Krome helped us deliver our luggage to our shuttle gate. Then she led us to the entrance of the most expensive University shuttle port restaurant, a place well beyond the means of the average student. I observed with dismay the crowded line of wealthy parents with their studious offspring in front. Krome led us on past, to a table in a back corner reserved for us.

Giem and I turned on our menus, and we tried to cheer up as we began to politely study an incredibly long, exotic, expensive list of offworld specialties. I suspect we both worried about what Krome could afford. Krome finally spoke up.

"It's been a rougher morning for you two than I thought, and I've probably been here long enough to know this menu better than you. I'll go ahead and try to select something you'll like."

That was a relief. The prices alone were scaring me into indecision. Krome knew what she could afford. A couple minutes later our identical steaming trays came up through the table, and we each slid one to our places. They smelled great, and looked faintly familiar.

Giem poked her generous vegetable quiche with a fork. "Made from quelsh eggs and cheese?" She looked back up at Krome, with the first hint of a real smile on her face. I did a double-take over my own large plate. Even the vegetables seemed familiar, and surely the brilliant magenta drink was krava juice?

"That's right." Krome smiled with pleasure. "No animals were harmed in the making of this dinner. And there's nothing like a ridiculously expensive restaurant meal to fight off a little homesickness. Plunge in!"

We set to work on the Big Maxson-style dinners, and for the next fifteen minutes or so, utter silence reigned except for the clatter we made with our utensils.

Krome paused over the last bites of her dinner and studied both of us intently. "You aren't going to tell Laki I told you everything, are you?" she said.

"Of course not."

"Never."

"Good. He'd probably disown me if he found out." Krome picked up her juice glass. "How about a human-style toast—to my friends!"

"And to our friend!" Giem said, raising her glass.

"Yes. And to the end of our last externship!" I said, as we clashed our glasses together.

"Right!" Giem said.

"The end?" Krome lowered her glass, and squinted one glinting eye, her version of a lowered eyebrow on her hairless, blue face, looking a lot like her uncle. "I'd say it's just the beginning, and you have the harder half to go. Laki tells me early promotion to senior status means daily morning rounds before appointments, even earlier scans and treatments, and more of the same with evening rounds, all night emergency shifts, plus weekend duties—"

"Laki told you too much!" I felt my food growing heavy in my stomach.

"Let's stun Krome now," Giem said. "We'll save Dr. Hako a lot of trouble that way."

"Hey, friends, remember?" Krome raised her hands, laughing.

"It's dangerous, being one of Giem's friends. Didn't Hako warn you?"

"And you have to be downright nova to get on Taje's list."

"Once more, with real effort and meaning this time." Krome raised her glass again. "To friendship, whenever and wherever it may exist in this demented universe!"

"To friendship!"

An hour later Krome waved goodbye to us at our gate, and Giem and I boarded the shuttle. I found just one very short, probably expensive message transferred to my deskcom in our measly cabin in the OOVTH. The message simply said, "Thank you."

Giem looked over my shoulder. "What is that from Nessel?"

"It's the end of this story." I smiled.

"You're still writing it?" Giem asked.

"Of course."

AFTERWORD

You might guess some of these escapades were borrowed from my backpack trips. On one, we did meet up with a park ranger, right across from that imposing peak in the photo on the back cover, at a great campsite. She wanted to claim it if we were leaving.

But first she asked about our trip so far, and we all agreed coincidentally that two of the lakes were kind of creepy.

The ranger didn't know about the leeches at one lake, which attacked my partner, when she waded into the water from a nice warm beach. She screeched, quickly snatched them off, and I yelled *"What is it, what is it?"* and bent over her to look. She got mad at me because all I cared about was my scientific curiosity. And she did go crazy and try to climb around that lake to see the trout better.

The other lake did not have a horse skeleton. Maybe a horse skull. I don't remember. The ranger told us a horse had died there, too far from a vet for help. Maybe that death was the source of the bad vibes we felt there.

The ranger also asked if we'd found a cabin in this mountain lake area, which she was looking for. She told us some crazy person had built little cabins all around the mountains. We hadn't found any of them in our explorations.

We did have a deadline to end our trip hovering over us and horribly dark clouds hovering over us, which would have trapped us in our tent. So we gave the ranger our campsite and we hiked on up the trail. And grumbled in the rain about our chosen careers over hers.

We did not have horses, only backpacks.

AKNOWLEDGEMENTS

I could not have completed this novel without the help of my best friend and husband, Brian J. Boudler, my fabulous editor, Jackie Melvin, and my awesome cover artist, Cricket Harper. Not to mention all those wonderful backpack trips in the South Sierra, the less than colorful but cute marmots singing in the rocks, and the grand ponderosa pines. All my mistakes are my own.

www.ingramcontent.com/pod-product-compliance
Lightning Source LLC
Chambersburg PA
CBHW072202130726
47910CB00011B/1790